First published 2016

Contact the author:

Face Book, Twisted Lanes

pphipps1@hotmail.com

Acknowledgements

Firstly, I want to thank my mum and dad. If it weren't for them, I wouldn't have written this novel because, obviously, I wouldn't be here lol.

Then I want to thank my loving wife and two daughters for putting up with me and pushing me towards my goal.

A big thank you goes out to J. Purcell; some people let me down when they said they'd help to edit *Twisted Lanes,* but she worked on it intensively like it was hers. She was also the first person to read this novel from cover to cover. So thank you – you're a great person.

A massive thank you to my boy Dean for knocking heads with me and designing my book cover. Check out his tattoo work on Instagram #deancutabove – it's fantastic.

Thanks to everyone who read bits of my novel while getting a sick haircut in my East Ham-based barbershop, Cut Above the Rest.

Last, but not least, a massive thank you to two friends who were a huge inspiration while I was writing this novel: Tracey Okonkwo and her sister Davina Okonkwo. Davina is also a novelist and you can purchase a copy of her book *RISE* from Amazon. There's an extract from it at the end of *Twisted Lanes*.

When I was 13 years young my teachers said three things would happen to me: 1) I'd meet my match, 2) I'd end up in prison, or 3) I'd end up dead.

Well, I've been waiting for all three and they've not yet come to pass. But guess what? I've written a novel! If only they could see me now ... lmao.

Look out for my next novel *All Eyes On Me*, coming soon.

TWISTED LANES

Patrick A. Phipps

TO KARL
NUFF RESPECT
FROM UNCLE
PAT

2020
STAY SAFE

It's All About Mumsy

Chapter 1
Morning Ritual

It all starts on December 18th, once upon a hood in the land commonly known as East Ham aka East Famz. It's one of the coldest winters I've ever known. The road men yank up their hoods, heads low, eyes firmly under shadows. This ain't good cause it means people are getting jacked even more than usual.

"Carlton! Carlton! Wake up! It's time to go to school. You're going to be late again!" mum screams from downstairs.

I want to scream back at her. Damn, blood, what's the point in this school crap? The day is way too long and it's so damn cold outside!

Trust me when I tell you I wouldn't dare say that out loud cause mum has zero tolerance for that kind of chat and I know the licks will come fast and furious if she ever hears me. I can't say much to mum about school. I really hate it, but I have to go cause it's all about making Mumsy happy and if that's what it takes, then this kid's on it.

"OK mum, I'm up!" I call back in a groggy voice as I crawl out of bed, trying to spend every second I can under my warm, thick, single quilt. I sit on the edge of the bed trying to wake myself up.

I hate this shit.

I'm so pissed off I want to punch the crap out of my pillow, but sleep's still in total control of my arms.

I suppose you're wondering who I am. Well, my name's Carlton Williams. I'm 15 and quite short and slim for my age, but I make up for that in other places if you get what I mean. My shoulders are quite broad, though; I think I get that from my old man. I'm a beautiful shade of light brown and well known for my big smile, but I don't smile too often.

I've got sexy, long braids that sit neatly on my shoulders. Mum occasionally cornrows them for me when she has time, but I'd rather get one of the girls from the ends to do my hair cause it gives me a good excuse to get up nice, close and personal with them for a couple of hours. You know, sitting between their legs, feeling all cosy and shit and occasionally laying back so I can cushion my head against their breasts; they just hold me there as if they don't know my mischievous intentions – now that's what I'm talking about!

Anyway, as I was saying, I grew up in East Ham which is the East Six side of London and I'm very well known in the ends. Mum's a single parent, so we value every penny that comes through our front door; she works in a bookies and has an afterhours cleaning job that allows her to pay the bills and buy food. Whatever cash she has left, she spends on me. So even though we haven't got much, I've never had to steal or beg like some of the kids I grew up with around here.

Although mum works for both of us, I do have a little job on the side because I like to look sharp in all the latest creps and garms. A boy like me can't afford to be caught slipping when the ladies are around. Truth is, all I really want is for Mumsy to be happy and spend more time and money on her instead of me, so I work fast and hard to get that paper and take some of the pressure off her back.

OK, I'm up, washed and dressed, looking fresh in my dark blue Funkwest jeans, plain, white sussmi T and plain, black Nike kicks. I always buy my jeans a little large at the waist so I can do as the ladies do. They leave their yards with their skirts down to their knees, but as soon as they step foot out the door and buss round the corner, they roll up their skirts just below their hips to attract us man and get us all excited and shit (some more excited than others).

But us man pull our jeans down low to show the designer label on the waistband of our normally clean boxers, so the peng chicks know What Time It Is. For now, I'll leave my jeans up since mum always walks my way to school and I don't want her embarrassing me in front of my boys. She always waits for the right time to make an example and that's usually when my friends are around.

Mum starts the countdown as she always does, holding up her hand and, starting from her thumb, she raises her fingers in the air, "three ... two ... one!" By the count of one my foot should be out the front door, but I always stand in front of it and let her get to *one* just to see the smile on her face when I step out.

"Too fast for you Mums," I say as she takes her best swing at me. "You feisty little boy!" she smiles as she closes the front door.

It's always good to see mum smile cause she ain't done much of that since my dad got a 'ten year government vacation' for selling class A drugs.

But what the hell do I care? He didn't do nothing for me or mum anyway. He was just like a thief in the night, popping in with his one arm, getting 'tings' from mum when he felt like it, then he'd just up and leave.

I used to hear her begging him to stay the night. I used to hear her say, "Delroy, why do I always feel like a prostitute when you leave me?"

And he'd reply, "Why are you always chatting shit?" He sounded just like a scratched CD, always talking the same old crap.

He never once put his head around my door to check on me, or to say hello or goodbye.

Dickhead.

Wasteman.

Well, I'm the man of the house now and when he comes out I'm going to be big enough and strong enough to kick his ass. He's going to come for his tings off mum, but he's going to get a beating from me instead. A damn good slap.

Anyway, let's not chat about him.

"Yo, Carlton!" I hear my boy call as I step out the door. Suddenly, the winter gets a lot colder, not cause I don't like my boy, but cause I don't know what's coming next.

"You going to come play computer later? Man just got the brand new footie game! Geeze! I'm going to kick your ..." He must've clocked mum walking out.

"Oh, hello Teresa," he says as he stops dead mid-speech, waving his crusty hand my way. Typical of loudmouth Rick. No manners whatsoever.

Rick's one of the boys I hang with on the sly, but don't get it twisted; the boy's got no swagger. He knows I'm a barber, but never once has he asked me for a trim. Trust me, he needs it badly. Rick's hair is all over the place. He's got a bit sticking out here, a bit sticking out there. His hair looks like it's running away from the police. It's as dry as roasted peanuts!

Talking about dry, when you look at his lips the word 'dry' finds new meaning. When he talks, the corners of his mouth fill with that white foam stuff crackheads get. I step back just in case some flies my way; trust me, if it lands on me that would be a darn nightmare.

Rick always looks like a thirsty brother. Every time I see his lips, it makes me want to drink two litres of Volvic just to remove the dryness from my own mouth.

He always wears the same, old stonewashed jeans. He washes them so much, they're two to three inches too short for him. Then there's that stupid, green, striped jumper. Light green, dark green, light green, dark green: it reminds me of a dirty zebra crossing. Whenever and wherever he walks, the front end of his blue, no-name brand trainers seem to open and close like a pair of lips.

Yeah, Rick has no swagger and he doesn't give a damn, but he does have all the latest computer games. Those that know me know I'm a sucker for a computer game. But having one ain't something I can burden Mumsy with cause she already has enough on her plate. Before I can say a word, her well plucked eyebrows become one, long unibrow as she throws a wobbly.

"Nothing like that," she says, wagging her finger in Rick's direction; she always speaks this way when some prick pisses her off. "He's going to work when he leaves school and you should find a damn job too. And pull up your jeans before you catch a cold in your batty. Furthermore, it's Miss Williams to you."

Rah blood, what can I say? I wish the ground would just open up and suck me in like a big, fat spliff. For real, I feel so ashamed for Rick, but it's funny as hell cause mum always comes out with something new and dumb arse Rick is the idiot that always walks right into it. I grumble at her under my breath. She just laughs out loud and I can't help but laugh too.

Here we go again. We stop outside the same clothes shop on High Street North; the cold's nipping at my bones through my thick, LV jacket. Feet are smashing into the concrete, rushing to catch a bus or dashing to get to school or work on time. Frosty air exits kids' mouths as though they're smoking dope spliffs. I look down. Why don't I ever see any dog shit on High Street North? It's as though dogs don't exist here. The scent of freshly baked bread and black coffee drifts from Percy Ingles' double doors, trailing from the sleepy mouths that suck on paper cups, trying to kick-start their day.

My day starts just as it does every morning. Looking through the shop window, I pretend to see what mum's looking at, but all I'm really focusing on is her reflection in the shiny glass. I can see the pain on her face, even though she's smiling, so I pretend to smile with her, but really I'm crying inside. I look at my £80 jeans, my fresh creps, my LV jacket. I'd give it all back to her to make her pain go away.

To start the ritual this morning, mum starts pointing and chatting away about how nice the jacket is on the mannequin and how she should be wearing it, not that silly dolly. I pretend to listen, but all I can see is the way she looks in her old, grey and black raggedy jacket. It's so ugly: grey and black chequered tweed. The damn thing looks like one of them old jackets from a black and white 1960s movie. It has big, black buttons and no hood to protect her natural, beautiful hair and smooth, brown skin from the cold. The big, flyaway collars remind me of the ears of an Indian elephant.

She looms in the shop window and some stoosh girl looks back out at her, cuts her eye and turns her nose up with a bitchy smirk on her face as she walks away. She knows something Mumsy doesn't know.

I know it too, but she better not even think it too loud, cause if she spoils the surprise I'll have to move to her differently.

"Bitch," I mutter under my breath. At least I think it's under my breath, but mum overhears me. I wonder if she's got some sort of magic power to hear through walls and read people's minds.

Wait for it … wait for it …

She throws a wobbly for the second time this morning. "What did you say Carlton?" Her voice gets louder as I get stuck for words. "Carlton! What did you just say?"

She holds me by the scruff of my jacket. Shame, man; I just hope she lets go before any of my boys come past and see mum having me up in the middle of East Ham. They'll never let me live it down; I'll be the joker for the rest of the day.

I've never really heard mum talk so sternly before. Maybe it's cause she's never heard me say something like that before. She's a little hard, but on point. That's why she always tells me it's not what you say, it's how you say it that makes the world stop spinning on its axis for a split second, but to the receiver it seems like a lifetime. Well, I'm the receiver and, trust me, it's the element of surprise that stops the clock.

I've got to speak quickly. "Sorry mum, but don't you see the way that girl looks at you every morning knowing you can't afford to buy that jacket?"

Mum lets me go and hangs her head. Her brown eyes settle on the clean sidewalk. "Who said I can't afford it?" she whispers. "I can afford it, but I just want you to look your best, so I concentrate on you. You're all that matters to me." She looks at me with hurt in her eyes; she can't hide it from me cause I know what she's really thinking. She doesn't want me to become like my wasteman dad, selling crack for the latest garms.

"Mum, I've got enough. Why don't you just cop that jacket? It's only three bills."

"Three what?" she asks sternly as her brow wrinkles.

"I mean £300 mum."

She rolls her eyes. "Carlton, you need to start talking properly if you want to get anywhere in life," she says as she wags her finger in my face. I know she's right, but I just shrug it off.

"Look mum, I'm going to be late for my first lesson. I've got to go and I'll be home late cause I've got to go work."

I walk away, looking back at the jacket. Only £120 left to pay, then I'll get mum out of that raggedy, old jacket in time for Christmas and into that fresh, new, cris one. I'll kill this morning ritual crap once and for all. I'm going to work hard cause I have two weeks left to get it.

Mum walks off. I call out to her, "Yo! Mumsy!" and she takes a well-deserved swing at the side of my head for the second time this cold morning.

I say, double-time, "Where's my kiss?" The blow stops in mid-air and with a smile she gives me a big kiss and cuddle that will last me for the rest of the day.

You see, man like me loves his mum and doesn't care about being a mummy's boy, for real, so she can kiss and cuddle me as much as she wants to, on the road or off; it doesn't bother me not one bit.

"Have a good day at school baby boy and keep your eyes on your books, not those tearaway girls in your class," she says with half a smile.

"OK mum," I say as I wave her off.

But as soon as she walks away, I get my swagger on for the other 'important' females in my life! Tearaways or no tearaways, as far as I'm concerned the easier they are, the easier I get what I want. So I just drop my trousers a bit low, rough-up my school tie, brush the waves on the side of my plaits and start swagging though East Ham with my garms, looking funky fresh.

What? Do you really think I'm heading off to school fam? Nah, blood. Man's got to make that P, you know, that cash money! And there's no time like the present as far as I'm concerned. More hours, more money.

I'm near my workplace and I can't wait to get them clippers in my hands. The buzzing vibration and sweet music of the blades fading are the only things that take my mind off the world and its madness. I'm just about to start my day when I hear yet another voice behind me, but this is a voice I hate. The bitter cold ain't so bitter no more as a bitter voice swiftly takes its place.

"Yo blood! Where you going? You going to the spot?"

I turn around and who do I see? Damn. It's Bulargi, aka Jacka. I can always tell it's him cause he has that fresh Nigerian accent with a horrible high-pitched tinge that doesn't fit his facial features or body size. Every time I hear him, I just want to burst out laughing in his face. His voice is complete confusion.

Bulargi's a street boy. He's a bit older than me, about six feet tall, but hench like he's pushing houses and eating elephants. He's all blacked out in a Nike tracksuit that he wears one size too small, so you can't miss his big arms and monster chest trying to bust their way through the seams to intimidate his next victim. He's rocking a plain, black t-shirt and black one ten Nike Air trainers.

Yes, Jacka's completely blacked out and that ain't good cause it means he's about to get up to no good.

He's mad dark-skinned and the whites of his eyes are red like when I just finish smoking the pengest spliff. Three tribal marks sit neatly on the left side of his face like he's sponsored by Adidas. He always crops his hair short and I hate cutting it cause he likes taking, but never likes paying. He sits in the chair, asks for the world and still walks out as ugly as he walked in with his money sitting neatly in his pocket, so I guess you know why we call him Jacka. He came over from Nigeria about five years ago, but he still has a deep accent. Imagine that! An African guy trying to talk street! LOL.

I don't really like to associate with him, or even stand too close to him, cause no-one knows when or where he's going to get lick down for robbing people. Yeah, Bulargi's a nasty piece of work and I don't want to be anywhere near him when the shit hits the fan.

He wears all the latest trainers and garms, but Bulargi's an animal in human clothing. I mean, check this out – the dude got shanked twice in his first two years of living in England, but he didn't care. According to him, his scars are trophies and, as he says: "It's all part of the game fam and I'm just going to add them scars to my tribal marks." He normally tells me this while grinning or laughing out loud so I just leave him to carry on and do his thing.

"Nah fam," I say quickly "I'm going to work, I need to start work early, need to make the rest of the P for my mum's jacket." His eyebrows knot and his big, dark lips curl upwards. I don't know if he pities me, finds me funny or if he's disgusted that I work for my money and don't just go out there and rob it like he does.

"What, blood? You still on this work ting?" he says, holding his belly and laughing like he's black Santa. "That's not for me son, I've got a brand new, shiny blade and I'm getting quick quid my friend. Bro, my quid's are so quick I should have my own TV advert by now!" he laughs loudly.

"Quick quid's what it's all about fam. So I tell you what, when you're ready to put down them clippers and that old, shabby broom I'll show you the ropes and get you some real dough.

"And oh, yeah by da way," he looks at me with a big smile as he points at me, "I saw your mum an hour ago."

My head's real hot. Blood's boiling in the back of my throat. That always happens when some prick pisses me off and I know he's about to spit some shit, so before he even goes there I look him straight in his beady, black eyes.

"What did you just say blood? Don't even go there! That's my Mumsy. I'd live or die for that fam so don't get it twisted!" He sees I'm dead serious, so he soon changes his tune. But knowing Jacka, that calmness won't last too long.

"Calm down Carlts man, calm down. No disrespect. You need to get on this jacking ting, I can see the madness in your eyes and I think you could be good at it blood."

He's pointing his phone at me and is calm for now, but before things get nasty I lighten the mood by throwing a stupid joke into the equation. "Well, if I start jacking, who's going to trim your hair fam?"

"Yeah, you've got a point."

Then he spuds me and we walk our separate ways. "She did look buff, though, fam. Jeeze," he says over his shoulder, not even looking back at me.

What can I say? I hear it all the time cause I must admit mum's a well-made woman. Don't get me wrong, I know she's my mum and all that, but I definitely understand what them boys see in her. She's all natural and never wears make up; her skin's a flawless dark shade of brown, her eyes are brown too, but a slightly lighter shade than usual.

In all my days, I've never seen her in a weave like them other want-to-be black women on the road. Mum always told me, "Carlton, love the skin God put you in and love the hair he gave you. There's not one race of people on this planet with our hair apart from us and that, my son, makes us unique."

So yes, her hair remains natural and well kept; sometimes she wears it out, other times she braids it, but most of the time she wraps it in cloth and keeps it safe. She often tells me she's hiding her crown from European thieves. She says it with a big smile: "If the queen can steal the jewels on her crown from Africa and Asia, what makes you think she wouldn't steal my natural, beautiful crown?"

Mum's a little shorty and I'm passing her in height each and every day. She's slim and very curvy, but she never puts her goods on show. Mumsy always remains well covered, not cause she's ashamed of her body, but she always points at younger and older women and says in frustration, "By the time them woman get a husband the whole world would've done seen what that man's getting. Carlton, pick your wife by the way she carries herself."

To me, that makes a lot of sense, but I can't say I don't like it cause them girl show off their bodies like Freeview TV! I for one could watch all day, so I walk off proudly knowing that out of all the boys in school I have the buffest mum and all of them look past that jacket. But obviously, all I can see is that damn, dead-out jacket and all I think is, *It's got to go!*

I'm going to work until my fingers bleed to get that money.

Chapter 2
Hard Work Pays Better

I finally get to work with one thing on my mind. Yeah, you know what I'm chatting about: the P. I walk towards the barber shop; I can see through the big double windows with the logo on both sides that reads 'Welcome to Cut Above the Rest – the Right Choice'.

Yeah, you're damn right it's the right choice.

All them other wannabe barbers are trying to shorten man's pockets by opening up right down the road from us trying to put a man out of business. Like that's going to happen! The shop's been here for too long and it's the cornerstone of the community.

Anyway, allow me to continue. I push the door open and before the music hits me, I can smell that barbershop flavour. You know the one: it's like bay rum, oil sheen and them nasty boys' body odour. *Damn! Can't those boys spell 'wash'?* Now comes the sweet sound of Bob Marley as *One Love* seeps from the speakers, separating me from the world of Lil Wayne and Jay Z.

I just love that shop like it's my second home. It's a safe haven that keeps me off the streets and from doing what mum doesn't want me to do. As a matter of fact, when I think about it, it really *is* saving me. I love that shop and I love the sounds, the smell and the harmony that you can't get on the streets.

To me, every head's a blank canvas and I'm the Van Gogh of the barber world. I look around to see who's trimming. Damn, it's my lucky day! There are at least six boys waiting on the green and black bench that blends nicely with the green and black décor. Patrick, my boss, is already cutting one; I know if I move fast enough I can cut at least two heads before he's finished the one sitting in his chair cause he seems to be slowing down in his old age.

Funny thing is, he doesn't even look his age; my boss is 45, but looks 30. He just hasn't aged one bit from the time mum used to carry me to the shop to get my hair shaped neatly around the edges. I think it's cause he doesn't smoke, drink or rave that hard and he spends most of his free time in the gym, so you can imagine how bleach he looks. He's quite short and he crops his hair real close to hide the bald patch that's just starting to peek through the crown of his head. But trust me, it doesn't age him one bit.

His swag's on point, but he doesn't wear name brand clothes. In fact, he laughs at the guys that spend all their dough on one tracksuit. He's dead against spending all that P on clothes, not that he can't afford them, but cause he knows how much they cost to make. He looks at all those young boys and brands them 'useless consumers'. He gets you thinking cause he's on point and you won't see anyone else in the ends rocking his look.

"Yes Boss," I say as my biggest Carlton smile spreads across my boat race.

"What's up, Carlton. It's a bit slow today and, anyway, why you not at school?"

I've already planned for this question cause I'm smart like that.

"Nah, the shop looks busy and our teacher didn't turn up, so they sent us home early. Thought I'd come in and give you a hand – by the looks of it you're lucky I did." I smile again, knowing that's a blatant lie, but I back it up quickly with "Who's next?" I'm trying not to think out loud the calculations running through my head. I'll be walking out of the shop at the end of the day with fat pockets.

Then I hear one of them little, picky head boys say, "Nah fam, we're waiting for our boy," as he points to the dot in my boss's chair. Bloody hell man, why do they have to walk in the shop with some big, fuck off entourage like that little, ugly youth is damn Jay Z? Kiss my fucking teeth.

I'm totally pissed off, but I can't show it cause Patrick doesn't like any kind of street thing in his shop. My boss looks over his shoulder with a slight smile. "I told you it's a bit slow." So I just say, with the lamest grin ever, "It's cool boss, we can't have it good all the time."

Damn, man. It's dead out. It's like a graveyard shift and I need to make this P fast.

****

Patience is a blessing that you'll only accomplish by exercising patience. I'll never forget that saying my boss always told me when he first took me under his wing in Cut Above the Rest when I was nine.

"Sweep the floor," he'd say, "and empty the bins!" he'd bark with equal force.

"When can I get paid?"

He'd reply, "When you're more patient and when you stand and watch me cutting like I told you to."

Why the hell would I want to watch that crap? I'd rather be Sweeping and slaving just for a bit of cash that I'd spend at the tuck shop in school so it would make me look like I had more money than any of the other boys, and make the girls fall at my feet just for a bit of chocolate.

Patrick really started taking the piss when I was 11. One time, he waited for the busiest Saturday of the year and I was at the back eating lunch.

"Carlton! Come go shop for me," I heard him call from the front.

"OK boss. What do you want me to get?"

I wondered why he spoke so loudly that day. I also wondered why people were smirking on the sly.

"Go to the hardware store and get me a left-handed screw driver."

As I walked out of the shop with money in my hand, the place was in uproar; I just shrugged my shoulders and carried on.

Ten minutes later, I bust through the door totally pissed off and in a crazy rage. "What's up Carlton?" my boss said, fighting to contain the laughter that was desperate to burst out of his mouth like a tsunami.

"There's no such thing as a left-handed screw driver!" I exploded. Clients fell to their knees, people spat out their drinks and I was a laughing stock. I'd had enough. I ran to the back, my tears flooding the shop floor. He'd broken me. I could hear his footsteps as he came in after me.

"Carlton, what's the problem? Where are you going?" he snapped as I gathered my things.

"I've had enough." That's all I told him.

"You've had enough of what Carlton?" he asked sternly with one eyebrow raised.

I slammed my things on the ground. "I've had enough of being your slave! I've had enough of your silly jokes, I want …"

Patrick cut in. "So what do you want to do?" He frowned like he was waiting for an answer that he thought would never come.

"I want to cut hair!" I felt a weight lift from my chest. I felt brand new, like the man of my house, when my boss handed me a pair of pristine Wahl super tapered clippers with words I'll never forget.

"If you want to fly like an eagle, you can't fly with pigeons. Now you know your worth."

It was a hard lesson, but looking back I can overstand why he was so hard on me.

****

Three hours have gone, but it feels like a year. I've only got £20 in my pocket. Shit, man, is this ever going to happen any time soon? Why does time always seems to slow down? Whatever I do, it just drags on.

Got to leave the shop, man, cause nothing's happening here.

"Yo, Patrick, I'm gone for the day is that cool?"

"Yeah, that's cool. I'll see you on Saturday Carlton."

"OK, cool." I head for the door like my life depends on it cause it does. I have to get to the shop to put this £20 down on Mumsy's jacket before it closes. When I finally get there, I feel so dumb with one, little £20 note, but it has to be done cause like it or not I'll just end up spending it on some crap anyway. I've got to man-up, walk in and get *that* look from that little pebble-nosed girl.

I open the door, walk into the shop and don't see anyone there. I look across the floor and I still don't see anyone, so I call out, "Hello ... Hello!" There's no reply. *OK, this is my chance. I can get this jacket right now and not pay another penny for it. After all, I'm a good boy; I don't really do bad stuff. I can do it this once, it won't matter that much.* I think deeper about it. *Mum deserves this jacket, so why shouldn't I just jack it? I'm not hurting anyone.*

I walk slowly towards the mannequin in the window that's still wearing mum's jacket. Little beads of sweat start to run down the side of my temples. This is not what I do. I mean, I'm not that sort of kid, but it's an easy catch man.

My heart feels like it's about to jump out of my chest as my breathing speed up times two. The muscles in my neck start to stiffen up on me as I keep breaking my neck to look back to make sure the lady isn't watching me. My eyes are scanning for cameras on the wall as I stretch my hands out to undo the zip, so I can peel the jacket off the dolly, still occasionally looking over my shoulder to make sure I don't get busted.

I hear a noise coming from the back. I hurry away from the mannequin, nearly knocking over a rack full of designer shoes. Yeah, this shop's full of the best designer gear and if it was any other day I'd just grab the first thing my hands landed on and get the hell out of here, but in this case all I want is mum's jacket and I nearly had it. "Damn!" I mumble under my breath.

That's when I see the same girl from this morning's ritual come through a little door at the back of the shop carrying three boxes of shoes. She places them on the desk then she looks up, nearly jumping out of her skin, arms across her chest.

"Oi!" she snaps in a not very welcoming voice. "You scared the hell out of me."

I don't give a shit; I wish the bitch would have a heart attack so I can take what I came for. Saying nothing, I walk over, put my hand in my pocket and slowly pull out this one, mash-up £20 note. "I want to put this down on my jacket please and that will make it £100 left to pay."

Trust me, she ain't happy. Not one bit. "Are you serious?" she snaps. "£20? Is that all you can pay?" As she grabs at the money, waving it around, her voice gets louder, her face is more crumpled than the money I've just placed as neatly as I can in her small, pink hand. Her face's so red it's as though she's stripped of make-up.

"Look, there are people with money coming," she says with a stinking attitude.
I stop her in her tracks.

"Who the hell do you think you're talking to like that? You don't know me like that, so you better breathe easy or don't breathe at all. Are you feeling me?"

She sighs heavily, but calms down. Now the wrinkles disappear from her forehead and I can see the bright colours of her eyeshadow and blusher.

"All I'm saying is that there are people out there with money that come in and ask about that jacket every day and it's the last one we have in stock."

"Hold on, blood! If that's the last one in stock why the hell is it still in the window?"

Then she hits me with it as she places her right hand on her hip with a slight *I'm in control* smile, speaking nice and slow, as though she's talking to a kid in a nursery.

"Well, if you don't come to collect it in two days' time then I will have no choice but to sell it to the next person who asks for it and you will lose your deposit. That's our policy and that's how it is." She shifts her head to one side, cocks out her right hip and says, "Are you feeling me?"

Feisty bitch! Did you see how she flipped that on me? Now I flip out. "You what?" I growl through clenched teeth.

"Look, there's no need to shout, that's how it is. I'll hold it for you for one more day and that's all."

I know I can't win this war so I have to eat humble pie. "Cool, blood, I'll get the rest of the money, just don't sell that jacket." With that, I head to the door. What I really want to do is tell her about herself, but, as I said to her, breathe easy. I take my own advice. I walk out the shop with my pride in my mouth and no money in my pocket. How the hell is man going to get 100 notes by tomorrow?

I could call on my best friend Patrick, but he'd just do some dumbness to get the dough and that's out of the question cause he's on his third strike and after that it's the bin forever. Then it crosses my mind. It not only crosses my mind, it hits my head like a massive echo.

Jacka. I'm going to have to call on Jacka. As I start walking, I pass Cut Above the Rest. I gaze through the window. *Raaass*, look at the shop. It's mad busy now, but all the barbers are in and no barbers' chairs are available.

Chapter 3
First Blood

I swing on to Saint Bart's Road, past the massive, old, green metal rubbish bins.

Damn, those bins stink like a nasty brew of rotten food, piss and shit.

I'm just about to pass the alleyway when I hear a desperate mumble.

It's muffled as though someone's in a dentist's chair getting a wisdom tooth pulled and can't speak or scream.

But no mashed up tooth can compare with what I hear next.

"Shut up blood, before I shank you bare times! Give me your money and your phone!"

The voice is rough and deep. Little hairs stand up on the back of my neck in ripples. I want to look, but can't bring myself to. My body's boiling and terror pumps from my skin in streams of sweat.

Then I hear a key sentence.

"Look, you dickhead, I've got a brand new, shiny blade and if you don't want man to duppy you, give up the fucking tings."

No way! It can't be! I quietly peep around the corner and down the alleyway, trying hard not to be spotted; fear's creeping in like it's me at the end of the blade. Wiping beads of sweat off my eyelashes, I see a man with a black hooded top wrapped around his head and face. That explains the mumbles. He's a short guy, about five feet six, wearing a white shirt, red tie and well pressed black trousers. He has shiny black shoes that are about to turn a nice shade of red if he doesn't empty his pockets fast cause standing over him, wearing a black t-shirt, is a very dark-skinned, six feet tall Jacka. And we all know Jacka's a spiteful little cunt.

What the hell happened to that squeaky voice?

"Give ... up ... da ... blood ... clart ... tings!" Each word's followed by a spot-on punch to the man's head. Now, you remember when mum said it's not what you say, it's how you say it? Well, you better believe that guy on the receiving end has his whole life flashing before him and is frozen in time.

"Is that all you got pussy, five bills an' a fucking iPhone?"

What does he mean, *Is that all he's got?* Forget the phone, that's going to get blocked asap anyways. But five bills! Five bills! Is Jacka crazy? Blood, that would be more than enough for me, so why complain? What the hell is this?

Here it goes again, my head gets hot and I can taste blood in the back of my throat. It runs through my head like a bull on smack.

I can do this. It's not so bad.

For some reason, it seems to turn me on, no homo. It flashes across my mind like bright A4 Audi headlights. If I do this, I'll be able to get Mumsy's jacket and have a whole load of change left over. Most importantly, I'll be untouchable.

I hear that deep voice again. It comes with intent; it comes with power and anger, spite and a touch of sarcasm. Jacka says softly, "Wet this for me blood."

Then I hear a scream. Not a girlie scream, but a scream that properly shakes me up. I look on in shock. Jacka got what he wanted, so why's he gone so far? Why?

Do you remember when you were younger and you used to pour blackcurrant juice in a glass of clear water and watch it spread and fill the entire glass, turning it deep purple?

Well, the poor guy's white shirt is turning bright red as his blood spreads out, consuming the right side of his body as it flows from between his ribs.

My legs are screaming, "Carlton! Run!" so I do just that.

This evening's hard for me. I'm finding it hard to settle. For once, I'm glad that mum works late. She won't be around to see the fear in my eyes cause she can read me like a book. I've seen my first ever stabbing and on top of that I still have the jacket problem.

I've got a couple of hours to calm down. I have to stick firmly to my plan to make my way down to the ends to meet up with Jacka. He doesn't know I'm coming and I don't even want to go. I heard he was a nasty piece of work, but seeing him in action confirms it. I know I need to get a link from him to make this P and I know he's the only one that can give it to me, but after what I saw, jacking's definitely out of the question.

I start to make my way to the strip, which is a little meeting place in East Ham outside the Hartly Centre where everyone gathers daily. It's good in a good way, but bad in a very bad way.

If you don't know anyone and happen to pass through, there's a strong possibility that you'll get shanked or just wrapped up if you're lucky. On the other hand, you can get anything here, from the latest smartphone to drugs, or even a brand new strap if the money's right.

I don't go there much cause those guys have no code of conduct and any one will try and move to a man if they're hungry enough. So when the drought is high, it's best to stay away.

I get to the strip and all I can see are bare hoodies huddled up like sheep trying to keep warm cause it's cold as hell out here.

As a matter of fact, it's the coldest winter ever, but the guys I'm about to meet are colder than any winter I've ever known.

Man, I can't spot Jacka. I look harder. Lo and behold, there he is, standing tall and darker than ever under that hoodie.

Chapter 4
Dancing With the Devil

"Yo, Jacka!" I call out.

He turns around, stone-faced. Boy, that guy's one scary dude. He looks over, not knowing who's calling him, like he's preparing himself for war or retreat. That's what happens when you live your life like you carry a spare one in your pocket.

I know there ain't time for any long talk with him, much less to stand too close for too long, so I walk over and make my face clear.

"Yo, Carlton, what you saying fam? Man could've got ghosted out here bruv. You got to move easy around me bro. What's up anyway? You finally come for your training, blood? LOL.

"What, that job not making you enough P fam? Well don't worry bro, when I teach you the art of jacking you're going to buy your mum a brand new wardrobe."

Damn, that guy talks a lot, but it's all a daze cause I can't erase that moment of madness I saw earlier from my brain. I can't even look at him too hard cause he'll clock that I know something and the question will be about *what* I know, so I try to act as normal as possible.

"Nah fam, I told you I'm not on that, but for real Jacka, I need P, bro, and I've got till tomorrow to make it."

Am I mumbling? Am I stuttering? I just don't feel right chatting to this freak. I know what he's capable of and I don't want anything from him, but I do need this.

I need it badly. If you were in my shoes, what would you do?

Jacka just looks at me sternly, like he's trying to read me. I swear I've stopped breathing. Does he know I saw him or something?

But then he smiles. Geeze, I thought I was a goner.

"Cool, fam. As you're my boy, how much do you need?"

"Only 100 notes bro."

Jacka bursts out laughing so loudly he makes me almost jump out of my skin. I'm not going to lie, I nearly touch cloth cause I think he's going to move to me for wasting his time.

"Ha ha! What? I'm sure you mean £1,000 bruv cause you're not talking about £100."

I have to act like I'm not scared and that I know what I'm saying. "Nah fam, £100 is all I need. No more, no less, but if more comes I'd be a dickhead to turn it down, you get me."

I hold my breath again as I watch Jacka rubbing his chin, looking to the ground in deep thought.

"Mmm, OK, look Carlts," he finally says, lifting his hands, "I'm going to line you up. You can do this two ways. Option one, I can teach you the jacking trade cause I know you'd be good at it ..." Jacka's voice is a distant echo as my mind goes crazy. I see the shank come down hard and fast before it ends up deep in that guy's side. I never knew the man, but I felt sorry for him, I felt his fear and it properly shook me up. It was a fear that I won't forget in a hurry.

On the flip side, it was a fear that I'd love to own and that's the worst fear of all.

Damn, what am I thinking? Snap out of it you fool.

Then Jacka loses it. That soon wakes me up.

"Yo! Blood! Are you wasting man's time, fam?" he barks through clenched teeth as his eyes almost cut me in two. "Cause unless you're feeding man's belly you better wake the fuck up and listen or fuck off and go cut hair or some shit like that!"

Rah! That came from nowhere; I swear my eyes nearly pop out of my head.

"Yeah, yeah, sorry fam, I was just thinking about option one. What's option two?" I ask to rush this shit along and not get slapped up in the process.

"OK, have I got your damn attention now? If you waste my time again your third option is going to be A&E."

I know he means it, so I'm wide-eyed and fully awake like I'm waiting for the winning lottery ticket numbers on Saturday night.

"You see them two olders sitting over there?" he gestures with his eyes.

"Yeah, I see them," I say confidently.

"Them man there are big fish in the game and they're always recruiting runners."

I don't like the sound of that, all I need is £100, not a prison sentence. "For what, Jacka?"

Then he loses it again. What am I doing here, talking to this bloody nutter? He's way out of my league.

"Look blood, shut the fuck up! Listen and I'm not going to tell you again." His face is screwed up and his eyes are turning from a dull shade of white to a deep, pinkish red; he's really getting mad and that ain't what I came for.

"Right. Are you done opening your mouth now?" he pauses for a beat, searching my eyes, "OK, them man move big amounts of food and they're always recruiting young blood to move it for them."

I think he sees my face seeking confirmation about what kind of food he means.

"You know: the hard food."

Fearlessly, I flip out cause that's the same shit my old man got banged up for.

"What? Crack fam?"

"Keep it down fam," he whispers, moving his hands to hush my voice. "Yeah, crack, it's big P right now and that's option two. Now choose one."

I'm thinking I'm going to end up just like my old man.

But it needs to be done, just one small move then I'm out of it.

Then Jacka says something real funny and I'm not talking funny in a laughing way.

"But Carlts, for real, I'd rather you go for option one fam cause them man there move proper dirty."

What, you mean dirtier than some dickhead who shanks people for no reason? Them man must move *proper* dirty then, but I try not to think that out loud.

"OK Jacka, I'm going with option two, so just line it up, yeah," I say as I brush him off. I can see that Jacka's a bit disappointed that I didn't choose to become his little apprentice, or, should I say, goon.

"OK, OK, cool bro, but just know that whatever happens, it's your choice and you owe me a drink for this, yeah."

"For real, Jacka, you should know me better than to tell me that. Blood, just link me."

"OK, cool. I'm going to go chat to them, wait for my call. But you see the real skinny guy?"
I look across. "Yeah I see him."

"That man there got OCD, so whatever you do, don't even try to spud man or he's going to take you to a next level, you get me?" Then he walks off with that lame swagger.

Chapter 5
I Smell a Snake

I watch him speak to them. Damn, they look so shady. A lot of countries think us English boys got no balls, but I'd never want to be caught slipping on a dark night with them breathing down the back of my neck, even if I was their family, and you better believe that.

Why is this guy taking so long? Argh man, I ain't got time for this! Finally, Jacka gives me the signal to come over. About time too.

My gut's telling me my life's about to change and not for the better.

It seems like only yesterday that mum was crying when the judge gave my dad ten years in the bin and I can hear her saying, "I just want the best for you Carlton. Go to school and get a good education, but most importantly stay away from all those bad youths out there."

I knew what she was really saying: "Don't end up like your dad."

I can see her eyes streaming tears from losing dad and if I don't play my cards right, there's a high possibility she'll lose her son. Yes, the walk is long and what should be ten seconds seems like a lifetime. Now I see it's not just words that can stop time, but actions too and the activity I'm about to willingly partake in will soon make me realise my life's about to change forever.

As I get closer, I take a look at the thugs I'm about to meet. I scan them hard; they're both olders, about 20 or so. One of them is short, a bit stocky and light skinned. As I get closer I can just about make out his hazel eyes.

He looks mixed race or some shit like that. His garms are proper on point, apart from that big ass afro sticking out the side of his black snap-back cap. He's in sportswear, all blacked out from head to toe. All them mans in the ends who get up to no good wear black like they can't be spotted.

He's sporting a black tracksuit; it looks like it's fresh off the racks and his trainers are amazing with a matt black tick. I've never even seen them before, but they're looking too sharp for him and I know *I* could kick them better.

What stands out most is the big gap between his front teeth and his constant smile. He just smiles all the time. I can see his mouth moving as he talks, but he keeps smiling with them big ass lips. That's some messed up shit. I mean, with a gap as wide as that why the hell wouldn't you try your best to keep your mouth closed?

I'm getting closer. *What the fuck am I getting myself into?* Like I don't already know.

Now, the next guy's the complete opposite. This guy's a little bit shorter and he's just like some yardie, fresh off the boat. By the look of his ashy-pale, dark skin he's been getting high on his own supply. He's also wearing black and has a number one hair cut with a bald fade.

He's trying to cover up the fact that he has a little sunroof thing going on; in other words he's going bald. He looks crazy, like an old man with discoloured teeth that blend nicely with his gold tooth. His dark skin merges with his black tracksuit and on his feet are plain, black Nike trainers.

When I was a younger, Mumsy used to warn me that if I pulled a face and the wind changed my face would stay like that forever.

I wonder whether his mum ever warned him about that cause his face looks like a monkey sucking on a lemon while watching a horror film. Or maybe he's mistaken me for some dude that lashed his girl. Either way, his face ain't changing for one second.

But the main thing that stands out about him is the strong stench of skunk. It's getting stronger and stronger and the closer I get the more I believe that my eyes are going to bleed.

This guy can't have any money cause he looks like a top of the top tramp. He's well skinny and about eight stones. There's no smile and no expression on his face at all. He simply stares into space with his beady, black eyes.

As I get closer, I can see he's holding a packet of wet wipes. He's constantly cleaning his hands like he just finished playing in mud – or just finished killing someone.

Even though he's like a total crackhead, the closer I get, the faster my heart races. It's pumping as fast as the funky house tune I listen to on my smartphone.

Rah man, I thought Jacka was scary. He just lost his position.

I try to break the ice firmly, so I walk over to the scariest looking alpha male.

"Wah gwaan blood?"

I extend my fist to spud him, totally forgetting that Jacka warned me not to. From nowhere comes a loud, thick voice followed by the strong smell of skunk.

"What fam? Do you know me? What am I, your fucking old man? Step the fuck off before I duppy you blood!"

What the hell did I do? This guy just switches up differently, spitting and all sorts. You know what? I'm going to keep my mouth shut till I'm spoken to.

Remember, I've never run with the wolves. I may have skanked a cab here and there, but these are big boys I'm dealing with now, so I can't afford to slip even an inch.

The one who seems like the second guy in command calms my fear with a smile.

"Peace fam, peace. Snake don't like to be chatted to by peeps he don't know. But I'm cool like that; as long as man don't pass his place. You get me fam?"

Just as I get comfortable, his face changes and that crazy ass smile disappears.

It's replaced with a brisk *I'm going to kill you if you cross the line* look. Then that big smile explodes again. Jeeze! I think Christmas has come early, I'm so happy to see that dumb, fake smile.

"They call me Smiley," he says as he extends his fist to spud me, "and that guy who wanted to shank you, they call him Snake."

I hear him, but I just want to keep conversation to a minimum. "OK, cool, Smiley." I smile back lamely, knowing these guys don't deserve a big Carlton grin that only belongs to Mumsy. Then Jacka butts in.

"Yo man, I'll leave you all to it. Good luck, Carlts. Yo, Snake, ding me when you're ready, you get me."

Snake nods. "It's cool. When we cross over the tings, man will ding you."

Snake looks at me and smiles for the first time since I saw him, which feels like forever.

Why's he smiling?

Is it for a good reason, or is it the smile of a clown? You know a clown's smile means sarcasm and pain.

Snake's too laidback for my liking, but Smiley doesn't waste any time. He dives straight into business and that's great by me cause business is all I want, as much as I want to get the fuck out of here.

"So I hear you want to make dough fam?" Talk about space invader, man's all up in my face with that big, dumb ass smile.

"Yeah I do," I say sternly, moving my face back and trying my best to act like I'm some kind of bad man. But before I even finish my sentence, Snake starts to wile out yet again.

"What da fuck is dis, huh? A family, fucking reunion? Jus take da pussy troo da ropes!" He strolls off, mumbling under his breath, "If man slip up, man's going to get ghosted quickly."

Smiley just laughs; I think he wants to keep me cool.

"Don't watch him blood. He's a big softy, but only when it comes to any of his eight kids. Anyone else don't stand a chance apart from me of course, you get me. So what's your name fam?"

"Carlton," I say, still trying to keep my eye on the nutter as he walks off.

"Carlton what?" Smiley asks harshly as he raises an eyebrow.

"Carlton Williams." Why all these questions? Something tells me to get the hell out of here, but I'm curious. You know what they say don't you? Curiosity killed the cat. I hope that's all it kills.

"OK, cool Carlton. So where you live?"

"I'm from the ends, bro, just down the road. Why?"

His face and that big ass, dumb smile are too close for comfort. "Don't watch that, it's calm. Just take me there, innit."

Now he's got my back up. I feel like I'm about to do business with me, him the nutter and mum and I don't like the thought of that.

"What for fam? I just need to make this dough. I just need a quick fix-up blood, so what's that got to do with my yard?"

"Well, Carlton, the first line of business is to meet mum innit?"

"What da fuck do you need to meet my mum for, blood?"

"Look Carlton, calm down man. Jacka told me you're a bit of a wild one when it comes to your mum, but I didn't think it was that bad. Look, cut the crap innit. So do you want to make P or not? The decision's yours."

That serious look crosses his face yet again like some game show host who really wants me to pick the right question to win the big cash prize.

Now, who's the maddest nutcase out of this pair? Is it the guy that smiles for nothing or the one who only smiles for something?

By the looks of him, it's not anything good to smile about at all. I'm baffled, believe you me. I'm bloody baffled.

Wouldn't you be? Would you call it a day, or would you run with the wolves?

I decide to run with the wolves.

"Yeah, I do want to make this money bro."

Then that big smile returns like it never left. So we take a long walk on a short path, if you get what I mean. This was by far the longest walk ever.

We were better off taking a cab, but even if I wanted to take a cab I couldn't get one.

The amount of cabs I've skanked, I can't afford to be caught slipping.

I only live like three minutes down the road but, man, it's a long walk. My mind's racing. Why does he want to see Mumsy? I'm truly lost now for real. I hope mum has a late night at work, I hope she stops for a game of bingo or goes to Calabash to buy some hard food for dinner. I just hope she's anywhere but home. Usually, I'm always hoping that she gets home before dark, but not now.

Then the worst of the worst comes to light.

Chapter 6
Meeting the Parent

"Carlton? Carlton! Where you going?"

I turn around and who do I see? Well, put it this way, it's the last person on Earth that I want to see. It's Mumsy.

"Hi mum, I'm going home."

Smiley's eyes are like fireworks on bonfire night.

"Rah fam, is that your mum? Blood, she's …"

Before Smiley can say another word I flip out. I tell him calmly, but forcefully through clenched teeth, "Blood, don't disrespect. That's my Mumsy an' if you ever dis, it's going to have to be a next ting."

It's amazing how you can change your voice when you want someone to properly take notice of what you're saying. Now I see and understand why Jacka changed his voice when he shabazzed that guy.

"Cool fam, I was *just saying*."

I reinforce my position. "Nah, bro, you don't need to *just say* anything. Trust me, when it comes to my mum just don't say a word." I think he's got the message. Well, I hope he's got it cause if he hasn't what will I do? Don't forget these are the big boys I'm tangling my insane self with now.

"Cool bro. It's good you got a lot of love for your mum, it makes my job easier."

What the fuck does he mean *it makes his job easier*? Before I can ask him …

"Hello Miss Williams, I'm Jason, but they call me Smiley."

Smart bastard, I'm going to pull him up on that later, trust me.

"Oh, hello Jason. I can see why they call you Smiley," says mum then she only goes and says what I'm dreading. "Carlton, are you going to invite your friend in for a drink?"

Sometimes, I wish mum wasn't so damn polite. But how's she supposed to know? She always thinks her good boy only keeps good company. How wrong is she? Trust me, I don't feel proud, not one bit. I try to put my foot in the door.

"Nah mum, he's ..."

Smiley blurts out, "Oh, thank you Miss Williams, I'm really thirsty."

And as he does, she falls for it. "He's very polite isn't he? That's good, Carlton. These are the friends you need to keep around you. He must have a lovely family."

"Yes mum," I say in a huff.

Smiley just looks at me with that big, old fake smile as mum rubs it in a little bit more. "And look at him Carlton, he hasn't stopped smiling since I met him."

Smiley puts one foot through the door and I can't help but think I've just let a nutter into my yard. Will he ever leave and why's he here anyway?

Smiley sits on the sofa and I sit on the chair opposite him, so I can keep my eyes firmly on that big smile. "Nice house Miss Williams." He just keeps rattling on, trying to make intelligent conversation – not.

"Yes Jason, I worked hard for it and it's not easy," says mum as she walks in and hands Smiley a glass of squash. "When you grow up, leave school and get a good job, you'll know what it's like to work hard."

"Yes Miss Williams, for me school comes first," he says, downing half of the juice, "and making money comes later," as he downs the last half. "Thanks for the drink," he smirks, handing the glass back to her.

"You're welcome Jason. Any time you want to pass and see Carlton, just feel free to pop round."

Smiley looks at me with a different smile. *Bloody hell*, I better get this guy out of my yard before mum tells him it's too late to walk the street at this time and he can spend the night if he wants. Why she spoke to him about school only God knows cause he looks older than she does. I'm just about to flip out and tell him to leave, blowing everything right out the water, when he saves the day and the mission that will help me cop mum's brand new coat. "Thank you Miss Williams, I'll definitely do that. I've

got to go now, got homework
to do."

Damn! The guy's good and I mean real good.
He nearly had me thinking he's my age for a minute.
Smiley looks into my eyes, deep into my eyes like
he's trying to tell me something and I know it's
something I don't want to hear.

"Are you going to walk me to the door
then bro?"

With a strong sense of relief, I blurt out, "Yep
let's go!" Truth is, I can't get him out the door fast
enough. He takes one more look at mum before he
walks out and then turns his attention to me. "Yo,
Carlton. Meet me at the strip tomorrow at 12 and
don't be late or I'm going to have to come back and
knock for you and maybe mum will give me a stiffer
drink next time, you get me."

"OK, I'll be there. Just leave."
At this point, I just want the freak to fuck off. He
turns one more time as though he's trying to rub salt
deep into my eyes so I can really see what he's
saying.

"Bye Miss Williams. Hope to see you again
real soon."

"Bye Jason, go straight home, OK."

Chapter 7
Same Shit, Different Hour

The night's flying past, maybe cause I don't want to do this anymore.

That's what happens when you try to slow down time: it just gets faster.

I leave my yard reluctantly and I'm on my way to the strip. Why do these short walks still feel like a lifetime? I reach the strip, but I don't see Smiley anywhere.

Where's this guy, man?

It's as cold as hell out here. With my hands deep in my pockets, I keep walking in the hope that he's near. Then I hear a voice again, but it ain't Smiley's.

"Yo! Pussy hole!... Come here."

Why, why, why does it have to be him?

I turn around and see the devil himself swagging in the shade like the snake he is. I keep my head held high and look him straight in his face as I walk towards him, struggling to maintain my composure.

"Don't try it blood, I can smell the fear on you … it smells like a virgin bitch about to take cock."

Why ain't Smiley here instead of this mad man? I walk over to him; every step feels like my worlds about to shut down.

"Come closer." He raises his voice. "Closer!"

I could smell the strong skunk on his breath, but what happens next nearly stops my heart. I hear a click and feel cold metal against my temple.

"Do you know what this is blood?" he says slowly as he presses the barrel against my head.

Now I know what fear really is. It's like a snowman standing in the middle of a park, frozen, as a wicked little kid stands in front of him holding a bucket of hot water.

"Yeah, I know what it is."

I get the shivers, but with all the shit swimming through my head I don't know if it's cause I'm scared or cold.

"What is it fam? What is it?" he snaps through menacing teeth.

"It's a strap." I'm shaking like booty meat.

"That's right. It's a nine-milly and it ain't no reborn. This shit makes a lot of noise, bitch, but it attracts a lot of attention and that's why I choose to use *this* instead." He reaches down as he pulls out an old, long ass, rusty machete; he holds the blade just under my neck.

"Now, dis don't make any noise – only when it cuts through bone." He looks at the blade like it's his best friend. "I like dis cause I can get up nice, close and personal wit' dis shit an' I can tek my time," now he turns his attention back to me. "Do you know what I mean?"

I can't get the words out fast enough: "Yeah, I get you fam!"

"I hear your mum's a peng ting."

Why does he have to bring mum into it? The thought of him mentioning my mum with his skunk-smelling breath properly pisses me off. I speak to myself like a mad man. *Carlton get that taste out your mouth and get it out fast.* I know it's Mumsy, but this fucking dickhead has a machete and a 9mm handgun to my head.

I swallow hard and let him talk. He reaches into his man bag. What's this mad bastard going to pull out next? But as his hand comes out to play yet again, I see it's a plastic bag and he holds it out towards me.

"I'm going to give you this charlie. It's worth two bags, that's £2,000. I'm going to give you an address; all you do is drop it there an' pick up the cash, but know this ..." He looks directly into my eyes. "If you lose it you pay, if you get sucked you pay, if you get nicked you pay cause if you don't pay I'm gonna to take a trip round your yard with Smiley.

I'm going to fuck your buff, little mummy with this blade. After I've fucked her, Smiley might get some as well cause he can't stop chatting about that bitch."

It dawns on me why Smiley wanted to meet mum. He came so he had not just my life in his hands, but hers too. If I even think about crossing him or Snake, it will be all over before I get to spend their drugs money. But that wouldn't have crossed my mind. All I want is enough money to get my mum's jacket before that bitch sells it to the next person who asks for it. Now I know if anything happens to their stash, I'll have to pay no matter what happens.

Jeeze. This guy's flipping out again! "What blood? You got something to say? Well, have yah? LOL. Nah, I didn't think so. Deliver and you get five bills. Don't deliver and mum gets fucked, then *you* get fucked. Here's the address. Now fuck off!"

I grab the stash and can't get away fast enough. But then he calls me back.

"Oh yeah, you forgot something."

I turn around. Baw! The slap comes hard and fast, lights flash in front of my eyes in different colours and directions. I felt like my nose was about to pour with blood. That dickhead! I just want to kill that wasteman! *Should I go for the 9mm, or should I just look at the bigger picture*? And what's the bigger picture? Am I fast enough to snatch that 9mm or not? *Think. Think. Think Carlton*. Er, nah I don't think so.

Patrick A. Phipps

"Now, you prick, that's called a bitch slap and the next bitch to get slapped is gonna be your mumz! Now bring me my dough."

I put my head, my ego, and everything else in my mouth and just walk away. Never in my life have I ever been boyed like that before. But as long as I'm the only one that knows about it I can live with it. I walk away and hear Snake shouting, alongside the ringing in my ear drum.

"Take the ting straight to your yard, drop it off tomorrow and don't forget that slap!"

I look back. He's on his mobile making a call. I push the drugs deep inside my jacket pocket. Blood, I'm never going to forget that slap and he better believe it like his life depends on it. But that thought only echoes through my head.

Reality hits home. *What the fuck am I doing?*

The one thing Mumsy tried to steer me away from, I've just jumped into headfirst. Is that jacket worth it? Cause I'm beginning to think that my mum looks great in that old, raggedy jacket, but I know she can look and feel like a rock star in the new one. The way things are going, is the jacket still going to be there when I go for it? Argh! Now this is more than a jacket, this is our life. Big up. Kmt, blood, how hard can this be? All I've got to do is turn this corner, walk two minutes then I'm home safe and dry.

Chapter 8
Triple Darkness

Have you ever been at home watching your favourite TV programme or playing your PSP and the lights just cut out cause no-one put money on the electricity key? Let me put it this way: *Who turned out the damn lights in da middle of the street*? That's right, the lights are out and I can't breathe, I'm shouting, but it's muffled. What the hell's going on?

I hear a voice.

"Free up da tings blood!"

It's the same voice I heard in the alleyway; it's the same voice that made me too scared to look.

It's the same fucking voice that Jacka used to jack that guy.

Oh fuck. I'm dizzy with fear, my heart doesn't even beat on time, it skips like a kid on Christmas day waiting to open his presents.

Please don't say it, don't say it. Then I hear that voice again.

"Blood, give me da tings before ..."

Time stops as I wait for his next words. *Please don't say them, I beg you*. But then they creep out like thieves in the night.

"I shank you bare times!"

My legs crumble. The nightmare's reality. I can see Jacka shanking that guy in the alleyway; it just plays over and over like a bad tune. The last thing I remember is a voice, a messed up, squeaky voice, "Pussy hole." I feel a sharp pain in my left kidney. The pain's so violent, then there's darkness and I mean triple darkness. I pass out.

After what seems like hours, I wake up on the cold, concrete floor. I feel my side, frantically searching for any sign of blood, but there ain't any. That dickhead must've hit me hard cause my side hurts like hell, yet more fear's to come, fear that I've been dreading. *Where are the damn drugs?* I start to panic. Damn, man, where?

I pat myself down and check the floor around me, under cars and anywhere my eyes can see. But they've gone, along with my jacket.

You're dead, you're dead echoes through my mind. Then the voice corrects itself. *I mean you're both dead, LOL.* A hollow feeling seeps into and around me as clarity crashes into my brain like a hostile meteor.

Wiping the sweat from my eyes, I look at my watch. Rah blood, how long was I out for? It's coming up to 8pm and Mumsy must be at home by now.

How the hell am I going to get in my yard without my jacket? I can hardly walk cause my side's killing me. Then my phone rings that stupid tone that separates it from all the rest, that stupid Blackberry tone. Why didn't Jacka take my phone? And that makes me start to think harder.

"Hello!" I say in a half loud, half pained voice.

"Hello son. Is that how you talk to your mother? Where are you and what time are you getting home?"

Trying to keep as calm as I can and trying to take the pain out of my voice, I say, "I'm out mum. I don't know what time I'm getting home."

Now the shock comes.

"Well Carlton, you better get home soon because your friend is here, him and his brother have been here for hours.

"I've being ringing your phone, but it kept ringing out and going to voice mail. Are you OK? You don't sound good to me."

You damn right I don't sound good cause apart from the wicked pain in my kidney I just signed our death warrants. Those dickheads are in my yard and that makes every single hair on my body scream.

"*What friend mum?*" I snap, then I catch myself. "Sorry mum, I've had a real bad day. I mean, what friend?"

"OK, I'll let you off this time. It's your friend Jason."

"Who?" I say frantically. Now my insides rise into my mouth.

"Your friend, Smiley. He's here with his brother."

I can hear the concern starting to rugby tackle her mind.

"Carlton, what's the matter with you?"

"Mum, I'm OK. Please put him on the phone."

"No Carlton, just come home. They're both eating."

I lose the plot, forgetting mum's the best when it comes to throwing wobblies.

"Mum! Just put Smiley on!"

"Carlton, who the hell do you think you're talking to?" she yelps. "You better mind how you're talking cause you're not too big to hold licks. Do you understand me Carlton?"

I'm lost for words.

"Do you understand me Carlton Emmanuel Williams?"

"Yes mum. Sorry."

Without her saying another word, Smiley comes on the phone.

"Yo! Carlton man, where you been? We've been waiting for you for hours and why you upsetting your mum?"

I freak out. "Cut the long talk. What da fuck are you doin' in my yard and who are you wit'?"

Smiley tries to act cool like it's OK to be sitting in my yard drinking out of my cup and eating out of my fucking plate.

"Yeah Carlts, it's just me and my bro Snake. You remember Snake don't you?"

Blood rises in the back of my throat. "Get da fuck out my yard fam! I'm being real. Get out now!"

Smiley starts to patronise me, I can hear it in his voice and I can see that big old smile spreading across his face. And I can see Snake just sitting there, looking at mum with those devilish, black eyes.

He's such a rude cunt. I don't even think he said hello to her, the prick.

"Look bro, we got them two tools you wanted. You know the ones? I think Snake showed them to you today at some point. Do you want me to give them to your mum?"

Now terror sets in. What the hell have I got myself into? What am I thinking doing this shit for some blasted jacket?

I've got to get them out of my yard. "No!" then I say it a bit calmer, "No bro, just leave." Is it possible to hear a smirk in someone's voice?

"Are you sure cause I can give it to her right now, you get me?" I can see that big ass smile beaming through the phone.

"No Smiley, please just leave."

"OK, but did you pick up the game from your boy that we sent you for?"

My heart skips a beat.

Should I or shouldn't I tell them the truth? Should I tell them someone's holding their stash? That someone robbed one of their runners? Would they want to get even to keep their rep or is it up to me to pay regardless?

I know I have to lie and I have to lie convincingly cause Snake's already told me if I fuck up, I'll have to pay.

I have to let them believe the shit's still in my pocket cause that mad man Snake is in my yard with my mum and only God knows what he's capable of. "Nah, I haven't delivered yet, Snake told me to drop it off tomorrow. But I will, I've got it in my pocket right now." I'm rubbing my fingers together hoping they'll fall for it.

"OK Carlts, safe. I'll meet you on the strip tomorrow at 10pm sharp. Bring the ting and don't be late, yeah." Sweat's pouring off me like heavy rain. I'm shaking like a crackhead going cold turkey.

"Now just leave my yard, please bro."

"Cool, but that's no way to talk to your friends, kicking us out of your yard in the cold like that is it now (giggle)? But it's cool, we're gone."

The phone goes dead. I have to get home quick. On the way, I start to put two and two together.

Why was Jacka chatting to them guys for so long on the strip before he gave me the link?

What did Snake mean by *I will call you when the time comes?*

Why did Jacka leave me with my phone and only take my jacket?

Why did he jack me in the first place when he knew I never had any dough and he must've known the drugs belonged to Snake and Smiley?

He knew I was using them to make dough to buy mum's jacket.

Most importantly, why did those two dickheads find themselves round my yard so early

when we planned to drop off the shit tomorrow?
Naahh ... how could I not see? ...It was a set-up.

Chapter 9
The Phone Call

Let's go back in time.

Snake slaps me, then as I walk away I look back and he's making a call. This is what he says: "Yo blood, what you mean who is it? Haven't you got my number saved? It's Snake."

"Yo Snake, wha gwaan? Did you give him the tings?"

"Yeah, the pussy got the stuff on him now. He put it in his inside jacket pocket, all I want you to do is jack the boy, but don't shank him."

"Why not?"

"What you mean, *why not*? Cause if you do, we can't get the fuckin dough dickhead."

"Oh, seen … I get you. Where is he?"

"He's on his way home, get it done, take everything, but don't take his phone – an' Jacka: …don't… fuck …up."

Do you see what those dickheads did?

****

Smiley and Snake leave my yard.

"Yo Smiley, let me call Jacka cause that pussy

hole says he still got the ting and I don't want the dickhead to check it and find out it's just baking powder."

"Yo Jacka, it's Snake."

"Yeah Snake, what's up fam?"

"What you mean *what's up*? Did you jack the boy or not?"

Kiss my teeth, "of course I did, long time man. I don't own this name for nothing, blood."

"Well how comes certain man are chatting about he's still got the tings?"

"Yo Snake, mans is bluffing cause I've got it in my hand right now.

"He's playing you fam and by the looks of it you're not the only one getting played out here cause you played him big time. It's like one big playground. I'm just sitting here laughing my arse off."

Snake starts to get real irritated. "And what do you mean by that, blood?"

"Come on, Snake. You know and I know this shit is baking soda, but it's cool cause man's going to shift that to some prick for fifteen hundred, you get me."

"Blood, do what you want. I don't give a shit about that. All I know is that dickhead's got to be shitting himself right now! So did you shank him? He sounded like he was in a lot of pain? I told you not to shank him."

"Calm down blood. I didn't shank him. He's my boy, why would I want to duppy him? All I did was put my size elevens in his kidney just to make it look good, you get me."

Snake starts to LOL, not the normal laugh, cause road man don't ever laugh normally, they just kind of pretend to laugh. "Oh, Jacka. He's your boy, yeah. So is that how you treat your boy? I tell you what, you was better off killing that pussy cause if he don't get my one and a half grand by tomorrow night he's a dead man walking. Do you get me?"

"Well Snake, it sounds like he hasn't got any choice now does he?"

"Exactly. Nice doing business with you. Your favour to me is clear now until next time cause you know there's going to be a next time. You're a nasty piece of work but someone's got to do it." Then Snake locks the phone off.

****

I'm outside my front door. I open it slowly and all the lights are off. I call out.

"Mum? Mum, you OK?" No reply. I get that taste in my mouth again and I'm switching to suicide mode. I call again: "Mum!"

"Yes Carlton! I'm in bed and I have to wake up early for work tomorrow. Make sure you reach home early, I may have a surprise for you."

Exhale. *What a relief.* And as for the surprise, I know it's going to be a big, homemade slap-up meal. She does that once in a while, but truth is I've had enough surprises for one day; I'm just glad she's safe.

"OK mum. Oh yeah, I forgot to tell you."

"Yes Carlton," she says in an irritated voice.

"I love you mum, more than you could ever know."

Her voice calms. "I love you too baby boy."

I'm in bed, lying on my back, looking up at my ceiling until the sand man takes me away for a few hours.

I don't know how I'll get to sleep with so much on my mind, but I've got to get up early for school and leave before mum does. Tomorrow, I don't want her to walk me to school, I don't want her to see the fear in her baby boy's eyes and I definitely don't want her to take me through that damn ass daily ritual.

I toss and turn in pain and fear and everything else that comes with being a dickhead. Whatever Jacka hit me with, he hit me good and proper, but tomorrow I'll repay the compliment.

Chapter 10
Taking Back My Pound in Flesh

I'm up and out the door with no time to play morning games with Mumsy, no time for that dumb morning ritual and definitely, most definitely, no time for school. I've got my hoodie on and my shank's deep in my waist. Guess where I'm off to? Well I'm not off to see Wizard the Wonderful Wizard of Oz if you get my meaning.

I'm going to Jackass', I mean Jacka's, girl's yard. I know he's there cause he always stays there after doing a hit on someone and with me the scenario was no different. I was just another job from the start. That dickhead's going to get it. He's going to pay for what he did. *Here we go again.* Everything slows down. I know he's coming out soon because his movements are like clockwork; you can literally set your time by him.

I have no plan. As I always remember a world champion boxer saying: "Fools come to fight with a plan until they get punched in the face." And that's a chance I can't take, so I'm going to let it flow. All I know is, I can't be seen by Jacka or I'll have to kill him cause it won't end there and, trust me, I'm not up for the killing shit. All I want to do is get the stash back. Damn! He's coming out.

I plot behind a red Vauxhall Astra and wait. I see the dickhead just walking willy nilly, like he's untouchable, not knowing he's about to get caught slipping. *Carlton, don't fuck this up, it's not what you say, it's the way you say it ... It's not what you say, it's the way you say it ...* I prepare to attack like a lion chasing his prey. My heart's drumming so fast I think I'm going to pass out. A second voice echoes through my head: *Why the fuck are you here bro, do you want to die?*

No, I don't want to die and I don't want my mum dead either.

I know I only have one chance and now my chance has come to make things right, I have to yank it with both hands. I get that taste in my mouth, the venom's flowing and I know I'm going to do a good job. My black Nike hoodie is off and ready. Heart: ten beats per second as he walks past. Without hesitation, I jump on him and wrap the hoodie around his stupid head.

How does it feel? How does it feel to be on the other side, bitch?

I lose composure. He nearly flips me. Fuck. I need to keep it together. I wrap my legs around him and hold on like my life and my mum's life depend on it cause they do. He desperately tries to shake me off, slamming my back hard into cars as he struggles to scream for help like a little bitch, but his voice and his calls are totally drowned out by my tightly wrapped hoodie.

Damn, this guy's strong! He slams me into

another car. I feel like my back has snapped in ten places, but I hold on for dear life. His muscles felt like a brick wall, but I know I can't let go cause if I do I'll be running for the rest of my life. I've got to feel fury; I have to think about something to boost my power to control this beast.

I think about my dad treating my mum like shit, but it doesn't do the job. So I picture Smiley and Snake sitting in front of my mum with their intentions. Yes. That does the job.

In a mad rage, I wrap my arms around his neck in a sleeper hold and squeeze with all my power. He grabs my forearm, trying to prise it from his neck, so I bring my left arm all the way down to Africa and bring my fist back to east London to punch him on his head side.

Damn, that feels good!

As he crumbles to his knees, I pin him. I'm totally possessed with rage and that rage completely changes my voice. He knows it's over.

"Give up your blood clart tings, you hear me pussy?" I reach for my shank and poke him – not too much, just enough to let him know this ain't a joke. I poke him and trust me there's blood. Fuck, man. That's a bit too extreme, but I've got to carry on cause it's all about protecting Mumsy, not that dickhead.

I've got to get the stash back; I've got to keep up the pretence.

Now Jacka can't talk, his voice is well muffled and I know he's feeling what all his victims felt when he put them through that shit. I'm glad. Again, I roar: "Pussy hole, you want me to shank you again?" I empty his pocket as he passes out in a pool of his own blood, but luckily none of it's on me. I pat down his pockets. The stash ain't there.

Where is it?

I look deeper. Bingo! A stash of one and a half grand. Now all I have to do is get another £500 and I'm home dry. I grab my hoodie and run and run and run some more. Jacka doesn't look good at all. But who gives a fuck? You live and you learn and by the looks of him he lived, but he didn't learn shit.

I get home, scrub my fingers until they bleed, change my clothes then I head back out. I have to find the rest of the money. This shouldn't be hard cause jacking Jacka was the easiest P I've ever made and if it wasn't for mum I could get used to it. Yet jacking comes at a price and that's a price I can't afford to pay. It's a shame about Jacka, but I had no other option.

Well I did have options, I just picked the wrong one. If I get through this, trust me, I won't make that mistake again. Now I've got to get the rest of this money and I've only got ten hours to get it. The time sponsored by 'the ends' is 12.10pm precisely.

I walk past Jacka's girl's road just to check if he's OK, but all I see is red tape and the entire street's blocked off. Police are everywhere. Jacka's definitely gone alright. I see his girl, so I calmly walk over to her to slyly get the info that I need. "Yo Carlene, what happened?" She turns and looks at me, distraught, and then breaks down. Carlene's a pretty girl, too pretty for Jacka, but crying makes her look so ugly.

"Jacka ... he ... he ... he's dead. He got stabbed this morning."

My heart sinks. Now, not only am I a drug pusher, I'm a murderer and no better than my old man.

"I'm so sorry Carlene," I say, trying to hide my guilt the best I can.

"What you sorry for, Carlton? You didn't do it." That makes me feel even guiltier.

"I kept telling him to settle down. We had an argument this morning and he walked out." She starts sobbing uncontrollably. I want to hold her, but I can't.

Guilt devours me like heroin gobbles a smackhead, so I just let her talk. But what she says next is yet another blow and it hits me hard.

"I tried to tell him ... I tried so hard to tell him, but ... he ... he just walked out."

"You tried to tell him what Carlene?"

"I tried to tell him that ... I'm pregnant."

Oh thanks! Thanks a fucking lot. What else can go wrong?

My pocket vibrates as my phone rings and I jump just a little bit.

I know who's at the other end of it and, trust me, I don't need to hear him right now.

I pick up ... it's that voice again. "Yo, pussy! Listen up. Did you hear about your boy Jacka?"

"Yeah, I did."

"OK, OK. So are you sad about what happened to him?"

"Well Snake, what do you think?"

"Don't be cause if I don't see you on the strip at 10pm sharp, you and your buff lil mum will be going to meet him. You get me?"

Now it's my turn to flip out and I have damn good reason to.

After all I've been through in the last few hours of my life, I don't give a fuck what that crackhead has to say.

"Look Snake, cut the shit blood. I know."

"You know what fam? You know what?"

"I know you set me up. You're going to make money off me and you got your food sitting right in your lap." Am I stuttering? Cause he is.

"What blood? Blood, you don't know shit and you better get that fucking one pound pizza taste out of your fucking mouth before I – "

I guess killing Jacka's given me some balls and that's just what I need to deal with this fool.

"Look Snake, shut the fuck up. You're going to get your money and then you can go and fuck yourself and leave me and mum alone, yeah! Now get off the fucking line you prick."

I cut the phone off. Now I'm really pissed. I get even more pissed when I walk past the shop and my mum's jacket ain't in the window. I storm into the shop. There's a lady I've never seen before. She's an oldish woman, her hair's totally grey and she

looks about 55. Her glasses seem to balance nicely at the end of her nose as she looks down
at me.

"Yo blood, where's the jacket that was in the window?" I barked as I try to catch a breath.

"Calm down sir or I'll have to ask you to leave the store."

She's quite polite, but I don't give a damn. I'm mad as hell. And cause I'm going through all this for a jacket that's not even there anymore her being polite doesn't mean shit to me.

"Look, fuck, calm down. Where is it?"

I start to make my way to the back of the shop, but she puts her hand out as though she's begging me to relax myself or she knows she'll have to call the police; for some reason I don't think she wants to do that.

"Please calm down. It was sold about an hour ago."

I draw the race card. "You bunch of racist motherfuckers. That jacket was for my mum. I paid good, hardworking money down for that jacket."

"Well young man, the manager told me to sell it because you've taken too long to pay the outstanding balance and for your information I'm not racist because my best friend is black." LOL. Just thought I'd slip that one in there for you. She's peering over her silver framed glasses and her eyebrows meet. "Now leave before I call the police."

Damn police aren't what I need right now. That's too bait, I know I have to just knock it on the head and take it as a loss. But I tell you something, if it was any other day I would just call my boys, rush that shop and take any and everything we want.

"Bitch."

I hoik up from the back of my throat and spit clean in her face, then I do a Missy Elliot (get the hell out of there). I want to watch my phlegm hang from her glasses, but getting pulled by boy dem ain't on my agenda. Now I'm really bloody mad. I ain't got enough money, no jacket, I've ghosted one of my guys and there are two fucking psychos after me and my mum.

Chapter 11
If I Could Turn Back Time

It's 9pm and I'm walking on the road when my phone rings. It can't be that dickhead cause we're meant to meet at 10pm. I take the phone out of my pocket and check the caller ID and see MUM flashing on the screen.

"Hi, sweetie, where are you?"

"I'm out mum, I'll be home soon."

"Well, I'm just coming home from bingo. I've got that surprise for you, so get home soon. Love you baby boy."

"OK mum, love you too."

If only she knew what her baby boy's been up to, would she love me then?

I wonder what surprise she has for me. Hopefully, she's won some big money cause she sounds mad excited.

I may be able to get the money from her, but then again that's a risk I can't take. I mean, say I go home and it's just another calabash meal.

Man, fuck it.

I've changed my garms and I'm back in my hoodie. I just need to do one more jacking; I know the last one went badly, but I'll just have to control myself this time. I know I need to find someone soft, someone that won't put up too much of a fight, someone that looks half decent and is bound to have money. I see one guy, but he looks like he won't free up his tings even if I hold a gun to his mum's head. Nah, leave that one alone.

I've got thirty minutes.

I turn a corner and can't believe what I see. It's a blue jacket with a matching bag and a big ass sussmi logo on the back. Yo! This bitch bought my mum's jacket and she's got the balls to wear it in the ends? She's going to pay.

I've found my victim.

That taste's in my throat and my head feels hot. I try to tell myself to calm down, but there's no stopping me. It's that fucking jacket's entire fault. I'm going to end this morning ritual bullshit, get my jacket and pay that crackhead his money. This bad dream's going to end. Crackhead will be happy, Mumsy will be happy, but I'll never be happy cause there's too much history under this bridge for me and I'm going to have to live with it for the rest of my days.

I'm getting myself ready. *Now Carlton, remember, it's not what you say, it's how you say it.*

I've made up my mind. I'm going to talk normally cause I realise you only change your voice when you're jacking someone you know and I can just be myself. At this point, myself and my anger are all I need and anyway I'm mad as hell. I'm going to get that jacket and I'm going to slap that bitch. Trust me, I'm going to slap that bitch hard for wearing my mum's jacket and that's standard.

It's going to be easy. Her hood's already up, covering half her face, and I'm ready. Fuck this, I was born ready.

You know what? Ban this waiting game!

I run up behind her and wrap my hoodie over her head, making sure I wrap it tight. I drag her kicking and fighting between two cars. I start punching her so hard on the side of her face I swear I break a knuckle. I know mum always told me not to hit women, but I just want to hurt this bitch. She's putting up a little fight so I punch her again and again, swinging as hard as I can. I'm so pissed off I black out for a minute as my body goes through the motions.

"Bitch, take off the jacket!" I growl

She stops moving for a bit.

Why?

Who gives a fuck? I try to pull the jacket off her. This bitch starts to wild out on man, kicking her legs and trying to scratch the hell out of me so I reach down my waist for my shank. Head. Hot.

It's going to go down nasty.

I couldn't care less cause she just won't shut up and I'm not about to get caught. So I start to shank her and with each swing of the blade I visualise Snake. I shank again and I see Smiley. One more shank and I see Jacka.

The moment lasts a lifetime. She tenses every muscle in her body each time the blade penetrates her. Oh, how mummy's little angel has changed into mummy's little devil. I don't give a shit. I just want her dead, so I shank with bad intentions. Her body's lifeless. No more struggle. No more noise and I know she's gone – gone by my hands. She's dead. My life's changed.

I grab the bag, leave the jacket and get the hell out of there. I run through the back roads like the little vermin I am until my lungs burn like hell fire, but I don't stop. *Stride … I'm … stride … a … stride … murderer.* Only yesterday, I was mummy's little boy. Who am I now?

My life flashes before me then in a split second the pictures stop. I'm a good boy turned bad. I need to clear my head as the deed's already done and I can't turn back time, although I wish I could. An innocent woman's dead, I didn't get my mum's jacket, but hopefully I got enough money to clear this debt that's worth selling my soul for.

Chapter 12
I Can See Clearly Now

I'm in an alleyway frantically opening the bag. I know that some people put their PIN numbers in their phones; I always tell mum she shouldn't save hers that way.

Man, where's the raas clart money? This better be worth it.

I open the purse. Bingo! Did I strike it lucky or what? Four bills - £400. Yes! Now all I need's £100 more then this nightmare will be over. Damn! There's no more, but hold on, I dig deeper in the purse, just dashing everything and anything over my shoulder. There's got to be something. Nah, nothing, just some old bingo slips. But hold on. Bank card. It's TSB, easy peasy. I pull out the card, hungry to see the details. My eyes blur with excitement, so I rub them a little until my vision clears. That's better.

Huh?

Can't breathe. Dropping everything. Falling backwards. Legs whispering run, run, *run*. Everything slows down ... stops ... my head's ringing ... the traffic temporarily deafens me and life's a faint breeze in the space of time.

That's my heart beating.

I'm the only person on the planet.

My breath escapes from my nose and mouth and the cold turns it into vapours. It evaporates and floats heavenwards.

Let's go back just a few hours. And ask yourself. Was it really worth it?

****

"Legs eleven, number eleven!"

"Bingo! I've won! I've won!" *Nothing like this ever happens to me!*

"There you go Miss Williams. You're a lucky lady. You've won the big one: £600! Give her a big hand! I hope that's going to make a massive change to your life."

"Oh my gosh! £600! I know just what I'm going to do with it. I'm going straight to that clothes shop and finally getting rid of this jacket." I reach the shop. Carlton will be shocked!

"Hello, can I try on that jacket in the window please?"

"Sorry Miss, but someone has put a deposit on it already. We have other jackets just as nice. Would you like to see them?"

"Er, no thank you, this is the jacket I want and if someone's put a deposit on it, why is it still in the window? I have the money for it right now, so can I buy it? I can't tell you the amount of times I've just been standing at your window looking at it."

"Oh, you're the customer I see every morning with your son. I wasn't meant to tell you as I think it was a surprise, but your son has put a deposit on this jacket for you.

"He's been going crazy trying to pay for it, bless him. He only has £100 left to pay, but he's taken so long we have to sell it by tomorrow. It will only cost you £100 if you want to take it now and maybe you can give him the shock of his life."

"Oh my gosh! He's such a darling! No wonder he's been working so hard. I'll take it now. Can I buy that matching bag too? You're right! He's going to have the shock of his life when he sees me."

"OK Miss, the jacket's £100 and the bag's £100, so that's £200 in total. Would you like to try the jacket on?"

"Oh yes please! Better still, can I wear it now? And can you get rid of this old jacket for me? It's no good to me anymore. I was going to give it to charity, but they would've just thrown it in the bin and I know my son hates it with a passion." I slip the jacket on. "So how does it look?"

"Miss, you look drop dead gorgeous. Your son will be well impressed."

"Thank you and have a great day. I feel so good in this jacket! I've got £400 left and when I get home I'm going to give it to my baby boy for being such a sweetie. But first, let me go and show off my new jacket to Miss Jackson."

It's 9pm. Let me call Carlton. "Hi sweetie, where are you?"

"I'm out mum, I'll be home soon."

"Well, I'm on my way home. I've got a surprise for you, so get home soon. Love you baby boy."

"OK mum. Love you too."

I can't wait to see Carlton and show off my jacket. Ha!

Oh my God! What's going on? Huh? Who turned the lights out? Aah ... What the! I can't breathe. Ooh no! No! Please let me go! I need to go home to my son! Who are you? What's happening? Please!

"Bitch, take off the jacket!"

Oh my God! It's Carlton! No, it can't be. My Carlton isn't capable of doing something like this! I lash out and try to say his name. *Carlton it's me! Carlton, it's me! It's mum! Please stop! Stop! That hurts ... ouch! Please stop ... the pain!*

A bitter blade penetrates my side as he stabs me at least three times. One stab punctures the womb that carried him into this world. Now it's getting dark, really dark, as I start to pass out. I stop fighting for a moment as my last memories of him flicker. What's causing the most pain? Is it the blade entering my flesh? Or is it the pain of realising that my only son has turned out to be worse than his father?

Mmm, let me think. No, no, no, it's too late ... Exhale.

Chapter 13
Look at Me Now

My name's Carlton Emmanuel Williams. I'm standing outside a little clothes shop, going through the morning ritual and the time is 12.15am. It feels like I've been standing here forever. I'm looking through the clear window.

I'm looking at my mum's jacket in the reflection, but this time she's wearing it. Her top's covered in blood and my hands are covered in my mum's blood. She's no longer smiling. She's looking at me with more pain in her eyes than she did when I stabbed her.

She fades away … she's gone.

Someone's tapping my shoulder. It's Carlene, she's crying. "Carlton. Carlton I have bad news." Her voice is a faint whisper from a far distance. "Carlton your mum's … Sh … she's dead." I take £1,900 out my pocket and give it to her and her unborn child. I take my phone from my pocket and dial 999.

"Hello, I need to speak to the police."

The voice sounds loud and clear. "Hello, what's the problem sir?"

"I've killed my mother."

Now I know making money the hard way would've been the easiest money I could've ever made. But I had to go and try to make it the easy way. Look at me now.

****

January 16th, Brixton Prison.

"Carlton, I'm out of here son, but I'm going to send you a present, gift wrapped. It's going to be a big one, so just be ready. And when it comes I want you to open it nicely."

"OK Dad, I love you."

"Love you too son. Be strong."

****

Ok stop it gets worse let's do some quick calculations. Snakes gives me the stuff, it's worth £2000 he say give him £1.500 and I get to keep £500, I take £1.500 from Jaka that's enough to pay snake so I didn't even need the £500...DAM

A wise man once said:

"They who are of the opinion that money will do everything may very well be suspected to do everything for money."   George Savile, 1912

Daddy's Little Girl

Chapter 1
Welcome to the World

7.55am on June 18th 1965 at Forest Gate Hospital.

"Miss Jenkins, push. Push!"

"I can't! It hurts! It hurts! Get that little bastard out of me! It's trying to kill me, just cut it out!"

"No-one's trying to kill you Miss Jenkins. I know it hurts, but I need you to push. I can see the head – one last, big push!"

"I hate it … get it out! Get it out of me *nowww*!"

"One last, big push … push harder! It's out. Great! You have a beautiful little boy. Here you go, you can hold him now if you want."

"Get that bastard away from me!"

Her spiny hand came down hard and fast. All she wanted to do was hit the pipe or get it in the nearest syringe she could find. She was alone, so alone and her best friend was in the back pocket of Biffa, her heroin dealer and pimp. All she could think about was when they'd meet again.

Heroin was her best friend, her only friend. He was the one who truly loved her, so she embraced him like she embraced a long, lost lover.

The nurse cried, "Oh my God! I think his arm is broken!" She'd never seen anything like it. "Get the doctor! Now!"

****

My name's Delroy. I'm 13 and addicted to morphine. I was supposed to have weaned my way off it by now, but cause of the shit I go through on a daily basis you could say morphine is this kid's best friend as it keeps me sedated through all the crap and pain that's going on around me.

I'm 5 feet 6 inches tall and weigh 11 stones – yeah, 11 stones – so I'm quite big for my age. I'm kind of scruffy, but my mum tries her best to make me look as neat as she can.

Let me put it this way: I'm neat on the way to school, but after school I'm the scruffiest kid on the block.

I'd say my best features are my almond shaped, dark brown eyes. That's about it really. Nose: too big. Lips: too big. And to top it off, I'm what they call bleak, as in *really dark*. My hair's an uncombed rug as no barber wants to cut or even touch it and my parents can't control it, so I often just pat it down to keep it low and out the way.

My parents often find it funny to say I've got a wild animal sitting on top of my head. They say it as a joke, but I don't find it funny. Still, I know they mean no harm cause they're the only ones who truly love me.

My name's Delroy, but they call me Lucky. I got that name from the doctor who had to amputate my arm just at the elbow as infection settled in after my mum threw me on the hospital floor no less than two minutes after I slipped out of her decrepit, heroin infested womb. Well, that's what my adopted father told me. The doctors said I was lucky to be alive so they named me Lucky cause, apart from losing my arm and being a heroin baby, I should've died from the force I hit the floor.

But I say "I died the day I was born"

My parents named me Delroy – it's the only black name they knew cause back in the day, there was only one black person in our little town they call Stratford, aka Stratty. That was the bus conductor whose name was … yeah, you got it right: Delroy. They adopted me and that's the only black name they knew. I'd rather be called Lucky, but Delroy will do, I suppose, cause it's much better than sooty, wog, nigger, chalky and coon. That's what the teachers call me on an everyday basis. I mean, it's got so bad they put *Nigger* on the register and when I don't respond I get detention. The female teachers love that as you'll get to understand later.

Yeah, the Seventies are hard for me, I can tell you.

They say if you call a person a dog long enough, they'll respond to that name – but not me. I hate the fact that they've got so much power over me they can call me whatever they want and get away with it. Trust me: my one ambition's to make them call me by my proper name.

I think you must've got it by now: yep, my parents are white, but they're as nice as pie.

Even though adopting me was a massive strain on their marriage cause of all the racism in our area, before I leave for school they always say: "Sticks and stones may break my bones, but names will never hurt me."

That's a fucking lie cause they hurt and hurt bad.

But bless them cause they just want the best for me. I'm the only black kid in the area – and in my school. I don't know my real parents or anything about my culture, plus I've only got one arm. I guess I'm blessed in a way as it's my right arm I'm left with. At least I can fight.

I'm going to change my nickname by force. Well, I have to cause all the white kids only go to school when I'm there so they can kick the shit out of me on a regular basis on the way home and on lunch breaks. When I don't go to school, they just bunk off as there's no black meat to pound after the last bell goes.

Then again, there's always Pritpal Singh, aka Prickpal, the little Asian boy, but he doesn't last as long as me so it ain't any fun for them cause they love a challenge. Believe me, I'm a big challenge. I'm not going to be beaten easily and with the morphine running through my veins, I don't feel as much pain as normal kids so they've got to recruit more racist cunts to even out the pace. Now, little Pritpal always leaves school with a smile on his face. That's OK by me cause the more beatings I get, the stronger I become and they don't know they're creating a monster that's about to be unleashed.

When I come to school I make sure everyone knows I'm there and when the bell goes I take a slow walk home. I want that beating so badly or, should I say, I *need* it. I'm under construction and my time's coming to start dishing out the punishment.

I can just about hear the good guys shout, "Run Del! They're coming! Run!" But that's just air brushing my eardrums and I'm not about to entertain it for a second.

I remember the teachers once placed bets about how many punches it'd take for me to hit the sack cause I always try to stay firmly on my feet.

With one arm, there ain't much protection when I've got five or six white guys pounding on my head, trying to see who can cause the most damage and knock me unconscious first. I stay standing as long as possible and the more beatings they give me over the months, the longer I stay on my feet. The longer I stay on my feet, the slower my walks home become and the fewer beatings I get.

****

I'm totally addicted to Kung Fu magazines. Every time I get a beating, I go home and practice my moves. I push my body for long periods, trying to touch my bollocks on the floor by sitting in splits and doing kick after kick, sometimes 2,000 a day. Last night, I heard what I've been waiting to hear for a long time: my hips pop.

Now my hips are ready, flexible and free. I'm free cause my construction's complete.

Back to school with a big smile on my face and today there's blood, lots of blood, but for once it ain't mine apart from the blood trickling out of my right knuckles and the pain in my feet after kicking heads all day.

I went to school with very, very bad criminal intentions. As the bell rang, there were eight of them kids; all I remember is stamping viciously on the biggest one's head.

"What's my name you cunt? What's my name?"

As my foot came down, I could just about make out the words bubbling through his blood. "It's Delroy ... It's Delroy ... Please don't kill me!"

"Yeah, that's right. It's Delroy, but you can call me Legs." One more stamp then lights out. Poor Billy. He won't be the same after that beating, but I had to break some heads to get my point across. It's a nasty job, yet someone's got to do it and I enjoy every bit of it.

So now my name's changed to Legs cause of the lack of use of my one arm. I've trained my legs to be my arms. Trust me, I can kick ass like you could never imagine. My motto is: *I don't fight to win, I fight to survive.* Now all them kids don't want to come to school when I'm there, guaranteed, or your money back with interest and believe me, I like the sound of interest. How the underdog's changed cause even the teachers look away when they see me coming – apart from the females. Their eyes are firmly stuck to me like glue.

Yeah, I have total control. Is that good or bad? Let me tell you, it's a very bad thing cause that little black kid with a massive, picky afro has just found a thing called strength and that leads to pain which breeds fear, then extortion with interest. Yeah, at the tender age of 14, I'm making more money in a week than my mum and dad make in a month.

I'm a pretty good size for my age and that makes me ruthless. Now my name echoes through east London's schools like a ghost riding on a winter's wind. Before I know it, I've got at least eight schools on lockdown that I'm extorting money, fags and all sorts from, including girls, on a regular basis. I'm so busy and there ain't enough of me to go around. The more my rep grows, the more violent I become. I just love the violence more than any amount of money, girls or morphine, but not as much as stealing cars.

That's another thing I'll talk about a bit later.

Anyway, as I was saying, oftentimes when I have these kids wanting to join me, I'll just ask them how far they're prepared to go to be on my right hand side. I wait to hear their response and it's always: "As far as you need me to go Legs." That's when I reach into my pocket and pull out my little friend. His first name's Stanley and his surname's Blade. Yeah, you got it: Mr Stanley Blade. When he comes out to play, he's not to be fucked with (big grin).

I say to them in a real calm voice, which is quite hard as my voice is deep like them old car engines I nick, "Put your hand on the table." If they're reluctant I give them a slap, rob them and tell them to *fuck off* as I know they'll be fast to rat me out to the pigs or just set me up. But the ones who do put their hands on the table ... well, I open the blade slowly as I love to hear my friend click ... click ... click when he comes out to play.

But what really turns me on is the look in them tin soldiers' eyes cause that's priceless!

I take the edge of Stanley and push the blade slowly under their thumb nails until they pop right off like spinning coins (heads or tails!). I look deep into their eyes and say softly and calmly: "That was fun. Can I do that to the other nails please?" They often scream loud, "No way!" or some shit like that, but sometimes, and I mean only sometimes, they say, "Yes Legs, you can."

"OK, but say please," I say with a big smile.

"Yes please Delroy."

The pain's written all over their faces, but at least I know they're my soldiers and they've got balls, but my balls have to be bigger to keep them in line. I remember one day I had five soldiers and five fingernails of my own. Now I've got twenty soldiers and no fingernails, if you get my meaning. I allowed my five soldiers to pop off one nail each and I didn't flinch. After all, I deserved the pain as punishment for not dying on my birth date.

I set the standard and it's a standard that's unattended, unmovable and not to be fucked with.

My army's grown and I've gained more control of schools in and out of the ends, so that means I've got to start recruiting more workers. I put the word out and now I've got a chain of little white punks kissing my ass just to stay on my good side and get some of that rep.

I've got a chain of little white bitches sucking my dick just to make me happy. I've become the most feared kid in east London.

Oftentimes, some kid will bring his sister to make me happy so he can get some of the high life. I even have some of the female teachers keeping me back for detention to see if it's true what they hear about black guys really knowing what they're doing. Trust me, I know what I'm doing and I make them pay for my services and that's more money in my bin.

I get more detentions than most of my year put together, but it's been worth every minute, even the times I went to piss and it felt like I was pissing out razor blades – yeah, razor blades. I carried that shit around with me for three months till one of the teachers gave me a tiny, green pill and, trust me, that's the best pill I've ever taken. Being the guy I am and the way I love money and pussy I'd be a fool to turn any of it down, but I'm a bigger fool to accept what's about to become part of my downfall.

Chapter 2
Skanking With the Devil

I died today. Let me tell you about it.

I'm 15, it's Monday at about 1.35pm. I've just left some bird I was linking in the school playground and I'm busting for a slash, so I run to the school toilets and burst through the door.

That's when I meet the devil himself.

Now I think, and everyone else thinks, I'm a proper geezer, a real jack-the-lad and all that malarkey, but this guy has some shit that makes me feel like the little afro-headed 13 year old who used to get the shit kicked out of him on a regular basis.

Anyway, I burst through the door and I see some boy; he's about 18 and as skinny as a rope. His eyes are bluer than blue and his hair's so blonde, it's almost white.

I mean, I can't even see his eyebrows cause they blend into his skin! His hair's cropped very low like them skinheads that used to chase me home once in a while. You can just about make out where his hairline starts and where it ends as it's so blended into his skin.

There's depth in the way he looks at me; no fear whatsoever. He just stares at me with glazed over eyes as if someone's popped two shiny marbles in his head.

The whiteness of his skin's like he's powdered his face, but later down the line I'm going to find out it isn't his face he's powdering.

Apart from all that, what concerns me most ain't who or what this guy is, but what he's got in his hand. What's he sniffing up his nose? Why ain't he scared shitless when he sees me? Cause everyone else is! I have to approach this guy with caution, even though I know I could K.O. him with one punch. So I open the conversation firmly.

"What you doing bruv?" My voice is deep, my eyebrows meet.

"What you mean, what am I doing? Who da fuck are you?" His voice sounds bigger than my balls and trust me, I've got some big balls.

"I'm Delroy, but they call me Legs," I fire back at him.

"Oh, Legs," he says with a slight grin. "I've heard about you, you're the guy that's got everyone running shitless, but I'm not running. Do you see me running Deeeelroy?"

I've got to think for a minute cause he's right. He doesn't even flinch. I know a pussy when I see one and for some strange reason I know he ain't one. He jars me out of my thoughts.

"OK Delroy, let's cut to da chase. I bet you're going to ask me what I'm sniffing up my nose, yeah?"

I raise my eyebrows in confusion. "Er, yeah that did kind of cross – " this guy just cuts in.

"Well I say fuck the questions, just try it, you might like it." He hands over a £10 note all rolled up tight like a tube with just enough opening to see through. Damn, man. This guy's carrying a lot of dosh and I want some of it, but I want to try this shit more, so I guess it's his lucky day.

"Cop hold of this for me," he says in a proper cockney accent. "I need you to do something for me before you dance with the devil. Can you do something for me Deeeeeelroy?"

I fucking hate the way he keeps dragging my name from the back of his neck to the tip of his tongue, but fuck it, there are more important things to think about. So I ask, quick-time, "Yeah, what is it?"

This feels like an interrogation. Shit. All I really want to find out is what this guy's sniffing cause whatever it is makes him totally comfortable about the fact that I'm thinking about kicking his nose right to the back of his brain.

"Well, what the fuck do you want me to do?" I snap at him. "And while you're talking to me like I'm your long lost brother, I still don't know your name."

He just watches me with them eyes and from nowhere he says: "All in good time bro, but first punch me. Go on, punch me in my face as hard as you can. Come on! Do it! Do it Mr Fucking Delroy!" I'm totally confused. What the hell is this guy on? I need to know and trust me, I'm about to find out.

Now, you know I said I like violence? Well, in this case I'm reluctant to hit this guy cause judging by how bulimic he looks, one of my punches would have to kill this dickhead then I'd never know the devil I so desperately want to dance with. He gets up in my face.

"Hit me, you fucking wog!"

Well that ought to do it. My hand never moved so fast. Crash! My knuckles connect with his jaw. Smash! Right cross to his nose. I feel myself going ape shit. Bang! I follow through with a roundhouse kick to the temple. In my rage, I don't even see the massive smile on this guy's face. Now I know I just initiated myself into tasting the devil.

"Damn, sonny boy! You're quite powerful ain't ya?" he says as he rubs his chin and spits out a mouthful of blood.

"Now we got that out the way, and you know this lad ain't no pussy, come over here and let me introduce you to my little friend called charlie." He spits another mouthful of blood into the nearby sink. "Charlie's my friend what kept me on my feet when you gave me your best shot."

What the hell's this guy on? He doesn't feel a thing. For some strange reason, I know this is going to be a long friendship, but an even longer day.

"Oh yeah, by the way, it's Wayne."

"What's Wayne?" I say in a huff, clenching my fist, trying to stop the pain in my knuckles. All I want to do is get this crap up my nose without any disturbances.

Furthermore, I'm still dazed by what I witnessed, but I'm more stunned by the way my knuckles feel and the fact that this kid's still standing.

"My name, bro: it's Wayne...Wayne Brannon Now where's that ten quid I gave ya?"

I open my hand and the note's now totally crushed where I hit Wayne as hard as I could. So naturally I'm a bit stuck for words. That's a first. "Er ..."

"Don't worry bro, give it here."
Wayne takes the note and starts to reroll it then he puts his hand in his pocket and pulls out this clear bag full of sugar.

"Yo, Wayne. Why you walking around with a bag of sugar in ya pocket?" I say, trying to contain myself from falling on the ground in a fit of laughter. "If you think I'm going to sniff that up my nose, you got to be pissed mate."

We both start gassing like we're old friends. He puts his hand back into his pocket and pulls out a razor blade and small mirror.

He looks at me with a sly grin. "I love razor blades. You can't see them till you're gushing with blood." Is he hinting something cause no-one loves their choice of weapon as much as I love my Stanley and it's only this bag of sugar that's keeping Stanley clean right now.

He pours a little bit of the powder on the mirror and starts to form two almost perfect lines with the razor blade.

"Bruv, come and get acquainted with Charlie. It ain't no sugar, but it's as sweet as fuck. All you do is hold one nostril, put this ten quid up the other one and sniff. Take it easy! This shit's got a kick like a mule."

Say no more!

That sounds good to me as all this morphine's working its way deep into my system and I'm getting used to it more and more every day. The kick's wearing off fast, so as far as I'm concerned a good kick's what I need. "Just give me the shit man. I'm down with whatever," I snap.

"Legs, it's your first hit so take it easy, just do one sniff first. Bro! Just one sniff! Are you crazy?"

That's the last thing I hear. You know when they say your life flashes before your eyes just before you die? I see everything – and I mean everything. I see my mother's face plain as day. As I meet her for the first time, she holds her arms out to me and I'm not scared anymore. I know what love is and I don't care if no-one's afraid of me anymore. The main thing is I'm no longer afraid of myself or who or what I'm destined to become, so I just drift into my mother's arms, no longer lost. She's got tears in her eyes for what I'm bound to become. Her voice is like cool, running water. It's as though I've never left her side. She holds me close to her breasts and rocks me in her arms like a baby.

She whispers in my ear, "Son, I'm so sorry for not being there for you and for what I did to you. I was in a dark place and I don't ever want you to be in that place, not even for a minute. I've got something very important to tell you. You must listen and listen keenly."

She draws her lips closer to my ear. "I know you're hurt and I know I did you wrong, but you must do something. This will help you in years to come."

"What is it mum? What shall I do?" I'm desperate for her wisdom; I'm desperate for her love, her hugs. I'm desperate for my mum. She looks into my eyes.

SPLASH!

I'm woken up in a freezing rush by my form teacher, Mr Goushard. He comes into the toilets, fills up a bucket of cold water and just flings it on me like some kind of water torture.

I return to consciousness violently, reborn on the toilet floor.

It's 12.18pm on a Tuesday afternoon. I've been completely out all that time, but the worst thing is I never got the chance to know what my mum was trying to tell me. I have more hate in my heart for everyone and everything as my mum was snatched away from me by some prick, so-called teacher.

Where's Wayne?

I want charlie more than ever before. I want that feeling again and I know morphine can't cut it for me.

I want to see my mother; I need to know what she was trying to tell me and if I have to die again then feel free to say I'm addicted to death.

I hear that tea-drinking, stinking voice again. "Clean yourself up! Your lesson starts in 30 minutes." I dry myself off with that hard, cheap, artificial toilet paper that's meant to be bog roll, but cuts up your asshole if you wipe too hard. I'm out the door, whispering *silly, fat cunt.*

Chapter 3
My Black Beauty

As I walk out into the playground, I feel the breeze penetrating my wet shirt. Something in the playground catches my attention. I look up and it's like *déjà vu*, a bunch of kids in a circle just shouting and screaming, "Nigger! Wog! Coon! Black bitch!" Hands fly into the centre of the crowd and I hear a female voice scream.

I'm shouting, "Oi! Oi!" at the top of my lungs. The maniac kids part like the Red Sea and that's when I see her for the first time.

Is this another dream? Is it charlie or am I really looking at a better looking female reflection of myself?

She's got smooth, dark skin, she's a little shorter than me and her hair's in cornrows so neatly done. She's afraid and I don't like that as it brings back memories of when I first joined this hellhole they call school.

Now I know nothing's changed behind the school walls. They're still a bunch of racist assholes and they think I'm just like them cause, like it or not,

I'm a bit of a coconut having been brought up around them for all these years. Truth is, I've been yearning for someone just like me. So I pick my victim cause I'm raging and someone has to pay, somebody has to get knocked out. I pick my victim from the bunch of racist bastards.

"Oi Jack! Get over here – now."

Jack's a redhead, his nickname's ginger minger, but I call him by his real name just to put the fear in him. He walks over very slowly and I can see he knows he's going to get it, but he just doesn't know how badly he's going to pay.

"Er ... You OK Legs?" His voice is quivering like a little bitch, but it's too late for him now.

"What da fuck... you think... you're playing at?"

"N-nothing Legs, just breaking a new one into our school. You know how it goes."

I black out. All I remember is pulling Stanley and when we were done there was blood everywhere.

My rage is well spent, but there ain't any way of sewing up poor Jack's face to hide the teeth that's now showing through the three inch circle I carved in his right cheek.

"Talk shit through your new mouth now, you little prick." I survey my playground. "Did anyone see what happened to him? *Did ya*?"

Fear rules as everyone replies in synch: "No Legs, we didn't see anything." It's like they all counted to three and say it at the same time.

"Good. Now Fuck off you bunch of bastards."

I turn my attention back to my black beauty. *Is she what my mum was trying to tell me about?* I have a strong feeling my life's about to change and I'm more excited than I've ever been. I look her dead in her eyes as I extend my hand and she just grabs it like she's hanging onto a cliff edge for dear life and I'm her only rope, it's as natural as ever. I gaze deeper into her eyes. I can tell she likes the power and she knows no-one or nothing will ever hurt her again – or so she thinks.

"And your name is?" I ask gently with my deep voice.

"I'm Teresa," she replies with her soft, girly voice.

"Hi Teresa, I'm Delroy, but they call me Legs."

"I know who you are," she says with a shy, pretty, grin as shallow dimples sit neatly on her cheeks. "I prefer to call you Delroy if you don't mind."

"Nah, that's grand, call me whatever you want. So do you want me to walk you to class, or do you want to skip class and do something more exciting?"

I confuse her. Her brown eyes glow like street lights. *This girl's beautiful*, I think to myself as her generous lips grab my attention and I can't help but show my thoughts every time she smiles. Her cornrows are a little bit scruffy after the beating she got, but compared to my mop they're still neat. Her skin's a nice shade of dark brown. Her face is slim and girly; that's so cute compared to all those grown women I'm used to controlling.

"Yeah, that sounds good. I hear you're a good driver. Do you want to show me?" she utters under the beauty of her slim eyebrows.

I like her already. It's a bit much for our first date, but you know me: I never miss an opportunity to look good in front of the chicks, especially as this chick's special.

"Come on then Teresa. And you get to pick the car."

We walk through the school gates hand in hand like we've known each other for ages. We swing around the corner where there's a road full of cars just the way I liked it.

"OK babes, take your pick."

I so desperately want her to pick an automatic, obviously cause of my arm. She looks at me with a little smile again, but this time her neat right eyebrow's raised high. "So, Del, I guess you have the keys to all these cars yeah?" I'm speechless. She lets out a little laugh. "I'm just joking Del, you pick one!" I sigh with relief.

"What about this one?" I ask desperately as I peek through the glass at the automatic gear shift.

"Nah Del," she giggles. "I don't like the colour. What about this one?"

She's fascinated and excited as she points to an outdated blue Volvo.

Shit. They don't come in auto, but what can I say? I don't want to look an idiot on our first date now do I? "OK, if that's the one you want that's the one you will have," I say, shrugging my broad shoulders and wearing my best fake smile.

I walk over to the car. *Why this one?* I battle with the thought in my mind, but it's too late. She's made her choice and I've got one chance to make this happen. *Jimmy the door ... get in ... lean across and let her in.* She climbs in all excited, wiggling her bum, trying to get comfortable on the cold, leather seat. I've got a rough idea of how to drive stick, but it ain't something I've practiced a lot.

"Teresa, I'll steer and you change gear when I say ... Er, you do know how to change gears don't you?" I say with a smile, knowing full well she ain't got a clue. I'm just trying to make myself seem bigger and better than everyone else as I do.

"No, Del, I don't." She's biting her pretty, plump lips.

Crash course. I lean across and look into her adorable eyes, hold her silky brown hand and put it where I want it, pushing it into position.

"First gear. Second gear. Third and fourth, then fifth gear. Have you got that?" She looks at me with a massive smile and rubs her hands together.

"Piece of cake Del! Let's do it!"

First things first. I tear off the plastic panel under the steering wheel, then rip out the wires.

"Count to three babes!" I say, puffing my chest out just a tad.

"1 ... 2 ... 3!" The excitement's written all over her cute, little face as her dimples get deeper.

Vroom … vroom … vroom, the engine starts. "Good boy," she smiles, showing a perfectly straight set of white teeth.

Man, that's so nice to hear! No woman has ever told me that. I've never had a black woman make me feel so proud of myself, even though I'm doing something totally illegal. So I just give her a big ass smile back.

"You ready to rock n roll?" I ask and she just nods her gorgeous head, too brimming to talk. "First gear please."

I stall the car and we bust out in crazy laughter. I reach down and pull the choke out a little bit to make sure it doesn't happen again. I look across at Teresa. "You got to get this right or it could turn out very badly, OK." She knows I'm serious and we both know we have to do this right, so we buckle our seat belts and brace ourselves for the ride of our life.

"Start her up, Del!"

We're on our way. "Second gear... third gear... fourth gear." It's the most fun I've ever had stealing cars!

We start going 60 mph in fourth gear and I'm calling fifth gear, but Teresa just can't get the stick in place. I look down at the gear stick in panic. "Get it in gear!" I snap at her. "Delroy! Look out! Oh my God!" Teresa yelps as I look up.

That's when I see her, but it's too late.

I just about make out her grey tweed jacket as she flies into the air, then comes down with a *bang!* on top of the bonnet as if the car's playing catch.

Now I see her properly.

She's a black woman, well skinny. She looks like a proper crackhead. Time freezes as her wig flies one way and her shoes go the other. I slam on the breaks as hard as I can, but to no avail. She slides off the bonnet and crashes to the floor. The two front wheels swiftly run over her and the back wheels closely follow. I know she's dead and the worst thing is she's black just like me. Why does she have to be black? Black people have never done me any wrong apart from my mum, so if she got hit by a bus I wouldn't give a shit.

I've got to get me and Teresa away asap, so we drive deep into Wanstead Flats where we burn the car to get rid of all the evidence. The Volvo explodes in flames. *I've just killed someone's old girl... I've just killed someone's old girl* smashes through my brain. I've done a lot of bad things in my short life, but murder's pushing it too far.

Teresa can't stop crying as I hold her in my arm and watch as the sky turns dark behind the flames of the burning murder weapon. "Teresa, you need to calm down. It's done and we need to have each other's back. If we don't talk no-one will know. Have you got me like I've got you?"

Even though I like her a lot, I look deep into her eyes to find a weakness and fortunately for her I see none cause I'm not about to go prison for no girl. That's why I pick somewhere in the middle of nowhere with a lot of bushes so no-one can see or hear her scream if Stanley comes out to play. Then she blurts out, trying to control herself, "I guess I haven't got a choice, do I Del? I've got your back and this is our bond for life."

We stand there and watch the car go up in flames against the midnight stars. As we walk away, I realise my life has indeed just begun.

****

Teresa and me have finally got it on and it's great. I don't think you understand – it's *really* great. I don't want to let her go.

Oh how time flies! We're 17 and squatting in a derelict house and the years just seem to rush past us like an express train and on that train are a whole load of new black faces. Teresa has more black male figures on her case, trying to get a date and the ting that man would die for, the ting more precious than gold or any drug.

I know Teresa's loyal, but I'm not taking any chances so every once in a while I do the only thing I can to make sure she stays in line. Yeah, I know you think I'm scum and I'm thinking the same thing as I can't stop messing around with any girl who throws her knickers at me. I have to point the finger to lift and shift my guilt.

****

I'm 18 and starting to realise I'm not in love with this girl, I was just in lust. How long can lust last? You know what? I'm off. I can't stay in this shithole no more with a girl I don't like. I can't even hold her after sex. She always says to me: "Delroy, why do I always feel like a prostitute after sex?" I just kiss my teeth and walk out. I've got to get out. I need to get gone today.

I'm just going to tell her.

I walk into the house. "Yo! Teresa!" She doesn't respond, so I call a bit louder. "Teresa, where are you?"

"In the kitchen!" I hear her yell.

I walk into the kitchen, which is really one quarter of the front room.

"I'm here babes. What's up? Did you have a nice day? I've got a surprise for you," she says. She looks happy.

There's no easy way to say this, so I just force it out. "I'm leaving. I can't do this no more."

Her smile turns into a grimace and I know I'm about to break her heart. But who gives a shit?

Not me.

"Why, Del? What have I done? Whatever it is, I can change! Please just give me a chance, Delroy, *please*." Her tears flow fast as she starts grabbing at my Lacoste tracksuit like I found it on the street. She starts pulling and she won't let go.

"Get off me!" I'm trying to pull away without damaging one of my best garms, but she holds on and her voice gets louder.

"No! Please Delroy! I left my family and everything for you! I have nothing and no-one left!"

The seams of my brand, spanking new tracksuit start to come apart. She's even stepping on my white Gola trainers! I proper lose da plot.

"Get da fuck off me, you stupid, black bitch!" Here comes the right hand square to her jaw as another follows to her body. Teresa just looks at me in a way she never has before: her eyes penetrate straight through me.

"Go on then! Hit me again! Go on! Hit me again you bastard!"

I look at her. "Are you sick, dumb or stupid? I could kill you with one punch. Now get the fuck off me, I'm out of here."

Then she says, as calm as day, "Nah, Delroy. I'm not sick, dumb or stupid. But I am pregnant."

"You what?" I snap at her.

"I'm pregnant. I'm going to have your child. So hit me, punch me, kill me, but you'll only be killing your blood line. Hit me again. Go on."

I'm mad as hell. Why would I want to be a dad? I never had a dad. Man, I don't even know his name! I guess it was some dickhead that shot his load in my so-called mum and paid her £3 or some shit like that.

Why the hell is some girl trying to force me into being a dad?

As far as I'm concerned, if I didn't have a dad, I'm definitely not going to be a dad to some kid and that's for damn sure.

"Get rid of it," I say nice and harsh through gritted teeth.

"No. I'm not gonna get rid of it. If you're not man enough to be a man that's your business, but I'm gonna grow my child with you or without you, like it or not."

How the hell do I get out of dis one? Maybe the only way I know how I suppose.

BANG!

I hit her hard, right in da gut. Right hand followed by a front kick. *"Aim for the belly, aim for the belly" whispers in my head.* She crumbles to the floor and I feel no way cause I'm that kind of guy. I'm the beast from Hell who's danced with the devil and survived. I hurt women cause I was hurt by a woman and I was hurt badly. I have no respect for women and that could be my downfall, but I don't give a shit.

I grab a black bin bag, fill it with my best gear and walk out the door. I should've slit her fucking throat in Wanstead Flats the day we burned that car. As I leave, my prosthetic arm sitting in one corner of the room catches my eye. Fuck it. I don't need or want that plastic piece of shit. It's five shades too light for me anyway and I look more intimidating without it.

You know what they say: looks can be deceiving. So I just walk and never look back. I'm glad to see the last of it, just like I'm glad to finally see the last of her.

Teresa's screaming at the top of her lungs, but I just keep walking.

I'm pissed off right now and all I want to do is hurt someone. The first person I see I'm gonna go for it.

I clock a guy bowling towards me, but he's massive; he looks like he's pushing buses and eating elephants. Fuck it. I'm going to go for it. My motto is, 'The bigger they are ...' I know you know the rest. I'm getting closer and I can see this guy's built like a shithouse. When I get close enough, I start the banter. "Oi! What da fuck you doing around here son? You're outta your league and if you come bowling around here you're going to get left behind."

He speaks and what he says stops me dead in my tracks. "Ha! Shut up Delroy, you silly cunt! See you ain't changed."

How does this guy know my name? I look at him good. "Do I know you bruv? And how you know my name?"

With a big smile, he rattles on. "What? Del, don't you recognise me?" He stands there pulling faces like he's trying to wake me up. I look again. I'm so out of my head with this baby issue, I can't even think. "It's me man ... It's Wayne...Wayne Brannon!"

I don't know if I'm happy, surprised or in a dream. If it is him, he's come at the right time. "What? Wayne from school? No way bro! What happened to you man? What you been eating and where the hell have you been? You just disappeared."

"Bruv, I've been about. What happened to you? Last time I saw you, you was dressed sharp and out cold on the toilet floor. Now you look like a tramp. Back in the day your clobber was well tight. Now you look like you sleep rough and weigh about 8 stones."

He's right. I have to take it on the chin cause I really just want to ask him about one thing: charlie. I know it ain't the right time, so I chuckle a bit.

"Yeah, it's been rough man. I need to make some dough and I need a place to put my head, but what I really need is some –"

Before I even get to finish the sentence, Wayne cuts in as he always does.

"No bro, you don't need charlie, well not yet anyway. I've got something better than charlie and when you mix the two you're super human, you're going to be like a god!"

"What is it bro?"

The excitement's blatantly written all over my face. "Come on bro. What is it?"

"OK, OK, hang on Del," Wayne says evenly. "First of all, you can stay over at my pad till you get back on your feet. You need to have a long bath cause I know that ain't your skin colour!"

I can't help but look at the size of him. That skinny little boy who took them hard punishments from me what seems like yesterday ain't so skinny no more. We start walking and I know this is the walk of many more steps to come.

"So where are we going Wayne?"

His lips start curling upwards like I just asked him the £1,000,000 question. "Bruv, I got this nice pad in Forest Gate next door to Wag Bennett gym. That's where I got this monster size from." Wayne starts to flex his biceps. "Go on, bruv, touch it. Feel da power!" We both start laughing like mad. Wayne stops mid-joke.

"Oi! Get over here and run fast!" He starts the countdown, "3 ... 2 ... 1 ..."
I look up. All I can see is this real skinny, dirty guy running over like his life depends on it. Actually, I think it does cause the look on Wayne's face is priceless. This guy's a bag of bones trying his best to get to Wayne on time.

It doesn't seem to be the first time he's played this game with the devil.

He's got that smackhead limp, dragging his leg behind him like a little puppy dog being dragged on a leash. As he gets closer, I can see his pock-marked skin and a pathetic, *please don't kill me* expression clouds his face. The stench that trails him is diabolical; piss stains are spattered on the front of his black jeans and sick tracks are smeared across the front of his old black t-shirt that's at least five times too big. Poor dude. I hold my nose with every desperate step he takes to get to Wayne before he hits number one.

The guy comes over two seconds after Wayne's count reached one. "Wayne, I got your –"

"You're too late mate." Wayne slaps the guy on his neck and he drops like a ton of bricks into a dirty heap. Blood's spitting from his jugular as he flops around on the floor like a fish out of water, gasping for breath; I realise Wayne's smacked the guy with a razor blade he concealed between his fingers. Wayne walks over to a drain and drops the blade, making sure it disappears. And that, my friend, is called lack of evidence.

"Come on Del. Let's go. Just walk normally. Don't look back. Just walk."

My mind's saying *Run you prick, get the hell out*! But I can still hear Wayne's voice: *Stay calm and just walk*. So I do. Every step feels like it's my last cause I know if the old bill catch us, it'll be me in the slammer and not white, blonde haired, blue-eyed Wayne.

There's silence for at least half an hour. I'm shitting it so much, I don't even notice I'm sitting in a brand, spanking new, mark-free Ford Cortina. I've smashed people in, I've hurt some folks real bad, but never have I gone as far as taking a life – apart from the car accident.

"Legs, what you think of the ride, man? Pussy puller or what?"

Is this guy for real? He's just topped some tramp and he's here, cool and calm, talking about his fucking car. It's too much. "What da fuck was that about? Killing a man in broad daylight."

"So I take it you don't like the car then Delroy?"

"Wayne, stop pissing about! Why did you do it?"

"Well Del, if you calm down a min I'll tell you. Blimey, you sound like my old girl!"

"I'm calm, cool, I'm calm. So what was all that about?"

"The crackhead wanker owed me money."

"How much?" Wayne stays silent, so I ask again: "How much?"

Wayne says casually, "Oh, ten quid."

I'm gearing up to kick off big time.

"Calm down, Del, calm down."

"Nah! Wayne, you're not right. Stop the car! Stop the bloody car! You're crazy!"

The next words that emerge from Wayne's mouth will stick in my head for the rest of my days.

"Look, it doesn't seem like a lot, but it's the principal bruv. If you let one get away with it all them crackheads will take you for a pussy. And you don't see me with a tail crying meow now do ya?"

I'm interested. "What do you do exactly, Wayne?"

With a big smile, he says, "You know charlie?"

I shrug my shoulders as if he just asked if I can spell cat. "Of course I know charlie. I can't wait to meet him again. So, what about him?"

"Let's just say there are a lot of people that depend on me to keep them happy and they'd give an arm and a leg for this shit, no offence Del. Rich and poor people, they're all on it and it's big dough mate, trust me, big dough.

"That dick I plunged owed me and he didn't pay so he had to get it."

Wayne shrugs it off. "It's not the first time or the last time this is going to happen. It's the name of the game my son and I'm going to bring you in, if you're not too pussy that is."

I'm real intrigued. This sounds right up my street cause I love violence like a smackhead loves charlie. So I make my point to Wayne.

"My name's Delroy AKA legs and there's no middle name called pussy. Cut me in bruv. Just tell me how much money I need to get in on this."

Wayne laughs out loud. "Money? Money? You don't need wonga my friend! I get that shit for free and that's 100 per cent profit."

I'm perching on the edge of my seat. Shit! *Money, money and more fucking money.*

"How bro?"

"Door work bro," he says, nodding his head like the little, brown nodding bulldog sitting on his dashboard. "It's all about the door work."

"What door work? Wayne, come on bro. Talk to me."

"Look Delroy, we're at my drum now. First, we get you in a bath cause you smell like cheap aftershave and I'll fill you in later alright?"

I'm getting really irritated now. "Come on Wayne. You're always keeping me hanging man."

Wayne smiles and looks at me with them deep blues.

"Yeah, but trust me it's going to be well worth it. Now let's get out and go inside. I'm going to introduce you to my old girl."

I look out the car window at his yard. The place is massive with double glazed windows and white bay frames. The walls are white with cream window seals that look like some poor bugger cleans them every day.

As I walk through the black steel gates, there's crunching under my feet, so I look down to see that I'm walking on: little black and brown pebbles.

This guy's living like royalty and whatever he's doing, I want a slice. A big, fuck off slice. I have to show my appreciation. "Fuck about bruv, is that your drum?"

Wayne looks at me as proud as Larry. "Yeah, but when we get inside mind your fucking language OK?"

His face shows no expression, but his eyes gaze at me like they're about to climb into my soul remove it and move in. But he doesn't scare me – it takes a lot more than that to scare me. I'm 8 stones, but I've got heart.

I can see he's deadly serious, so I give him the benefit of the doubt. "Wayne, don't worry bro. It's cool."

He puts his key in the door and calls out. "Precious, where you at? Make yourself respectable. We've got company, babes."

****

I don't know whether to wipe my feet, or just take off my trainers cause the beige, deep shag pile carpet that's about to swallow my dirty feet looks too good for anyone's bare feet, let alone filthy trainers. Wayne bends over to take off his shoes so I just follow his lead.

Something's twinkling in the corner of my eye and as I look to my left I see a massive mirror with a thick gold frame surrounding it like a well-made tailored suit. The twinkle I see is the reflection of a massive crystal chandelier that hangs from the ceiling, looking down at me as though I'm the cleaner who's about to rub the dust off its shiny, round balls.

Down the hallway, a door is ajar on my right. I peep through the crack. It's the front room. Up against the wall is a giant wood veneer cabinet that houses a 25 inch screen. Alongside it stands an all-in-one Amstrad music system which is playing the smooth voice of Jimmy Cliff singing one of my favourite tunes, *Many Rivers to Cross*.

In front of the tv set stands a glass table that balances an Atari games console, two joysticks and a VCR player. Stretched across one side of the wall is a white, Italian leather sofa with two matching armchairs. I know they're Italian cause everyone knows all the best shit's from Italy. Everyone also knows you've got to be loaded to afford it.

There's another door directly opposite the front door; that door's wide open. It's the kitchen and it's bloody massive, but I know I'm not going to see much of this room so let's move on.

Chapter 4
Meeting the Family

Precious comes down the stairs. Fuck.

She's a polished, dark skinned black woman and, damn, she's fine, just strolling down with her long, slender legs. She caresses the bannister with one hand, flaunting her smoothness through a split in a Chinese silk red robe that stretches from her feet to just about the top of a curvy hip. Her butt's so round you can't help but see it from the front. Her hair's a neatly shaped afro with a slight centre parting so neat it's like the black foam around the microphone we use in our sound clashes. It makes her neck seem longer and her skin sleeker.

That's a natural black woman from head to toe!

Her exquisite, dark brown eyes dazzle as though they're competing with her skin, but they complement each other effortlessly. She's flawless. *Fuck.* It's a thought yet my eyes scream it out loud. Wayne sees straight through me, but luckily he just smiles proudly and shrugs it off. It's weird how naturally she falls into Wayne's arms as he gives her a big kiss.

"Hi baby girl, you OK?" Wayne whispers gently, as though he's a little boy about to ask for a slice of chocolate cake.

Without saying a word to Wayne, she turns her attention to me ... and in a huff she blabs without any consideration about the trampy, one-armed black dude standing on her nice, clean carpet with a bin bag for a suitcase: "Wayne, you bringing home strays again?"

I look at Wayne's cheeks as they slowly turn red. I love being black cause only my eyes give away weakness.

"Del, this is my wife Precious," he turns his attention back to her. "Aw babes, this is an old friend of mine. He's on a bit of a low, so he's going to be staying over for a bit. Is that cool?"

She turns to me and grumbles. "Well, first things first: bath cause he smells like cheap aftershave just like you did when we first met. And sir did you leave something in the car?" she asks, arching her perfect eyebrows.

"Precious, what do you mean?" I say to her in my deepest voice, trying not to look at her too hard before *he* gets hard, cause by the size of him he won't have anywhere to hide.

"Where's your other arm? Did you leave it in the car?" *Feisty bitch! I don't give a shit who you are. No bitch chats to me like that.* I'm going to get stuck in.

But before I start, she breaks the ice with a cheeky giggle and that calms me right down as I was about to lose myself in madness. "I'm just joking. What's your name?"

I don't really want to answer as it may be a trick question and if she pulls another stunt like that, I know, and Wayne knows, it will have to go down dirty. "My name's Delroy," I say reluctantly.

She places one hand on a well-rounded hip and raises her left eyebrow, looking even sexier, and snaps as she moves her head from the left to the right.

"Well, remember this Delroy. I'm the queen of this castle." She sticks her head out to elongate her lovely, dark skinned neck. "And whatever I say goes. Isn't that right Wayne?" Wayne mumbles, "Yes babes, it is."

The little boy comes out of him, not like when he slapped that smackhead with a razor blade. You can see in his eyes that he loves her strength; it's as though she keeps him grounded, she's the battery that powers his motor, she's what he works so hard for. But what I like the most about Wayne is he never acts black just cause he has a black woman.

Imagine a white, racist dickhead coming out with some shit in front of him not knowing his pride and joy's black; that's when he'll pull out *two* razor blades, not one and you know that's a straight mars bar, well not that straight mind you "lol"

Precious glides back upstairs to run my bath. She's strong and sexy as hell. By the way Wayne's admiring her, I know he worships her so I have to erase those ideas from my head fast. He's putting me up in his yard for nothing. I want to smash the part of my brain that's making me want to bang his wife.

"Wayne, she's beautiful and she's black. I never for one minute would've thought you'd have a black woman on your arm let alone in your yard."

Wayne looks at me like I'm crazy. "Bro, once you go black you never go back! I'm going to work, so get in your bath and make yourself at home. When I come back, I'll fill you in on the business." Just like that, he walks out the front door.

Either this man's testing me or he's just a good guy. He doesn't really know me, but he's willing to put me up in his house and trust me around his wife. For those reasons, I'll never betray his trust and I'll stay loyal. Then I hear her voice.

"Delroy! Your bath is ready. Come up before it gets cold." That's the same thing Teresa used to say, but there's no going back to her now. I totally burned those bridges to ashes.

I enter the bathroom. Shit. It's so clean, you could eat your grub off the black marble floor tiles.

Lavender and rose bath salts, mmmm. I get in the bath and submerge myself in the hot, steamy water, totally leaving the world behind me. It feels like the only bath I've ever had.

My eyes are heavy, my body's light, all my stress is ebbing away and I'm out for the count.

Chapter 5
The Business

It's 3.45am and I'm in a deep, coma-like sleep. Wayne's knocking at my bedroom door. I wake up still sick with tiredness from the bath I had earlier; I could just sleep for a year and some.

"Yo Del, you OK man? I'm back and I got something to show you. Look at this bro!"
I rub the sleep out of my eyes, desperate to see what goodies Wayne has to show me. Wayne starts to dig deep into his pocket and pulls out at least five wads of ten and fifty pound notes.

Now I'm awake and I mean wide awake.

"Damn bro, is that what they're paying you? That's crazy. What do you do? Look after the queen?"

"Nah bruv, that's the little hustle I was telling you about."

"Well, by the looks of it Wayne you need to tell me more."

Wayne shrugs his massive shoulders. "I'll fill you in tomorrow bro, it's late and you're going to need your sleep for what I've got planned for you in a few hours."

I'm frustrated, but I try to keep my voice down. "No Wayne, tell me now or I'm not going to get no sleep at all ... just tell me man."

Wayne shrugs his shoulders again and huffs reluctantly. "OK bro, I can see you're up for it. This is how it goes. I'm the head doorman of all the nightclubs in east London, so anything I say goes. I control who comes in and who stays out. I know all the dealers on the circuit. So I let them into the clubs and I get my runners to keep a dog's eye on them.

"Obviously, it's only a matter of time before they start selling their shit – weed, crack and all the rest of the hard stuff – and that's when I step in and give them a slap. I take their gear and anything else I can get off them little punks. They don't grass cause they know who I am. And who they going to grass to anyways, the pigs?

"Now here's the twist. The same stuff I take, I give to one of my young dogs. I usually use my guy Smiley cause I don't have to pay him. I just feed him when he's itching if you get my drift. Then he sells it on, he gives me the dough and I keep track of the buyer by using Snake. He tells me what club this guy's going to hit then I make sure I'm there, or one of my soldiers is there, to let them in with the gear.

"I keep a dog eye on them and as soon as he makes a sale I pull him and take his shit. And that, my friend, is 100 per cent profit cause I get their money and my shit back. Plus I get some nice stuff for my

Precious, and if she's happy, I'm happy and that's what you call *brilliant* my son."

I can't believe what I'm hearing; Wayne's a genius, a fucking legend.

"Wayne, that sounds like easy money, my friend."

Wayne just says with a smile, "It's all in a day's work mate and I tell you something else: working the doors pay just as good. So it's double bubble and if you like a bit of a rumble. The doors are the place to be."

I get real excited like a fat policeman eating Krispy Kreme.

"What about the girls bro? You must see a lot of skirt."

Wayne looks shy, his eyes shine differently and what he says next stirs up emotions, memories and a little bit of the green-eyed monster in me. "Yeah, there's a hell of a lot of skirt: black, white, even Chinese. There's all kinds, but none of them can beat my Precious. They can't even come close. It's all about my Precious, bruv, so when I see that door open and them punters come through all I think is *Show me the money*, show me the fucking money. That's just me but I know it's going to be right up your street."

I try to shake off the jealousy. I mean, why can't I have that feeling for a woman? Will I ever have that feeling, or am I just going to keep using my fist against myself, knocking myself out of the game every time a girl falls in love with me?

I find myself sharply saying, "OK bro, I'm up for it. When do we start? Can we start tomorrow night?"

Wayne's quick off the mark. "You ain't ready yet. First, you need to put on some weight cause judging by your looks, you're about 11 stones now. We need to buff you up to about 18 stones; that'll be great for your height."

I can't argue. I'm very skinny for a 6 feet 5 inches guy and I'm not feeling myself at all. One thing's good though: 11 stones! I thought I was three stones lighter. I need this badly cause all I'm doing is getting dribs and drabs of money here and there.

I don't want that life. I surrender to what Wayne's telling me like a duck to sauce.

"Alright Wayne, but how long will it take?" Wayne just smiles that big smile, like the one he used when I tried to kill him with that punch the very first time we met.

"With the shit I've got for you bro, it's going to take three months and you better be ready; it's going to be a lot of hard graft mate. Now get some sleep and we crack on early tomorrow."

He starts to walk out the room, leaving three wads of notes on my bed.

"Yo Wayne, you forgot your dough bro." I never imagined I would've said that to anyone who left that amount of wonga around me, but I guess it feels as natural as anything.

Wayne turns around and says proudly, "Bruv, that's yours. Tomorrow, go and buy some new clobber and some decent aftershave." He chuckles and starts walking out the room.

I can't believe it! There must be at least a grand or more just sitting on my bed, looking at me. No-one's ever done this for me before. "Thanks man, for real." I'm trying to restrain a big smile.

"Del, it's OK son. We're boys and that's just the start cause we're going to be gods this time next year. Now get some sleep cause tomorrow I'm going to introduce you to my friend called steroids, but you can call him Roids for short."

Then he disappears behind the door and I fall back into a coma sleep, not knowing if this is a dream or reality. I don't want it to end. Is this guy a God-send or too good to be true? I'm out for the count.

****

A massive hand's bouncing me around like a basketball on my bed. "Delroy! Wake up bro, wake up!" Oh shit. That voice sounds familiar. It's a dream. I'm going to open my eyes and be back in that same, crappy, old squat with Teresa waking me up for a crappy breakfast like she always does.

"Delroy! Wake up man! Wake up!" I open my eyes and the first place I clock is the dresser. The money's still there.

This ain't a dream. I exhale at the thought of spending it. Wayne's voice: "Damn bruv! You were well gone man, get up we got to go gym."

I wipe the sleep from my eyes and look at the big red clock that's neatly placed on the wall, all colour coded to match the black and red stripy velvet wall paper. "Wayne, are you two quid short of a fiver? It's 6am in the bloody morning."

Wayne chuckles. I can see he wants to belly laugh, but he doesn't want to risk waking Precious.

"That's the way we do it bro, nice and early, get it done and dusted. You know, the early bird catches the worm and all that bollocks. But before you get up I got something for you." He pulls out a syringe, a long, bloody syringe.

I back up. "What the hell you think you going to do with that bro? What the hell is it?"

Before I know it, the needle's sitting neatly in my right bum cheek. Bloody liberty! But it's the first time with my new friend called Roids and most definitely not the last.

I'm out of bed and we hit the gym, or should I say the gym hit me. Yes, it hit me like a bad smell with a lot of steel, muscle and a ton of bricks. I'll never forget walking down that alley between a lot of trees and bushes as we stroll through the old, black door.

I say to Wayne, "Yo, bro where you taking me? This isn't a gym, it's a house."

"Just wait till you get inside," he chuckles.

The first thing that hits me is damp mixed with sweat and hard work, like man verses B.O. We step inside and there's a guy standing behind a short, wooden counter; he's old, but you can see through his washed out Wag Bennett's gym T-shirt that he was a lump back in his early days. There are a few pictures on the wall of all the top body builders with their countries and dates printed on a once gold, now off-gold, plaque.

Arnold Schwarzenegger, Austrian-American, 1947: The Austrian Oak.

Stephane Caron, Canada, 1970.

Michael Kefalianos, Greece, 1970.

Fouad Abiad, Canada, 1978.

Tevita Aholelei, United States, 1969: Stone of Tonga.

Damn, I think to myself, this is the real thing. But the best is yet to come. "Hi Wag," Wayne greets the old man behind the counter. The old man looks at me with a slight grin.

"So Wayne, you've brought a new body to kill. I hope this one survives."

What the hell does he mean by that? I guess it makes sense. No-one can really train with the monster that's about to kill me.

Wayne chuckles, "He'll be safe as houses."

"Wayne, where's these bloody weights?" I'm trying to remind them I'm standing right here.

Wayne walks and I follow carefully. "Come on bro, what you scared of? Come this way."

Wayne's like a god. All the way through the gym people stop their workouts to shake his hand. I'm surprised to see his picture on the wall alongside the late greats.

We pass through another door that takes us into a garden that's covered with a plastic roof; it's full of flowers and little statues of naked men with their dicks out. I bite my tongue and say nothing. We walk through yet another door.

Where do we start?

There are machines and weights as far as my eyes can see. To my right, there's a big cardboard cut-out of a life-sized Arnold Schwarzenegger standing proudly on an old stage, as though he's keeping a dog's eye on the gym. Amazing! It's going to be my second home.

We start training: legs, back, shoulders, chest, biceps, triceps abs, one-arm chin ups and one-arm press ups.

This guy's trying to kill me, but I can feel the steroids coursing through my veins. I'm an animal, untouchable. It's the closest thing to death, apart from my interview with charlie and he's one friend I can't wait to meet again.

Yes, the training's good, but there's a problem. I must also reacquaint myself with a mate I don't ever want to see again. Do you know who? Well, take a wild guess. OK, you can't? Let me give you a clue: I've only got one of them and every other lucky bastard around me has two. Yeah, that's right: my plastic arm.

Wayne tells me I can never get one side of my body balanced with the other if I only have one arm. I need to get my prosthetic so my body will grow properly, or at least look half decent. He says he has a guy who can reinforce it with steel rods so it won't snap under the pressure of the weight as I get stronger.

Getting the arm and using it ain't really the problem. The problem's going back to that place and facing Teresa again. After a long, hard slug in the gym and a well-deserved bubble bath I'm anxious to go to Stratford to buy some new garms. I know exactly what I want: a Gabicci top, a pair of Farahs and a pair of moccasins cause when you rock that kind of clobber the girls love it. As I'm leaving, I call out to Wayne.

"Yo! Wayne! I'm going to take a trip down to Mr Byrite to cop some garms. You coming or what?"

Wayne tries to change my mind; he's worrying too much about me and I'm not used to that kind of thing.

"Del, why don't you get some rest then go out man? You're going to overwork yourself and your body needs to rest."

I didn't have a daddy and I don't need one, so I call back calmly, trying not to bark at him. "Nah, bro. I'm cool and I'll be quick. I'm not going to buy much cause I can feel myself growing and I know I'm going to need to change my wardrobe again pretty soon." I know Wayne's right, but I've never felt this way before. Whatever he injected into me is already working. I love every second of the sensation; I'm too hyped and I want to go, tired or not.

And I'm glad I did, cause if I listen to Wayne I would have never meet Sandra ...

Chapter 6
My Soul mate

I walk into Mr Byrite and clock her right away. I love dark skinned females with full lips and strong features cause in my eyes they're gorgeous, but, damn, *this* girl is especially fine.

I know I said the same thing about Teresa, but I mean it. This girl's damn sexy. She's about 5 feet 5 inches tall and size 10 to 12, but her breasts are as big as my head and her ass balances out the weight of them. She has thick, curly, light brown hair; it's slightly frizzy and I like it ... I like it a lot, the way it just bounces alongside her tits as she walks is amazing. She probably doesn't even have to comb it, she just wash and goes.

She's wearing a light blue polo t-shirt that says 'Hello, I'm here to help' in big letters. *Damn, girl, you can help me any time.* Just get a spanner and fix my heart cause by the looks of me and by the looks of her I know she's about to break it. She's walking over. As she gets closer, I notice her eyes are a stunning green-grey. I fall smack, bang into a trap and it seems like she set it up. I'm in love. She's getting closer and I'm struggling for breath, trying to stuff oxygen in my lungs like that smackhead Wayne opened up with a razor blade.

I really don't know what to do with myself and by the look on her face she knows it. *What's she going to think about me only having one arm?* Will she want me? I want her badly. She's standing right in front of me. I've died and gone to heaven. Yeah, fat chance of that. I feel like a little boy. She speaks.

"Er, hello are you looking for something in particular?"

Silly me, I just come straight out with it. "Yeah, your number please. I mean ... sorry ... I mean, I'm looking for a Gabicci top and a pair of strides, I need some new aftershave please cause Jah Shaka and the Mighty King Tubby are having a sound clash tonight at Stratford School and I've got to look sharp."

"OK then. I'm not really into dub music cause I'm a soul puss, so, apart from my number, I'll show you where they're kept. Follow me please."

Damn. I've blown it. She smiles. She leads and I follow like a little puppy dog just begging for a bite to eat and a place to sleep.

I'm walking right behind her and I can't keep my eyes to myself. That bum has legs of its own, it's just bouncing from side to side trying to demolish everything in sight. Shit! She's as fit as hell. Oh my God, if only ... if only. A little voice in my head says

Back up, Delroy. She's out of your league. What's she thinking about my arm? Does she think I'm less of a man, or does she know she's getting acquainted with a fighting machine? She turns around as though she's moving in slow motion, totally throwing my mind off balance.

"Here we are, trousers are over there and tops are to your left. I'm not going to show you any aftershaves cause I think the one you're wearing smells great. It's Brut isn't it?"

This girl is good.

"Yeah it is. How do you know?"

With a smile she says, "I can smell a good man when I meet one. Hope you find what you've been looking for." Then, just like that, she walks away.

I call out to her, "Yeah I have," but no amount of money can pay for her so I guess I'm going to go home empty-handed. She looks back and with a big smile she disappears between the Adidas tracksuits.

I buy my garms and walk slowly to the door, eyes cast to the floor, heartbroken. Why didn't I just persist about the number? Now I'm never going to see her again. I'm so stupid, acting like a little girl. Now confidence starts rising in my chest. I'm going to find her and get that number. As I turn around, she's standing right behind me.

"Did you get everything you wanted sir?"

"I think so." Aaarrgh! If I had two hands I could punch my own face here and now, right on the spot, so it's a good thing I have bags in the only hand

I own. Then she says with a smile, "Well, I think you forgot something." She stretches out her hand and slips a piece of paper into my side pocket.

"You look harmless, so I guess you having my number can't hurt."

Is she taking the piss or what? It doesn't matter cause she has me hooked.

"I'm just joking. As you can already guess, your arm doesn't bother me at all so stop trying to hide it cause you can't hide something that's not there. Anyway, it looks like you need a hair specialist to plait that messy head of yours."

She lets out a slight giggle which is so cute cause I can see dimples dancing on her face like the magic jelly beans I used to play with when I was back at school.

"This is the number of the phone box at the end of my street. Call me tonight at seven sharp. I'll be waiting there for your call. I know you won't be late cause by the looks of you, you have a house phone, so call me later. You're so shy and sweet and I like that," then she walks off.

I'm left standing here gobsmacked. If someone else had cracked that joke I would've cracked a rib or two. Anyway, next stop phone shop. Need to get a phone by tonight as I don't recall seeing one in my bedroom. Then I need to pick up an old friend called arm. But first wimpy sounds good cos I'm proper hank-Marvin.

Chapter 7
Living the High Life

Twenty years old and living the high life, everything's going great. I've made it to head doorman. Still working under Wayne, though, but that's cool cause me and Wayne are inseparable.

One punk put the word out that we're an item, but that's OK, we dealt with him properly with the help of his mum who held him down while we peeled bits off him. She had no choice but to do what we told her unless she wanted to end up on the table alongside him. When we'd finished inside the kitchen, we covered the boot of Wayne's old runner round Capri in plastic, broke some glass bottles and dashed some spanners in just for small measure and a bit more pain. Then we dragged the prick kicking and screaming as we shoved him in.

His mum was screaming and crying like a good one, so I spun round, grabbed her by the neck and whispered, "Calm down, he'll be back home real soon. One more thing: if you like your ears and nose where they are just try and calling the old bill and I'll come back and swap them around for you after we bring your son home in an open casket" It didn't take her long to dry her eyes.

We took a drive down to one of them bed and breakfasts on the Romford Road, stepping hard on the brakes from time to time and raging the car over any humps we could see.

Next stop, we had to pick up batty boy Steve on the way. No-one likes batty boy Steve cause not only is he gay, he thinks he's one of them bad boy yardi gaylords. But in my book you can't be a shirt lifter and a bad boy all rolled up in one. We don't like to associate with guys like that, but on this occasion we needed him to make an example of the cunt in the boot and show him what being gay was all about.

We knew about Steve from the gym. He's about five feet six, built like a tank and has long dreadlocks which he ties back with a blue bandana. He wears bottle-thick glasses that make his eyes look massive; that's some scary shit.

We heard he swings both ways, is hung like a horse and at that time he had a touch of the old VD, so yeah, batty boy Steve was the man for the job or, should I say, the gay for the job.

When we pulled up outside the bed and breakfast Wayne said, "Here you go, two hundred quid, two boxes of doms and a stone to rub on your dick." A stone keeps your boy hard for hours. "Your new bride's in the boot. He's a bit bloody, but I'm sure you're going to make him bloodier than what he already is." So Steve took the stuff and he was gone. I couldn't help but think, *That poor bastard, he ain't going to shit right for weeks, but maybe he'll keep his mouth shut in the future.*

****

Anyway, as you can tell I'm still the same old Delroy, just bigger. Height: 6 feet 5 inches. Weight: 20 stones. Arms: 20 inches. Chest: 52 inches. Waist: 34 inches. One arm dumbbell dead lift: 80kg. Bench press with prosthetic arm: 120kg. Squat: 200kg.

Yes, I'm still on the roids and built like a shithouse. As for charlie, I tried him again, but the effects were too much. Mixing it with roids sent me crazy and I can't bring that shit around Sandra.

Yes, I'm still with Sandra and we're totally in love. I never thought I'd say this, but it's true: the day I saw her it was love at first sight. My mind's drifting back to my first encounter of real love ... I'm there.

I knock at Sandra's door, my heart racing, not knowing what to expect. I remember the first day I saw her in the shop.

She just floats into my life. Her precious feet don't even touch the ground. She moves so elegantly, trying to disguise herself behind that shimmering, gorgeous smile. So elegant is her movement it's as though she's about to melt into my arm. I replay that thought over and over again in my mind. When she laughs, it's like the Pacific Ocean gently hitting and taming the rocks on the edge of midnight.

Does she know she's beautiful, or am I the only one that sees the rose petals fall at her feet as she glides deeper into my soul? Her work uniform appears to be the finest silk cuddling her curves. How could she have another man with that body?

Her body's perfect in every way – it should be mine and mine alone. I wish I was the tight, blue polo shirt that's wrapped snuggly around her breasts cause my embrace she'll never forget!

Tight black trousers are firmly moulded around her sexy, full ass which tops off her thick, healthy thighs very nicely indeed. Envy settles in. How can those garms hold such beauty?

Her body should be for my embrace only! If only I could stop time for one second; the way I feel about her, that second would be 1,000 years of kissing her full lips cause her body looks too pure to desecrate with the mad tings I want to perform on every inch of her body.

I get to Sandra's house and push the front door open.

"Sandra! I'm here! Where you at?"

She calls faintly from a faraway room. "I'm in the kitchen Del."

I feel a mad rush like I'm a virgin about to lose what was once mine. I can't wait to see her, so I race towards the kitchen, totally forgetting it's the first time we're meeting with no-one around to stop me from smashing her back out. Consequently, I'm a little bit surprised when Sandra gasps and steps backwards.

SANDRA

I gasp, not out of fear but cause of the way my pussy hurts and moistens when I see him again.

DELROY

"Sorry Sandra," I say sharply. "I forgot myself for a minute, I just couldn't wait to see you." She smiles that great smile I love so much. "It's alright Del, I couldn't wait to see you either." Bet her pussy wants to see me even more. She's trying to be modest, rattling on and on about work and how the customers are so full of shit. Man, this talk is long cause all I want to do is feel that tight ring around my cock. I know it's tight cause she hinted to me on a couple of occasions that she only wants to open up for me, so I know she's a V reg, waiting for me to take her for a ride …

I don't even hear Sandra speaking anymore; I'm just looking at what she's wearing. It's that pleasing, little red nightie I still love so much. Damn! Every time I see her wearing it, it's like the first time I see her wearing it if you get my meaning. I look closer. Fuck. She's totally bare underneath. I can just about make out two little chocolate buttons on the end of her big breasts, hard and peeking through her nightie. They're peeking at me like they're waiting so desperately for me to pop them into my mouth and suck them into oblivion.

What happens next shouldn't come as a shock cause everyone does it, or thinks about doing it. I slowly walk over to her as she's still chatting away, not even realising I'm about to nail her right here on the spot. I seize my chance. Bang! Her left leg is up on the sink and I'm on my knees licking her well shaven pussy. Thank God she ain't wearing any panties.

SANDRA
My God, what's this guy doing to me? is all that's rushing through my head. The way his full lips are sucking my clit is amazing. I can't even suck on a lollipop at that rate and if he was sucking a lollipop, he'd have popped it clean off its stick by now. Shit. I'm drowning in lust. I need his tongue to go deep, deeper inside me, so I take my thumb and forefinger and spread my lips wide. I pull on the back of his head, roughly rubbing my wet pussy in his face, not caring if he suffocates for a few seconds. His tongue pushes deeper inside me as I fall deeper in love with him. "Good boy ... you're such a good boy," I whisper.

DELROY
This is the first time I'm eating her, but the way she tastes, I know it won't be the last. Oh, guys are always trying to get head from girls. Why don't they try giving them head too and see the result? Do it

properly and the girl you want will be totally locked down, hook line and sinker.

Anyway, I'm here flicking and sucking on Sandra's little friend, desperate to make her cum deep in my throat as she stands grasping at thin air. I insert one finger gently into her ring; I'd love to put two fingers in, but I want to keep it as tight as possible for my boy to penetrate. I start to nibble and flick her taut, erect clit with my tongue. Fast then slow, hard then soft. Her breathing is picking up speed. As she gasps for breath, I glimpse up and watch as she pulls at those firm nipples and rolls them between her fingertips. Now she stops breathing and bites her bottom lip. Her eyes are rolling to the back of her head. I think she's going to pass out.

"Yes it's there ... it's there, please don't stop. Oh my God! Please ... Please ... Don't stop Del!"

She grabs my head, forcing me to suck her clit harder as she grinds her pussy, violently violating my mouth. Finally, after crossing many rivers, I reach the heart of her ocean and like Niagara Falls she bursts her banks, squirting in my mouth. Her right leg crumbles as she desperately tries to muffle her cries by biting on my fingers as I slip them in and out of her mouth. I try to keep her steady with my chest and shoulders. I try desperately to catch every drop of her water like a thirsty brother, not wanting to waste a bit. I need so desperately to show her this isn't a one night affair. This is one of many nights to cum, I mean come.

SANDRA
This isn't the first time I've ever cum, but it's the first time someone else ever made me orgasm and it's definitely the hardest I've ever cum. After this, I know I'll be addicted. I want to breathe, but I don't want to breathe. I want to scream, but I want to hold my screams in my chest to intensify my orgasm. I want to crumble, but my legs hold me firmly in place to fully taste the madness. I don't like to call the Lord's name in vain, but – Goddamn – his lips are *good*! I can hardly wait to feel his dick.

DELROY
After composing herself and brushing her hair away from her eyes with her well-polished finger nails, she kisses me gently, sucking on my tongue as though she's trying to taste herself. She whispers gently. "Now take me to my room and take what's yours."

She wastes no time; she just grabs me by the hand and pulls me up the stairs and down the dimly lit hallway, leading me to her bedroom door. She hesitates there, as though she's trying to tease me. I look deep into her eyes as I pull her through the doorway. Sweet mango and lemon oil evaporates in an oil burner on her dressing table. She pulls back just a bit, but I can tell she's just teasing my now well firm cock as she presses her pussy against him. I land a well-aimed kiss on her soft lips, tasting lip gloss that makes her tender mouth glisten in the candlelight.

"Mmm, cherry flavour," I murmur.

The sound of Janet Kay singing *Silly Games* plays in the darkness on a cassette tape recorder that's placed on a little table on the right hand side of the room; that just makes me want her even more, so I start kissing her softly at first then more passionately as I lead the lamb to the slaughter. I push her up against the wall as I work my way down, kissing her neck, running my hands all over her body like she's the only woman left on the planet. I want her to feel as though every inch of her body is being caressed by 100 hands and kissed by 100 lips.

"Oh baby, you feel so good," she says as she rips at my top, trying to undress me and control her legs at the same time. I lift her nightie over her head, unable to wait to see the roundness of her plump, firm tits as I picture myself sucking on them while grabbing her tight ass, spreading it wide to reveal her well-trimmed, brown and pink beauty. Her skin shines as the candlelight flickers against her cocoa-buttered skin. I proceed to roll my tongue over her nipples, licking and sucking them equally, so neither feels left out. She gasps and holds on tight.

"Delroy, I'm yours baby boy, all yours." Her voice courses through my veins. I grab her hands and pin them against the wall. "Sandra, don't move your hands from there ... don't touch me at all ... just leave them there and don't make a sound," I say to her, in a deeper baritone voice. She gasps like she knows this little game, as though we've played it before.

SANDRA

"I can't, Del ... I can't ..."

And I mean it. I'm about to explode with tension, but he calms me down so he can continue his little game with my body that's now his playground. No swings, no roundabouts, but I know I'm in for a lot of ups and downs. "Ssshhh, baby girl," he says as my voice quivers. Now, intense frustration sets in and I know I'm about to cum harder than ever as he starts to kiss down, down, down the rest of my body, knowing exactly where he's going as if he's reading a road map.

He whispers, "I want to taste you again, baby, is that OK?"

What woman could resist? I command him softly: "Feed yourself, baby, feed yourself!"

DELROY

I obey. As I gently kiss her stomach, her legs spasm with excitement and anticipation. She knows what's coming. How could she forget after the way I nailed her in the kitchen? I look up at her. Her eyes roll while I carry on moving my lips down her body, kissing and licking her thighs as I gently spread them apart, admiring the beauty of her tight quim; my tongue rolls over her clit as she gasps in excitement, much louder than when I sucked her nipples. She moans as I start tasting her for the second time.

"Eat me baby ... please eat me all up!" She starts to wine on my mouth as I tease my tongue across her clit. I push it deep inside as I grab her hands and place them firmly on the back of my head so she can grab it tight and guide me to the spot that matters most.

"Good girl," I mumble. She tastes like honey, all warm and sweet. I slide down to the floor, bringing her with me as I lay on my back and invite her to sit on my face. My tongue goes even deeper inside her now as she rides me, forgetting, or not caring, that I can just about breathe. I hope it's not my tongue that's about to take her virginity as I try to penetrate her with every last bit of it. I grab onto her hips, making her grind on my mouth as I try to regain some control.

But she ain't having any of it.

She's in total control, riding slow at first then speeding up. Her body feels tightly coiled, as she rides my tongue I can feel she's about to cum, her whole body starts to tremble. She cums and I swallow it up, yet again not wanting to waste a drop. I spin her around, placing her firmly on her back, wanting so desperately to fuck her pussy while her clit's still delicate, not giving her pussy time to recover from the way she came. Now it's my turn.

SANDRA

Tiny beads of sweat run down my chin, past my neck and down my breasts. Delroy just wants to lick me dry as though he's trying to get as much of my body fluids in him as possible; I chew my bottom lip as I know what's coming next. Fear creeps in as he pulls out his cock. I pant as I see the length, totally forgetting about the girth. *Where in the hell did he get that from?* Now I know why his confidence is sky high! His manhood compensates for his arm and now he's about to prove it. I'm scared and have to buy some time, so I do it the only way I can think of. That's right. I repay his kindness in full.

DELROY

Sandra grabs the shaft of my cock and fear twinkles in her eyes as she pulls me towards her, guiding me into her mouth. I just follow the end of my cock as it penetrates her generous mouth. Hmm, what the hell is she thinking? *How long does she think I'll last without gushing?* She starts by placing my hood between her lips and wraps her hands around my bum cheeks, pulling me deeper into her throat. She gags a little, but she's not stopping. She tries again.

I swear she thinks she's in some competition with me and by the way her lips feel i should be coming first as my balls are about to blow up and kill everything within a five mile radius. She senses my body stiffening as I'm about to cum and slides my cock out of her mouth, from shaft to tingling tip.

"Not yet baby boy," she whispers. "I got a lot more, be good until mummy says so OK?" she says as she pumps my foreskin back and forth then grabs at my nipples. With two hands, she places me back into her mouth and starts to suck violently as though she wants to drain me of every bit of my life force. The sound of her lips moving me in and out is too much to bear. Thank God she pacifies me as she slips me out and runs her lips down the shaft of my cock as she starts sucking on my stiff balls.

Her hand finds its way to the end of my boy as she starts to pump him back and forth again. "Let it go baby ... let it go," so I do as I'm told. She hurries her lips to the end to catch all she can.

Only seconds pass and my cock's already knocking at her entrance. "Please don't hurt me Del," she says, not realising that this just makes me even hornier as pain is my playground and my playground is everyone's hell. I never knew anything about heaven and I never really cared, but tonight I will as I'm about to take my Sandra there.

SANDRA

He's teasing me with the tip of his cock, only pushing the head inside. My pussy opens as I start to back up, trying to get away from his weapon, so he wraps his arm around me, holds me there, teasing her and giving her cock inch by inch. My pussy blossoms open like a sunflower in the early months of spring. I beg Delroy to stop teasing my pussy and give her what she wants. So he does, as he bites me hard on my shoulder to confuse the pain and forces his cock deep inside her like she's one of his enemies. I feel a small pop inside me as Del's cock breaks my hymen. Now, she's definitely open and his. By the look on his face, he knows it.

DELROY

Sandra digs her nails into my back and bites my shoulder to stop her from screaming the house down, but I don't care, the pain's good and well deserved, so I give it to her hard and fast, just how she wants it. I love the way she moans after every deep stab with my hard cock that's already so desperate to cum again. But being the man I am, I hold it in my well stiff balls. She wraps her legs around my waist as I wind my cock deep inside her to the rhythm of *The First time I Ever Saw Your Face* by Marcia Griffiths on the tape recorder. Her legs are up in the air and on my shoulders, so every jook I give her pussy is deeper than the last as our position shifts.

She's tearing deep marks into my back, but I'm still not caring. Her moans have turned to screams, calling me *Baby* as she cums again, but I don't stop or slow down. I just keep working her harder. I want her ... no ... I *need* her. Her skin against my skin is the best thing that ever happened to me and the sound of our sweaty bodies slamming is the best tune I ever heard. I flip her over on to her hands and knees and start deep fucking as I grab her hair. I pull and go even deeper inside as she looks around at me, unable to talk. She can just about catch her breath. Her face tells me to stop, but her eyes tell a different story, so I listen to her eyes and fuck her deeper.

I lay her on her belly and wrap my big hand gently around her throat, as she finds time to reach under and grab at my balls, telling me she wants me to cum with her yet again. I wine my hips in time to the sweet sounds of Janet Kay singing *You Bring the Sun Out*, then I lose track of the music and speed up, fucking her hard and fast. My whole body stiffens as I cum and she squirts all over my cock and balls, wetting my pubic hair. Now she's mine. At least, I think she is as she falls into a deep sleep. She disappears into the darkness wordlessly. Damn, I'm good. I pick her up, lay her gently on her bed and cuddle her. This is where the night ended and the morning came.

****

Yes, Sandra's my heartbeat and I made a pact with myself that I will never flinch towards her, not ever. I've never laid my hand on her. I love this woman to death and back and I'm not about to allow my hand or legs to make that mistake again. The money I bring in is great; we live in a big house and drive the latest top spec Ford Granada. We have our ups and downs, but it's nothing I can't handle, I just go out, kick the shit out of some poor bugger, get it out of my system, then I go home, make love to Sandra and play happy families.

She thinks I'm just a doorman, but if only she knew. But she's great cause she don't ask any questions, and she loves the gifts I get her. She's never seen the pile of gift boxes I stash in the boot of my car. When I pull some guy for shagging some bird in the toilet, I take his cash, her jewellery and kick them out. I clean the jewels and put them in one of the boxes. They look brand, spanking new and I give them to Sandra like I brought them from a swanky shop (little chuckle).

She's happy and it works great for me. I give her anything she wants, but there's one thing she wants that I don't ever want and that's a baby. She goes on and on about it, but I just brush it off, I'm not interested. I've already got one son but I've never seen him. I heard he's a boy called Carlton, but I'm not interested, not one bit.

Maybe I can't get past the ghost of my mum that hunts me so badly. I don't think I ever will to tell the truth. Sandra got pregnant once before, but she lost it. I didn't want it in the first place, so her losing the baby didn't bother me one bit, but keeping her happy is all I think about. I'm in a catch 22 ain't I? The thought of having a child makes me sick to my gut. I mean, imagine if it's a boy! It's just going to be another bastard like me and if it's a girl she may end up being kicked out a nightclub for getting smashed in by some dude in a dirty club toilet. So when I think about it, I'm not in a catch 22 at all.

But things are about to change tonight. Wayne's gone over to France to make a pick-up, so he's there for the weekend and I'm left to keep the ball rolling. I have to get to the club at least three hours early, so I can brief the rest of the doormen. For some reason, Sandra's totally getting under my feet and, as you can imagine, being 20 stone and over 6 feet I need all the space I can get.

"Delroy, we need to talk."

"OK babes. Can't it wait till I get home from work? I'm going to be late and you know that can't happen," I say gently, but she's persistent.

"I know Del, but can you come downstairs for five minutes please?" I can tell she's frowning.

I'm at the top of the stairs and I really can't be arsed, plus I'm starting to get irritated. Don't get it twisted. I didn't *say* that to her.

"Sandra, just come up cause I need to get out of here." I can't think straight, I just need to go. Before I know it, Sandra's standing in front of me at the top of the stairs. I hold her head with my big, scarred-up hand and kiss her gently on the forehead.

"Babes, what can be so important that you can't wait till I get back?"

What she says next knocks me straight out of the game. She holds my hand firmly and stares up into my face. "Delroy, I know who you are, what you want and what you don't want. But I need you to keep an open mind and heart about what I'm going to tell you. This is what I want."

I look deep into her eyes, trying to keep the beast contained as I know exactly what she's about to say. I need to get to work without a major argument erupting.

"What do you want Sandra? I've given you everything and anything. What do you want so badly that you can't wait to tell me and make me late for work?"

She expresses herself firmly, "A baby Delroy, a baby's what I want."

"Oh come on Sandra! Not this again. We've been through this a thousand times. I don't want or need a baby."

She just looks at me with those big, bright eyes. "It's too late Del."
My heart jumps clean out of my chest. "What do you mean it's too late?" I try to keep calm, I try to hold down the beast that's now raging inside me and trying to claw its way out of every bone in my body. "Sandra, what do you mean?"

"I'm pregnant. I'm going to be a mum and you're going to be a dad. We can do this, Del, we can do this if we stick together."

I put my hand over my eyes as if to hide my past ways of getting what I want. I'm trying my hardest to keep my hand and feet to myself. After all, I love this woman and I made a vow never to lay hand on her. I have to get out and fast.

"Look, Sandra, it ain't the right time to talk about this. I need to go, so please move out of my way."

She puts her arm across the stairway. "So when is the right time, Delroy? When do you want me to tell you? You're going to be a dad for God's sake."

It's too much. "Sandra! Just get out of my way!"

I push past. It ain't my fault. All I want to do is get out of here, I don't mean any harm. I gasp as I see Sandra rolling backwards down the stairs like a scene from a bad film that will never end.

"Sandra!" I yell at the top of my lungs.

I dash down the stairs, trying to catch her to break her fall, but I'm moving in slow motion and little do I know something else is about to happen, something I can't change even if I was the strongest man in the world. I slip and tumble. I try to stop myself, but 20 stones, one arm and the law of gravity aren't a great concoction. I end up smack, bang on top of her. The combination of my full weight and the speed I fall pin her up against the wall at the bottom of the steps.

"Oh my God! Sandra, are you OK? I'm sorry, I didn't mean it. I'm sorry ... please get up! Open your eyes!" She seems dead, but after five minutes she slowly opens her eyes so I try to pick her up from the floor.

She turns on me and snarls, "Get off me!"

"Sandra, *please*, it was an accident."

"Don't touch me! Stay away from me!" she snaps again.

Now I'm begging. I can see everything we've built fading away fast. I'm looking at the woman I love so deeply, the only woman I've ever loved, slipping through my fingers and I have to make it right. But how? I'm not used to fixing things I break.

"Sandra, I'm sorry. Just let me help you up and I'll leave you alone. I just want to make sure you're OK." But she ain't having any of it.

"Delroy, if you care about me you'll just leave me the hell alone!"

What can I say? My heart's shattered. If only she knew I'd rather cut off my one arm than ever hurt her. "Alright Sandra, but I'm going to call Precious. Is that cool?"

"Just leave me alone," she groans, clutching her belly and sobbing like a little child.
All I can do is walk and hope for the best, but something dark's spreading across the back of my brain: *I wish she'd lose that little bastard child cause this is all its fault.*

Sandra spends half an hour at the bottom of the steps till Precious arrives. She hears knocking on the front door.

"Sandra? Sandra! Open the door! It's Precious!"

Sandra pushes herself off the floor and flings open the door, bawling hysterically. "Precious, I don't know what happened!"

"Sandra, stop and sit down." Precious gently wipes the water from Sandra's eyes.

But Sandra goes on. "I don't know why he did it; I think he's trying to kill our baby."

Precious tries to explain to Sandra, but she's too disorientated to hear her. "Sandra, you better sit down babes ... sit down now."

"Precious, I'm fine, I just need to get away from Delroy. He's not the man I thought he was, there's something about him that's not right and I'm getting scared, real scared. The way he looked at me when I told him I'm pregnant … He wanted to kill me there and then and if he tried, how the hell could I have stopped him? He's abusing the steroids and they're going to his head! Please help me! I just need to get out of here."

Precious raises her voice a little. Firmly. "No Sandra, you're not fine … look down." There's blood everywhere.

"How did I not feel it, how long have I being bleeding?"

She grips her belly and limps to the bottom of the stairs where she was sitting and the nightmare hits her. There are clumps of blood and sickening pain sets in. It's so bad that she remembers the pain from six months ago. Another miscarriage. She falls to the ground, curled up in a ball then all she sees is darkness before she passes out.

Three hours later, I'm at the door in the club, still calling my house phone every five minutes and still getting no love from Sandra.

The voice in my head is asking, *Delroy do you blame her*?

But another voice is talking to me, a voice I haven't heard for at least two years: *Forget her man, look at all these chicks. Just bag one of them, sniff some charlie and enjoy yourself. Sandra ain't going nowhere and if she's still acting like a prick when you get home, give her something to cry about.*

Guess which voice I listen to? Well, let's put it this way, I wake up at 1pm the next day lying flat out on the stage in the club with a nicely powdered nose.

Damn, man! I totally lost it last night. My shins and fist are hurting, so I guess I must've kicked off after taking charlie. I'm topless and my trousers are wrapped around my ankles, just the way I like them. What the hell happened ain't really important. What's important is getting home to Sandra.

She must've calmed down by now and what's happened made me realise how much I totally love this woman. If it's her life's dream to have a child, then that's what I'm going to give her.

So yeah, I'm in my car, speeding down the road, slowing down every time I see a bully van then flooring the pedal to the metal. I pull up outside my yard and sit in the motor for a bit; I'm shivering, not cause it's as cold as hell out here and certainly not cause I'm scared of what Sandra's going to say when she sees me, but cause I'm petrified that I finally made up my mind that I'm about to tell her I'm going to be a dad and I'm going to do it to the best of my ability. I put the key in the door. I hear that voice in my head again. *Come on Delroy, stop acting like a big girl's blouse.* That voice really pisses me off sometimes. I finally get the key in the door, shaking like I'm in the North Pole, rolling around naked in the snow. Anyway, I'm in my yard now.

I call out, "Sandra! Where are you babes?" No response. I call out again. She can't still be mad at me. "Sandra! Sandra? Where you at babes?" I look down at the ground and jump back. Rah … what the hell am I standing in? It looks like a hell of a lot of dried blood. I'm in shock. *Where the hell is Sandra?*

I run over to the stairs where I left her laying, shouting at me, and to my horror there's more blood, a lot more than at the front door. What have I done? She might be in the bedroom. Judging by the amount of blood, she could well be dead. I sprint upstairs as fast as my legs can take me and burst through the bedroom door, knocking it clean off its hinges, hoping for the best.

But the worst is yet to come.

Something's lying on the bed, it's just there looking at me. Reluctant to touch it or pick it up, one hundred and one things race through my head as if they're trying to catch up with the tears streaming down my face. Now I know what people mean when they say *My blood ran cold*. I walk over and gradually persuade myself to pick up the note lying there on the bed. It says:

Delroy, you've got what you wanted as you can see by the blood that you spilled yet again. I can't do this anymore. You've killed our baby and now I'm dead to you. Please don't try to find me. Just let me go. Love always, Sandra.

She's out of my life. I look in her wardrobe and there's nothing left. Everything's gone apart from the Gabicci top and Farah trousers that I bought when I first met her. I can't believe she kept them for so long and I can't believe they once fitted me. But I do believe I've lost the love of my life and there'll never be a replacement.

I sit on them stairs all day, hoping that Sandra will walk through the door again.

****

One day becomes one week; the week becomes a month, then a year. Five years have passed and I'm reckless, abusing drugs, steroids and alcohol. None of them can get Sandra out of my mind. My violence tops the charts and in my book, I'm officially crazy. My life's spiralled out of all logical control and only Sandra can tame me, but she's long gone. I create any reason to beat the hell out of some poor guy. Oftentimes, when football's playing I get drunk out of my head, walk into a pub full of rival fans and sing our local football songs just to get a good beating, *"I'm forever blowing bubbles, pretty bubbles in the air,"* but there's nothing pretty about any of it.

I deserve to be punished.

I know I can kill these guys, but I must be punished for what I did to Sandra. I guess you could call me a self-harmer. My life's totally spiralled out of control and Wayne's just about had enough. I'm cramping the entire system. On my bad days, and trust me I have a lot of those, I'll stab people in the leg just cause the mood takes me; sometimes, they come back for me ten and 15-strong. I've been plunged up a few times, yet they never win. They always come off worst, but I'm attracting a lot of blue lights and that's bad for business.

Wayne told me I had to take some time out, so I did, but money's low cause I just blow everything on drink, drugs and women. I need to make some papers and I need to make them fast so I can feed my habit. Wayne gives me some dough here and there, but he won't let me back on the door. Who can blame him? I'm a menace to society and I don't want to get Wayne banged up. After all he's done for me, I don't think so. I've got to make some cash of my own, so I do it the best way I know how. And that's my first ever time inside prison.

It happens like this.
I go out on the road and start recruiting foot soldiers. There are long days and nights of spying on where they live and meeting their loved ones, you know, just so none of them get brave and try doing a runner with my shit. I know they're too scared to even think about that – but I always say it's better to be safe than sorry.

I've got my runners and I'm ready to send them out to work, but first things first – I've got to get the merchandise. I ain't got any money, so this is what I do.

It's a dread black night. I go out barefaced and hit on ten crack dens. I rob them of all their stash and money. I kick off their doors and swipe everything they've got at gunpoint. I'm so off my face tonight ... as a matter of fact, every night. These so-called hard men drug dealers shit themselves. Literally. They even help me to carry their own shit to my car and put it neatly in the back of the boot. What a bunch of wankers! I just take everything, not giving a fuck about the consequences.

I'm driving down the A13 with £40k of crack, £20k in cash and two shot guns in the boot. I'm so off my head, I'm not releasing my foot off the gas and I'm clocking 110 mph. Now there are blue lights up my ass.

Damn. Are they flashing me or are they on call?

I slow down to 70 mph, hoping they'll just fly by, but no. Their flashing lights almost blind me. Sod this for a laugh! If I stop I'm going to eat porridge and if I don't, I'm still going to eat porridge.

Fuck it. If you want me, you're gonna have to catch me.

I put the pedal to the metal, now I'm going 90\100\120. Now I'm hitting sides at 160. Those bastards know what they're doing when they put their beams on. They shine straight through my rear view mirror and I can't see a damn thing. I reach out to rip it off, but how can I do that successfully with one arm? There's a flash of light, a sharp bit of pain, then darkness.

Am I dead again? *I'd be so lucky.*

****

I wake up two years later in a prison hospital ward. I didn't even get a trial, but I wake up to ten years in the slammer. Now I have to learn to walk again and put my size back on fast cause that and Stanley are my only protection. It doesn't take long as Wayne's getting me everything I need inside to make me the monster I once was. It only takes me a year to get back to my normal self, but it takes me another year to get my memory back. For some reason, Sandra's never left my head for one minute and every time she crosses my mind, charlie wants to step in and help me get rid of her.

But I have to use this time to get me off the white heaven and clean myself up before I get out of this shithole. I know that once I'm out, I'll never come back here again, not on your Nelly mate. I'm riding bird and I've got three years left to go, so I'm trying to keep my head down and do my time. I send Wayne a visiting order to see me cause he keeps rattling on about how he needs to see me asap.

I hear my number called: "AA6447! Visitor." It must be Wayne cause he's the only one I want to see. Even though Teresa has had my back most of the time I've been here, I'd give my right arm to have Sandra pay me a visit, but she never has. She must know I'm here. I mean, how could she not know? And if she does know, why hasn't she even tried to get in touch? For definite, it's over and that's a hard pill to swallow.

I walk out of my cell and into the visiting room. Wayne's sitting there. Damn, the guy's a lump; he's put on more weight. Even the screws look shit scared.

His massive chest looks like it's going to burst through his plain, white Lacoste t-shirt like some hulk. He sports that with plain, dark blue jeans and white Reebok trainers, but the best thing he's wearing is a long, black, leather mac that tries its best to contain his 22 inch arms. It's one of them thick jackets that you only use when you're trying to conceal a double barrel shot gun, but the only weapon under that jacket is Wayne.

I bound over, so excited to see him. "Wayne, what you done to yourself man? You're massive! Is it that new shit you keep banging on about, you know, the growth hormones? Wayne just sits there and I clock it. There's something not right. I know Wayne better than anyone and something's on his mind. Something big.

"What's going on bro? What's up? There's something wrong, it's written all over your face." Wayne just sits there, looking like he's just seen a ghost and is reluctant to talk. "Oh, for fuck's sake Wayne. What is it?"

One of the screws calls out, "Keep it down, or your visit is over!" Saucy cunt.

Wayne just stands up as though he wants to kill this guy and by the size of his arms he could with one punch. The screw looks away fast as I grab Wayne's arm.

"Calm down bro, just calm down. I need you on the outside, not in here with me. Sit down and talk to me. Is Precious OK bro?"

Wayne looks up at me with his big blues and finally speaks, "Yeah, she's OK."

"So what is it man? You really need to —"and before I can finish, he just blurts it out, as he does.

"It's Teresa man, it's Teresa."

I'm confused. "OK Wayne, what's up with her?"

"She's dead bro. Teresa, she's dead."

Wayne's eyes start to glaze over, but he doesn't drop a tear. As much as he wants to, he has a big problem showing weakness and he has to hold it back or it will show the other lifers weakness on my part. But I flip out.

"What? Nah she isn't! Why would you say that bro? Why you saying that?" Wayne tries to calm me down. "Wayne, you're for real aren't ya? What the fuck happened? Well, I don't believe you! She can't be!"

Wayne snaps back at me, his face totally screwed up like he's about to go into battle. "She's fucking dead Del!" Even though I don't feel for her like I feel for Sandra, I still have love for her and her death cuts me deeper than any Stanley or razor blade ever could. She had my back, she always did, but I only realise that when she's gone and it's too late. I've got a saying, *If you don't love me in life, don't ever try and love me in death*. Well, look at me now.

"What happened, Wayne? Was it an accident?"

"Nah, Del she …"

"She what bro? Talk to me man. She what?"

"She got plunged man. She got flipping plunged."

"She *what*? Plunged by who? Why the hell would anyone want to kill her?"

Wayne just looks at me deep in my eyes, then he drops his head into his unusually massive arms. Now I'm frowning. *What the hell's going on?* I grab his arm again in frustration. "Wayne! Talk to me! Talk to me!"

From the corner of my eye, I can see that one of the screws in his tight, fucked up uniform is looking my way. He's just about to open his mouth and I lose it: "Shut up you cunt, or I'll come over there and open you up like ha fucking cana Coke!"

Now I turn my attention back to Wayne, but nine screws are huddling together, getting ready to drag me out. Wayne looks at me.

"It was Carlton, bro."

Am I hearing things? "What was Carlton?"

"It was Carlton who killed her and he's on his way in here."

I crumble. No words can pass through my lips. I'm dead once again, but this time I'm dead inside. Why the hell Carlton would want to kill his own mum is beyond me. I don't know him, but I know he loves her more than life itself cause she always kept telling me how loving he was; I think she wanted me to get involved, fuck that, but now I wish I did. The screws are getting into formation, but before they rush me Wayne hits me with another bombshell.

"It's Snake and Smiley's fault. They set him up, but don't worry about them, I'm going to deal with them."

I look at Wayne; my eyes feel like they're bloodshot from forcing myself not to cry, but I can't control the anger, the heat and the madness in my mind: they're stronger than ever before. "What, Snake and Smiley? Those little cunts! Don't say a word to them; act like you know nothing. I want to deal with them myself when I get out and don't worry about Carlton. I'm going to deal with him too."

Then the war starts.

I see the screws marching towards me like some hooligans at a West Ham match. It's only natural for Wayne to want his pound of flesh, cause one, we've had each other's backs for years and two, he hates screws as much as we hate them dickheads Snake and Smiley, so I have to keep him calm by any means necessary. I need him on the outside, not banged up in here with me.

"Wayne, just walk away, don't get involved with this, I need you on the outside. Just get up and walk away."

Now they're running towards me with ill intentions. That's fine by me as all I want is blood and lots of it as my school days flash before my eyes.

"Come on then you bunch of pigs!"

Everything goes crazy. I wake up in intensive care, two weeks later. Status: two broken ribs and twenty stitches – fifteen in my head, five in my ruptured testicles – two black eyes, a broken nose and to top it off, an additional six months on my sentence. But it was worth it cause I think I did more damage than they did. I wake up to see some guy sitting near me on my right hand side. I can't make the person out as my eyes are still swollen and full of gunk, so I have to look a bit harder.

Chapter 8
Mirror Image

It's Carlton.

I know it's him cause I'm looking at the mirror image of myself before I became a monster. I can see the pain and the anxiety in his face. This is the first time I ever set eyes on him since he was born and the tears well up in my eyes as I stretch my hand out towards him, finally understanding the outcome of my selfish actions. It seems like a lifetime, but Carlton holds tightly onto my hand, just like Teresa did the first time we met, and I know he needs me.

There's no fire or life in his eyes, but I know I'm the spark to relight them. We just look at each other, scanning our faces like we've just seen a new species of human, but then I say it. I never knew I'd ever say this and it feels as natural as breathing: "Talk to me son. Talk to your old man."

****

Is it an accident us being here and meeting for the first time under these circumstances?

I really don't care cause now I know I have a reason to live and I also understand what my mum meant when she told me every disappointment is for a good.

After Sandra, I was heading for a massive fall, but now I'm a father and I'm going to be the best father I can be, according to our surroundings that is.

The look on Carlton's face is priceless. It's as though he's been waiting to hear me acknowledge him as my son for what seems like an eternity, but it's a crying shame he had to lose a mother to gain a father (shame on me).

He sits at my bedside any chance he gets; from the start of free time from his cell until lock down. He tells me the full story from beginning to the end of what happened with him, Smiley and Snake.

I make sure we share the same cell for our remaining time inside. It's great what you can do with money and a corrupt jail warden. I even get to keep my Stanley that I opened up many faces with. I put the word out in the lock-up that Carlton's my son so he's safe, no-one gives him any aggro, but as I train him I set him up for a beating just to toughen him up that little bit more.

****

I must admit, spending all those years in this shithole with my son have been the best years of my life, even better than the years I spent with my Sandra, but now I've got to go.

I've done my time and I'm getting released tomorrow, but I'm happy I made up the years I missed with my son and I'm proud of what I made him: he's a beast. Now, he's ready to take on the world. It's time for him to properly man up cause I'm out of here this time tomorrow. I don't want to leave my boy again, but I know I have to if I'm going to deal with Snake and Smiley. And if it wasn't for that, I would've just killed a screw and got 25 to life so I could stay with my boy. So now, I'm saying goodbye to my son for the first time in his life.

****

Throughout the time I spent in prison, I've never been to the barber on my prison wing. No-one in this joint can be trusted with a razor over my head, especially them dirty razors that have been through the heads of grasses, rapists and, worst of all, them paedos. Carlton's dying to cut my hair cause he keeps going on and on about how he was the best barber in east London when he was on the outside. So every day, he bugs me about chopping off my thick dreadlocks that now hang roughly about five inches below my broad shoulders. He's dying to cut them off before I get out of here. But sitting in a barber's chair is out of the question as my mane-like hair is my pride.

Even though Carlton's my son, and I know he needs me in this joint, with all the badness I did to him and his mum, I can't trust him either, at least not yet. My dreads make me feel strong like those big, old lions wallowing in the heat, giving orders to the females and not paying attention to the cubs that run wild in the African sun, occasionally nipping their father's tail with developing teeth that soon prove to be their most dangerous weapons.

Yes. I'm the king of this fucking jungle.

My locks are as precious as the fistful of beard that sits neatly on a Muslim brother's face, always clean and tidy, ready for their five times a day prayers. They always try to suck me into that shit, but God's the reason my life's so fucked up. It's His fault I'm sitting in this shithole, so obviously I know that ain't for me.

Anyway, I'm always clean shaven, that's something I can do myself and I definitely don't trust no man other than myself to take care of that.

I keep three or four of my dreads hanging in front of my eyes, so I can hide behind them and block out the mystery of my forever ticking mind. When I flick them back it's a sign that grabs your attention for better or for worse. Now, I flick them back for the last time in this joint and call out to my boy.

"Carlton! I'm out of here son, but I'm going to send you a present, gift-wrapped. It's going to be a big one, so be ready, and when it comes I want you to open it up nicely, just like a cold can of Coke."

I probe deep into Carlton's eyes: he's ready. I put my hand in my pocket and pull out Stanley. I lower my voice into a serious half whisper, as though I'm trying to hypnotise him.

"You see this blade? He's called Stanley, surname Blade. He's more famous than the king, the queen and even Bob Marley. He's brought me through a lot of wars. Stanley's been my friend for over 25 years and sometimes he's the only friend I have cause he does the job, no questions asked.

"Son, I've seen a lot of tools in my time in this hotel. Boiling hot water mixed with sugar and jam, three blades in a toothbrush, and you know that's a straight Mars bar cause you can't stitch that, soap or a snooker ball in a sock, razor blades in a bar of soap – that one's real messed up cause you can't see the damage till you finish washing your balls.

"But nothing, and I mean nothing, comes close to my Stanley. Now I'm giving it to you. You'll know when it's the right time to use him and when that time comes, go straight for the throat, if you get what I mean. Let him be your best friend. Get used to him son. Play with him and listen to the beauty of his voice when he comes out to play. Click. Click. Click. Do you understand me?"

My son's listening to me intently. I can see the blood in his eyes. He's grown into a man, or, should I say, a warrior with a desperate cause just like his old man.

"Yes dad, I understand. Love you dad, always have, always will. Get them for me."

I'm fighting the hardest fight I've ever had to fight in my life (my tears). After all I did to this boy and his mum, I now know that even though he never saw me he always loved me. Then I hear one of the screws call me out. "Delroy, it's time to go! You're free, but I know you'll come back. They always do."

But I know I won't be coming back to this hellhole, so I walk away. I never look back. I don't want to show Carlton any weakness as he needs all the strength he can muster. There are a lot of wankers in here that want to get to me cause I had total control of the drug trade. I had A, B and C wing locked, hook, line and sinker. Trust me, I turned over more cash in here than when I was out on the cobble stones! So they want to shut down my system, but they're too scared shitless to ever step to me. Now I've passed the link on to Carlton and they think he's a weaker target – so they believe. That's going to be a painful lesson for them to learn, a very painful lesson indeed.

Carlton has too much to live for and only one reason to survive. And I'm going to make sure he fulfils that reason by any means necessary.

Chapter 9
I Smell Freedom,
But Where Is It?

I walk through the gates, close my eyes and take a deep breath. Ah, I can smell freedom and it smells great. I open my eyes and look up at the sky; it's a brilliant shade of blue and not one dark cloud's in sight. The trees and freshly cut grass look fantastic.

Now you can see what ten years in the lock-up can do to a man. It's sad to think my Carlton may never see the beauty of the outside again.

Wayne's walking towards me and behind him is his brand new, blood red Rolls Royce Phantom. "Bloody hell Wayne, what did you do? Rob a bank?" I call out to him.

Wayne smiles that big smile. "Nah mate, pure, hard graft. Business is booming. Since you've been away, a lot of new shit hit the streets and it hit hard. Everyone out here's like the walking dead. I had to take Precious and Kimberly out of the ends bro, it was getting to be too much."

I'm a bit put back. "Precious and who? Who's Kimberly?"

"My little girl, Del. I didn't want to tell you while you were inside. I just wanted you to keep your head down and do your time. Anyway, she's in the car and she's dying to meet her uncle Del," he says with a big smile.

"OK bro. Damn! I can't believe there's a little Wayne on the loose!"

We walk towards the car and as we get closer the door starts to open. I see Precious step out first then I stall. Why is she here? I thought she hated me cause of Sandra.

Wayne sees the look on my face. "It's OK bro, she's cool. Trust me, just come on."

Anyway, let's just get to the chunky parts cause I know you know how it goes: I see Precious and she gives me a cuddle. I see Kimberly, she asks about my arm and blah, blah, blah.

I take my place in the front seat of the car with Wayne, knowing it's going be a long drive home, but even longer to get used to my newfound freedom. I crack the window open a bit, just enough to feel the fresh air blowing in my face. That feels and smells so different from my prison garden. I can't help but look around and think damn, cars are bigger, faster and prettier, but some are so small I wonder how the hell anyone can fit in them. I mean, they look like you can't even swing a cat in them.

My eyes close as I sink deep into the soft leather seats and the scent of Italian leather overtakes the smell of freshly cut, green grass.

****

We reach Wayne's yard. Precious and Kimberly get out the car and we stay behind; all that's going through my mind are Snake and Smiley.

"So Wayne, I intend to sort this thing out soon as bro."

"OK Del, but get in first, get settled and we can get cracking in the morning." I knew he was going to say that and I know he's right cause he always is. But that ain't what I want to hear.

"Nah bro, I want to sort it out now right now." I'm starting to get real pissed off.

"Alright Del, so what's your plan? Do you even have one? Look, things have changed out here since you've been banged up. It's not like before when you can just do some guy, bury him, and walk away scot free. You've been banged up for ten years bro; now cars are faster, there are cameras plotted everywhere and clubs are busier.

"There are more guns on the roads and little pricks that want to hear them go bang. The little punks that used to run for us ain't so little anymore; they all want to move up in the ranks so they do some crazy shit to get there.

"Those little punks have no morals whatsoever and they don't live by the code. So if we're going to do this, we need to do this in a way we can get away with it and I've got the best idea to sort out them little dickheads."

As I said, Wayne's always right so I have to eat humble pie.

"Alright then Wayne, what do you suggest we do? Come on. Spill the beans."

Wayne broke it down to me perfectly: it was genius. Only Wayne could come up with such a fucked up idea and I know it will do the job brilliantly.

Now my mind's at ease and all I have to do is wait, so I use that time and start to get my life back on track. I start my old job back on the door and I'm more reckless with the women. I have a different woman every night or sometimes two girls at a time. Champagne, fast cars and bling; that's me and they're the in thing. I think I'm trying to wash Sandra out of my mind, but I must admit it ain't working, not one bit. Them girls just cum and go if you get my meaning.

****

Time just seems to fly by. I'm 38 and I can feel that I need to settle down. Wayne and Precious are well settled; they're on their third child and happy as Larry. So now, Wayne never works much. He's recruited more foot soldiers to run the business; I'm head door man and I never do much, just make sure our runners do their jobs. With no lover and very little violence, I'm bored as hell.

****

Now I'm 39. Me and Wayne are doing everything: money laundering, debt collecting and if the money's right we take people on a long walk on a very short path. It's sad sometimes cause a few are people we know, but we like the money better than we like them so it makes life much easier. Half the time them bastards get what they deserve anyway.

When's it going to come to an end?

We've done some bad shit man, some real bad shit and you know what they say, what goes around comes back around, with a swift kick, deep in ya nut sack.

****

It's my forty first birthday, so I ain't going to work tonight. Wayne says he's going to cover the door for me, so I'm going to go to the club with my sad, lonely self and pull some old tart, drink, smoke, sniff charlie and live my poor, lonely life as I always do. I walk through the club door and there's Wayne.

"Oi! Del! Happy birthday old man!"

I look at Wayne with a fake smile from behind the three thick locks that hang in front of my tired eyes.

I laugh, "Thanks bro, I'm just going to go down and grab a few drinks and you know what else."

"Yeah Del, enjoy bro. You're only old once then you die!"

"Er, thanks Wayne you old bastard. You're not no spring chicken," and with that I begin to take that long, lonely walk down the steps to the dance hall.

I feel like I've done this a thousand times before – maybe it's cause I have. I get to the bottom of the stairs.

"Surprise!"

The lights turn on and there are decorations, balloons and a massive cake with my name on it plus the bonus: half dressed women. Just the way I like them!

But all I can see is her.

I'm totally hooked like a smack head with a syringe. She's just sitting there at the bar. Damn! Beauty has no place in the dictionary cause beautiful is sitting right here in front of me. With her bright eyes and caramel skin, she's wearing a slick black dress and I can just about see her cleavage peeking out of the V shape that sits snugly on top of her breasts. The light makes her skin sparkle as though she's covered in glitter. She ain't too naked, but let's just say she ain't dressed like a nun and I like that, it makes her stand out from all them other women that are dressed like a bunch of slags.

She's my only focus, but by the looks of it I ain't in her focus at all. She looks up at the birthday boy then turns to order her drink. As she reaches into her bag to pay the barman, I swiftly walk over.

"Pete, that drink's on me." How rude, I totally blank everyone around me.

She looks up at me, towering over her, one arm, dreads to the middle of my back and as black as you like: a sheer beast of a man. But then she says in a Manchester accent, "Thanks birthday boy."

Chapter 10
My Life's Just Begun

No, she ain't Sandra, yet I know she's the one for me. As I do with my fast mouth, flicking three, thick dreads away from my eyes, and in the deepest voice I can muster, I ask, "How old are you?"

She looks at me, eyebrows raised. "Damn, is that how you guys do it in London? Don't you think I have a name Delroy? And if you're trying to pick me up, cause I know you're trying to pick me up, don't you think you should at least ask my name first?"

This girl ain't your average bird. Does she have a gob on her, but I like it. "Er, sorry, what's your name sweetheart and how do you know mine?"

She curls the left side of her pretty lips, tilts her head to one side and says in the most sarcastic voice ever, "Er, Delroy, it's written all over your birthday cake and so is your age."

I look back for the first time at the big wooden table; it's covered in a nice white frilly cloth that just about hovers over the club's liquor soaked floor. There are two bottles of Dom Perignon champagne and I know Wayne brought that cause it costs a kick up the nuts. There's a big banner drawn in felt tip pen, saying Happy Birthday Uncle Del – I know that's from Wayne's little ones. The table had at least eight champagne glasses polished to the nines and party poppers everywhere and between all of that there it sits: a big chocolate cake covered with candles and Smarties. It says in white cream, 'Happy Birthday Delroy, You Old Cunt'. Written all over it, about 100 times in very small writing, is my age and I know Wayne did that to make a point: we're both getting old. I know it's him cause there's a big LOL written on it too.

"Don't you think you're too old to be chatting up someone half your age? You're old enough to be my dad!"

And on that note, I back up with my tail between my legs and head for the door. I hear one of the women call out to me some shit about cutting my cake, but I just keep walking and she knows not to ask me twice. Then I hear the beauty's voice again and it stops me dead in my tracks. "Age ain't nothing but a number – before you ride off into the sunset my prince, my name's Nadine. And you can take that look out of your eyes cause I hate being naked in public."

We both laugh, but I still don't know how to take her by the words she's using. But all I want to do is take her and take her I do, right back to my house. It's like we've known each other from time. We just connect. We have a connection and that connection's like I found God.

Everything I do for the next three months slows down. Nadine moves in with me, I stop the charlie and I know I just want to be a dad and settle down with her.

I'm not about to make the mistake I made with Sandra, no way, not this time. I want to be a father and I want it bad; I guess I just want to prove to myself I can so I do. I'm not surprised when seven months later after a lot of sex, Nadine calls me at work.

"Hi Delroy."

"Hi babes, I'm working. What's up?" I know something's up cause I can hear it in her voice and I know fear when I hear it.

"Del, I'm pregnant."

Man, talk about just coming out with it! She nearly knocks me off my feet, but I'm so happy! I don't even know what to do with myself. Even though it's happening so quickly, I'm over the moon. But I can still hear in her voice there's something not right. "How far have you gone? What's up? Aren't you happy? Cause I'm over the moon, I'm coming home right now and we're going to go shopping and we're going to celebrate big time!"

"I'm two months gone, but Del –"

"What's up babes?"

Then she says what I don't want to hear. Let's just say karma's come around at the wrong damn time and if I could get my hand on her I'd kick her ass. Karma's ass, that is.

"I can't keep it Del, I just can't. If my mum knew, she'd kill me. I was meant to be in university. I came to London for one night to celebrate getting into uni then I met you, got distracted and I lost my place. My mum's going to kill me if she finds out."

Now I know how Teresa and Sandra felt times ten.

"OK Nads, just stay there. I'm coming home. Please don't do anything stupid. Just wait for me."

I jump in my car and put the pedal down to the floor, *that brings back memories, memories I never, ever want to relive*, then I get to the house. I burst through the front door as softly as my big arm allows me to and I see Nads sitting there on the stairs, looking like a lost, little child in a big, bad world of her own.

But it's my big, bad world too and I ain't going to let nothing or no-one hurt her or our baby.

"Nadine, I'm here. We can sort it, we can make it right." Nadine just looks at me and from nowhere she just starts to scream, her northern accent gets deeper than ever. "How da hell can we? You're a 41 year old man with one arm and I'm 20! So how are we gonna make it work, ha? How?"

I'm heartbroken. "Nadine we can, we just need to stand strong."

"No, Del! I just want ... I just want it out of me. Just help me to get it out. Delroy, please just help me!"

I beg her not to say it, but she keeps going on and on and I crumble.

A big man like me falls to my knees.

All my fears and hate, sorrows and pain just come flooding back and even though I was only a baby when I lost her, I can hear my mum's voice, I can hear the hatred she had in her heart. Now, I'm on the floor crying like a baby.

I hear Sandra's voice, "It's OK Del, calm down." I feel her arms embrace me and hold me against her breasts. "It's OK, we can keep it. We can keep our baby, it's not going anywhere, I promise." I look up thinking Sandra's come back into my life, then I see Nadine holding me. She ain't Sandra, but she'll do.

I explain about my mum and my arm and like any good woman, she understands. I'm not saying she ain't scared, but she understands and that's all we need.

****

Nadine's eight months pregnant and the time's come to let her mum and step dad know what's going on. Wayne let me go, so I'm no longer at the door or doing the shit I used to do. He says I'm getting too soft. But he also says he gets it as he went through the same with his first little one and when I'm ready, I can come back on the circuit. Until then, I'm a liability.

I take it on the chin cause Wayne's always right and he only wants the best for me and Nads.

Chapter 11
Meeting the Parents

Nadine wakes me up at 11am for breakfast in bed; I can smell the fried egg, bacon and plantain. The fried egg went down nicely with the five slices of toasted hard dough bread and on my bedside there's a pint glass full of smooth mango juice.

She sits on the edge of the bed, looking at me with her big, bright eyes and perfectly round belly. It's like we know what each other's thinking. Then she starts talking to me with her full lips. I sit up in bed, cut into her conversation and tell her exactly what's on her mind.

"Nadine, I know babes. It's time. So when do you want to go and see them?"

Nads just sits there looking at me, dumbstruck as though a cat really got her tongue and after what seems like an hour and some she finally talks to me.

"We can go on Friday and tell them. Pending on the outcome we can either stay there for the weekend, or book into a hotel and come back on Saturday."

"OK Nads, if that's how you want to do it, it's fine by me. I just want to get this out the way, so you can have a proper, relaxing birth cause that's all that matters." But what I really want to say is *Pending on the fact that I don't crush her dad's skull.* I have to stop them kind of thoughts going through my head.

It's Friday morning and we're ready to go. Nadine changes her mind at least ten times in the space of two hours, but I convince her it will be OK. Personally, I couldn't care less if we go or not. I don't need to know them and as far I'm concerned Nadine's my girl and the mother of my unborn child – that's all that matters to me. She never talks about her family to me anyway; I don't know why, but maybe it's cause we're too busy loving each other.

So nothing can change the fact that she's no longer a mummy or daddy's girl, but she's my girl and that's for damn sure. I'm prepared to crush anyone or anything to keep it that way.

We take a long drive to Manchester with no transfer of words at all. I think we're both scared for different reasons.

Apart from everything else that's going through my mind, all I really want despite my age and my one arm is to be accepted, but I know there are a thousand and one things going through Nadine's poor little brain so I try to break the ice a couple of times to no avail.

It seems like the quietest time of my life. This is real solitary confinement and it makes prison seem like a nightclub. Nadine confirms that we're ten minutes away.

"Pull over Delroy," she says under her breath.

"But we're not there yet, Nads. It's just down the road now."

Her voice rises and she snaps, "Just pull over!"

I pull the car over to one side of the road. Nadine flings the door open and what comes out of her is like a tin of soup. She chucks up everywhere. We sit there for an hour and forty five minutes until Nadine looks at me and, with a deep breath, says, "I'm ready now. Drive. It's just around this corner."

I turn on the engine and start driving slowly around the corner, I mean very slowly, like it's going to make a difference.

"Pull over Del."

I pull the car over for the second time, hoping she won't take so long to get this over with.

"Look Del, I just want you to know, whatever happens now, just know that I love you and always will, just know this. I need you to be strong for me and for our baby and that means no violence. Promise me Delroy." She looks at me sternly, "Promise me."

I promise her reluctantly, but my adoptive mother always told me a promise is a comfort to a fool. That's a really old saying, but a true one. I know she needs me to be strong and I don't want to let her down. Then she kisses me on my lips with passion, more passion than in the short few months that we've been together. And yes, she rinsed her mouth out first …

"I'm ready now," she says putting on her bravest face.

We get out the car and walk towards the front door.

The house is massive; it's pebble dashed with white and brown stones, it has big, white bay windows and a drive for at least three cars. There's a black BMW and a red Jag parked up nicely; there's a spare place, but I park on the road for a fast getaway. Better to be safe than sorry I always say.

Why the hell did she leave here in the first place to come to the middle of that shithole called east London? Oh yeah, uni, that's why.

Nadine breaks down in tears, I hold her and tell her, "We're here now, let's just do this and get it out the way babes. Let's be strong and do this together." But deep inside I'm more scared than when I decided to tell Sandra I was ready to be a father.

As a matter of fact, I'm properly touching cloth.

We get to the door and Nadine rings the bell. We wait. Two minutes go by. There's no answer and in a way I'm glad. I'm just about to bottle it when Nadine goes for a second attempt, but then we see her mum through the foggy glass panels in the door walking towards us.

"Who is it?" she calls out and I step back in fright.

"It's me, mum. It's Nadine."

Nadine's mum opens the door and she's totally gobsmacked as she looks straight past Nadine and gasps: "Delroy!"

I can't breathe. My eyes open wide as I flick the three long dreadlocks to the back of my head.

"Sandra!"

Chapter 12
Born Alone, Die Alone

My name's Delroy. The doctors called me Lucky cause I should've died, but I say I died the day I was born.

I'm naked, my body's completely shaved hairless like the day I was born. I open up a brand new Stanley, one that's never been through a battle with me yet.

The battle he's about to go through is bigger and more daring than any battle I've ever fought.

A voice speaks to me: *Don't fight it Delroy, don't even contemplate it. You know you deserve every part of what you're about to get, so just get it done and don't make a sound.*

That's when I start to peel off every tattoo I ever had.

Every bit of ink has to go, apart from the one that reads Sandra in Life or in Death, which was the first tattoo I inked on my body and that's ink for life. So that's staying firmly over my heart, but the rest has to go cause I want to die the way I was born.

I've got to do this and I've got to do it fast before I pass out.

The blood's flowing fast. I'm in a daze then that voice comes back: *Now's time for the noose. Just get up there and wrap it around your neck.* I'm sweating like a good one, trying to keep my 13 stones, 6 feet 5 inches body balanced on the edge of a chair. I had to lose some weight for this moment as it takes a lot of rope to hold a 20 stones guy and I've only got one chance to get this right.

Anyway, I'm balancing on the edge of the chair and all I'm thinking is, *I've gained a daughter who's the mother of my son and grandson called Jamel.* I've lost my son, Carlton. Now there's nothing left to live for. The rope's firmly around my neck.

Before I do this I'm going to tell you something: if you're thinking about doing this, it ain't the way to go, trust me. Listen and listen well.

As I kick away my chair, hoping the rope will hold the weight of my body, I feel the noose tighten around my neck. My face starts to bloat cause of the constriction and I can feel my eyes bulge as the whites fill with blood. As my vessels explode, haemorrhages form on my face and other areas of my body as I spaz out.

I lose control of my bodily functions as I release all tension in the throes of death. Then the beauty of darkness creeps in like a thief in the night. I breathe no more.

So, I guess you're wondering what my mum was trying to tell me and I tell you this: she must've been trying to tell me to be a father to my child. If I'd paid more attention to my duties, I would've been a damn good father. I would've known my daughter and this never would've happened. But it's too late now.

The deed's done and all cause daddy didn't know his little girl.

****

A wise man once said:

"It is a wise father that knows his own child."
William Shakespeare

"The most important thing a father can do for his children is to love their mother."
Theodore M. Hesburgh

Once Upon a Night

Chapter 1
The Meeting

I'm going to tell you a story, but first let me tell you a bit about me.

My name's Phipps, aka Snake. I got that name cause I put in a lot of effort to reach this status, so I guess it quite rightly belongs to me. In my clique, I was the soldier responsible for setting up snake-like moves, feeding off other people's food and hard work; in some cases I had to duppy a brother out here, you get me.

If you've got an untrained eye, you'd never in a million years think I'm that kind of guy cause I'm as skinny as a bone. On top of that, I've got a bad case of OCD and a desperate need to keep everything around me clean, especially my yard and my hands. But let's not get it twisted: I don't take shit from no-one. I walk the walk and talk the talk and that, my friend, makes me a very dangerous brother. So when it's time to get my hands dirty, or if the price is right, OCD's got nothing to do with it.

Yes, I'm skinny like a bag of bones, but I'm running with the wolves so I'm well protected.

And if I can't dead you, you better believe I know a man who can.

Anyway, let me tell you my story. Maybe this will help you to learn to keep your grass cut low, so you can see snakes like me creeping up on you and catch you slipping. More importantly, what happens to a snake when it bites the wrong person? I've learned the hard way, so I hope you learn from my mistakes and never get yourself into a predicament like mine. Don't forget what they say, *There's more than one way to skin a snake*. Well, the saying's actually *There's more than one way to skin a cat,* but who gives a shit? Snake. Cat. Same difference: they're both cunning.

It all started once upon a night. I'm going to take you from the beginning.

It's 8pm and I'm just here, jamming on the strip. It's the wickedest summer in a long time, even though it's 8pm the heat's still beating down hard on my dry skin. So I'm just here minding my own business, watching a vampire movie on my smartphone when some dude pulls up in his fully blacked out Audi A3, bass to kill and wheels that keep spinning even when the car stops.

I don't know who this guy is as I've never seen that whip round the ends before, so I'm on heat as I reach in my waistband for my shank. The driver's side window slowly rolls down. Is my time up for all the bad shit I've done? Is it my time to pay the piper, or is it just some rich prick that wants a fix? I tell you this for nothing, if it's a rich kid, that whip's going to be mine quickly. Man would just jump in the car, stick my shank in his side and let the prick drive me to his yard to get the log book and sign it over to me.

The window rolls all the way down, now all I see are teeth and a big ass smile. Not too sure who this dude is as the darkness consumes his face, but the voice finally puts the icing on the cake.

"Yo Snake! You like the wipe fam? (giggle). Jump in, man's going to rave hard tonight. Come on, jump in the car fam! You on this ting or what?"

That big ass smile belongs to my co de, Smiley. I say nothing. I just jump in the ride, a little bit pissed off that it's my boy as my mind's totally on a jacking thing and I'm geared up to suck this ride. Trust me, the ride's proper peng. I love the red lights in the dash and the black heated leather seats with red piping stitched neatly around them. It's just crisp and to make matters worse, it smells of some peng skunk just the way I like it. This is my kind of ride, but I don't show it.

"OK Smiley, where we going and how hot is this ride cause I don't want boy them pulling man over you get me?"

I indicate to Smiley by tapping my seven and a half inch, black matt blade with a jagged edge for ripping flesh that's stuffed securely down the front of my sussmi jeans. Smiley rolls his eyes like he's never stolen anything in his life and the question I've asked him shouldn't have spat out of my mouth.

"Kmt, breathe easy Snake, the ride's clean bro. Look, I've even got the paperwork here so just cool yeah."

I settle as I feel the leather seat start to heat up. What a fucking show off.

"Turn the heating off bro!" I snap. "We're in the middle of summer you dickhead. Haven't you got any AC in this bitch? And you still haven't told me where we're going blood."

Smiley just looks at me as he flicks off the heated chairs and flicks on the AC, doing what he does best: smiling. Flash little prick. Yes, that guy can smile for Brixton. The boy smiles at anything and everything and he's starting to piss me off as there really isn't any need for all the smiling shit.

"Look bro, where the hell are we going?" I say a bit more loudly with my face screwed up like them ten pound notes we get shooting food to them crackheads on road. "Snake, calm down man. First, we've got to check Wayne. He's got some new shit he wants us to try out."

"What the hell's wrong with that guy man? We ain't lab rats. The last time we tried some shit for him, you thought you were super Smiley and nearly jumped out the fucking window. You know what we come like? We come like some birds that's being dashed in a cage with ten cats. Damn man, I can't wait to do my own ting cause them mans taking the piss. Where's that prick?"

Smiley knows I'm talking the truth, but what can he say? He ain't scared of much. Trust me, I've seen him knock out some big guys and that's why he's my right hand man, but Wayne's a fucked up dude and if you ain't scared of him that's a big mistake. Smiley's face is dead straight, no smile, nothing and being around Smiley for so many years I know that face means fear.

"Snake, we got to do what he wants. He's our older. What you going to tell him? No?"

Smiley's right, he knows it's the truth and I know it's the truth, but as long as I'm not in front of that mad man I can be as pissed off as much as I want.

"Alright, so where the fuck is he? And don't let me have to ask you again!"

Smiley's a bit pissed off with me now. I think it's cause we both feel like two, frightened, helpless wankers so we're trying to rekindle our manhood by taking it out on each other.

"Bro, why the hell do you always have to start getting violent? You're a violent little prick, you know that Snake?"

I look Smiley deep into his eyes and see his fright as I caress my shank. I guess him not knowing what I'm going to do next makes him a little bit on edge as he knows I'm a mad man. And friend or no friend, I don't give a shit. I look at him hard, then from nowhere I just LOL.

As much as he tries to contain the fear it's written all over his face, even as he allows himself a sarcastic smile.

"Alright Smiley, where's Wayne?" I say in a low voice.

"No Snake. Be nice and say please," he say as his grin gets bigger, exposing two missing teeth at the back of his mouth.

Cheeky little prick. "OK Smiley. Please. Where's Wayne?"

"That's better Snakey boy, LOL!"

Look, I know Smiley's my boy, but at this point I feel a massive urge to feed him with some serious licks. However, I don't want to get my hands dirty as I'm low on hand wash. Smiley looks at me for a second then he tells me what I want to hear.

"He's waiting at Stratford station for us and we can't be late cause you know what that mad ass man's like. So we got 10 minute to get there bro." I feel my chest tighten. "Well Smiley, what you waiting for? Put your teeth away and put your foot down bruv."

We drive like a bat out of hell, quickly stopping at the corner shop to pick up more hand wash.

Chapter 2
Say No to Drugs

We reach the spot in Stratford, under the long, gray bridge just by the bus station. We're five minutes late and I know we're both shitting ourselves. Wayne's sitting in his red Rolls Royce phantom, so we pull up alongside him, making sure our window's totally wound down cause trust me when I tell you it's easier to get deaded out here quicker than you'd ever imagine. And who'd care if scum like us went missing?

Wayne looks totally pissed off. I glance at the passenger seat. *Now there's a face I haven't seen in a long while.*

It's only Delroy and he's a one-armed nutter. Trust me, just cause he's got one arm, he's not armless so don't let that fool you for one minute. Everyone knows Delroy's a nasty piece of work and not to be messed with. Delroy sits there, he doesn't even look at us. He just keeps his head straight, eyes glazed over, firmly gazing out the front window and I can't help but notice the 9mm burner he's holding in his lap with his finger firmly on the trigger as though he's about to pop one off at a moment's notice.

Now all I want to do is get the shit and do a Missy Elliot. Wayne doesn't say much. He sits there for a moment like he's thinking about what riddle he wants to ask us, but it ain't a riddle at all. What he says makes a lot of sense to someone that's already shit scared.

"Time can be your downfall, you little pricks. Do you understand me?"

Me and Smiley almost sound like echoes bouncing off each other: "Yes Wayne, sorry it won't ..."

Wayne cuts in, talking so loudly and aggressively that I think his spit's going to hit me square in my face.

"Shut up both of you! I washed my ass this morning, so I don't need it licked clean by you little punks. OK?"

Then Delroy looks me straight in my eyes. He's lifting his hand as he points the nine directly at my face. Damn man, we're only five minutes late! I must say, I see death. My eyes open wide as I try to control my breathing. Why do peeps always put their hands in front of their faces when someone points a gun at them like they can block bullets? LOL.

But it isn't funny: I feel like I'm dead already.

Now I know what all them other pricks feel like when I put my gun to their heads and trust me it isn't nice at all. If the bullet doesn't kill me, that look

Delroy's giving me will. *Why's he looking at me like that?* Why is he pointing that gun in my face cause it looks like there's more to it than us turning up late, that's for sure. And why's Smiley halfway under his car seat?

Wayne looks at Delroy sternly and snaps, "Delroy! Put the gun down!"

Delroy freezes, like time's stopped.

"I said, put ... the ... fucking ... gun ... down Delroy!"

Delroy reluctantly puts the gun back into his lap like it belongs there. I exhale as Wayne reaches into his glove box and pulls out the fattest spliff I've ever seen in my life. I mean, this spliff's as fat as a Cuban cigar and neatly skinned up. Frankly, I can't wait to get my lips around it and suck on it like I'm sucking on my wifey's breast.

Wayne continues as he hands it over to me. "Now, this is a new drug we're investing in and we need to know how good it is before we spend any dough on it. So you take this and smoke it. And I mean *all of it*. I'll call you tomorrow for the s.p. If we buy it and it's shit you're going to be two dead little pricks, so don't fuck up. Now fuck off before I get Delroy over there to take that gun and blow a hole in your nut so big that he can jump straight through it."

He doesn't have to tell us twice.

I try not to look at Delroy, who's eyeballing me hard like I jacked his girl or something. I do catch a glimpse of his beady, black eyes behind them three, thick locks that hang down his face though. His eyes are all glazed over like a fat kid's cake. I tap Smiley on his leg to try and signal to him to duck out cause Delroy can get real nasty and I want to see tomorrow. Them mans have ways of totally getting shot of your body and I mean *totally*. No-one will ever find you.

Smiley gets the hint and we speed off down the road to breathe another day.

Smiley doesn't want me to notice that he's touched cloth? I know he has cause I can just about smell it through his jeans, but there ain't no time to go home and change. I want to spark up this spliff so I can get on this raving ting. The way that spliff smells, it's going to be a rave to remember. So, no time for Smiley to change his pants now.

I can still hear the fear in Smiley's voice. "Yo Snake, you know we could've …"

"Smiley, don't say a word. Don't say another fucking word. Just give me a light so I can spark up this bitch!"

And trust me when I say whatever Wayne put in this shit is just that: *a real bitch*. She's a bitch that's got me hooked; I'm sucking on her hard like a juicy nipple. Smiley's digging me from the side of his eye.

"Yo Snake, send that over here man, that smells Peng."

But I can't let this spliff go. It's stuck on me like a lizard on a limb. And it got rid of Smiley's bad smell neatly. "Just drive the damn car man, I'll save you some," I snap as I rock in another long pull.

"Well, make sure bro cause Wayne said –"

I lose it again, as I do. "You know what Smiley? Fuck Wayne and fuck that crippled ass, one-armed dick head. Every dog has his day and the way we're moving up in the game, they're going to be moving down real quick, those old pricks."

Smiley's eyes are set firmly on the sweetly rolled spliff I've placed neatly between my lips. "OK, take this man. This shit's crazy, it's kicking in already." I reluctantly hand over the best spliff I've had in ages.

Smiley reaches out with that big smile on his face and just as he's about to take a long awaited pull on the big head, some feds pull up alongside us and Smiley's proper shook.

"Snake take it back. Boy dem on my right!"

"Cool, just drive and you can have some when we reach the spot."

I happily take back my bitch cause since I was a little kid I've hated sharing. Anyway, I don't want Smiley's thick, smiling lips all over it. I remember when I was nine and I got a toy from my uncle, my first action man. My mum told me I had to share it with my little brother and that really pissed me off, but I had a plan. I sat at the top of the stairs and called my little bro up. When he came to play, I pushed him down the stairs and said he slipped. It was harsh, but at least I could play alone with my toy while he was crying his eyes out and getting over his cuts and bruises.

Smiley hands it back and looks at me aggressively.

"OK Snake, but make sure you don't smoke it all cause the way you're sucking on that ting, I'd have thought you was sucking on your girl, LOL."

He's right. I'm mad hooked. There are all kinds of bright colours and my mind's running wild like it's trying to escape from my ears. One minute I'm hot, then I get mad cold. I watch myself running in front of the car, looking back at myself as I tell myself to catch up. The roads and trees are ripples in a pond as they vibrate in time with the afro beat tunes blasting out the bass box in the boot of Smiley's new ride.

My body's real light as a blast of wind from the AC hits me in my face. Suddenly, I'm jumping out of an airplane, falling at 100 feet a second. It's the best feeling I've ever had. Freedom.

But then things start to go bad.
I look at Smiley and he's smiling as usual. I look again and there's one of them vampires from the film I was watching, just staring at me with some long fangs and I mean long, fuck off fangs. His eyes are bloodshot, like he's been smoking one of Wayne's fat zoots; his skin's white as snow and stands out starkly against his crisp, black vintage suit. I back up against my door, kicking out at Smiley.

The car starts swerving all over the road and we're going head on into an oncoming van at 60 mph. Is my life flashing before me? Hell yes! But not cause I think we're going to die in a fatal car crash. It's cause I really have it in mind my boy's going to be eaten by some maniac vampire and I'm next on the menu. I bet all Smiley's thinking is *Thank God he's a good driver*.

Smiley's totally pissed off. "What the hell's wrong with you Snake? Are you crazy?"

If only he could see what I see. "Nah bro, but whatever I just smoked has really kicked in man, for real. Damn. Sorry man."

"Yeah, damn!" he barks at me, "you can say that again, Snake. You never even saved me any of it. Typical you. But you said sorry, that's a first. Must be really fucked up, bro."

We reach the spot, but I'm not handling this shit very well. I'm hallucinating real badly, but it isn't anything nice at all, you know, like floating in the clouds or flying like Superman. Nah, trust me, it's far from nice.

Big, black bulls are speeding towards the car with huge red eyes and as they're about to smash their horns into us they disappear in a puff of red smoke. I rub my eyes with disbelief, hoping the vision will go away, but as I reopen them I see headless soldiers hanging from the trees. That really shits me up, but no more than the vamp who just sits here between me and Smiley with them blood shot eyes, looking hungrier than before. Smiley shakes me hard.

"Yo Snake! We're here man. Snap out of it, that shit can't be that strong."

I'm shaking like a leaf and there are big, black bats flying all around the car and I don't want to get out. I can't think. I can't move. I'm just fucking scared. What the hell's wrong with Smiley? Can't he see any of this shit? The vampire who's been sitting with us like he's part of the gang is closer to Smiley than any girl's ever been. His mouth's open. He looks at me with those red eyes and, with a sick smile, he throws his head back. His mouth widens even more and the fangs seem to grow longer as he leans in to take a lingering, hard bite out of my boy's neck.

I freak out.

"Get out the car, Smiley! Get out the fucking car!"

I kick Smiley out and I jump out after him. I roll on the ground for what feels like a lifetime, but all I want to know is if Smiley's been bitten.

"Oh God! Help me!" I say out loud, but I keep rolling. I can't stop.

I call out again with more passion, "God! I'm sorry for all the things I've done. Please forgive me! I'll never, ever do anything bad again!"

God must've heard me cause I've come to a grinding halt. But where am I? It looks like a scene from medieval days.

I can smell the dampness of wet grass, but it ain't cause of rain. It's something more sinister. The combination of smells is weird. I look at my hands through blurry eyes and there it is: blood, lots of it. I'm lying in the middle of what seems to be a feeding ground. I study my surroundings, trying desperately to focus on a way out, but all I can just about see through the fog is dark, dense forest. I don't know which way to turn. It would be suicide to try to make a run for it.

Then I smell something different, something sweet. I look up and thousands of red petals fill the air as they fall from the trees in abundance. As they touch the ground, they wither into black hash and die. Beyond the trees, I can see enormous, black birds. I think they're vultures circling, staring down at me as though they're waiting for a freshly prepared meal.

The pollution of death fills the air and a thousand eyes are on me, but for some strange reason I know these eyes belong to one thing and one thing only. Who, or what, it is I can't tell you. Hairs stand up wildly on my body. Fear's my enemy and hunger's about to consume me. God's no longer here for me and who can blame Him?

My breath's no longer mine as horror seeps into and around me. It's eating me from the inside out, like I'm terminally ill. Death's knocking at my door, but I'm reluctant to open my arms and embrace him. Smiley's my only brother, my only hope and I long to see that big smile once more as now I know that smile was food for my soul. But where is he when I need him most? It's the first time my soldier has left my side in battle.

A gust of wind brushes my face; the way it's blowing I think it's the last breeze that'll come in my direction. On the breeze, I don't smell roses, mildew or the green grass. It's death riding my way. Closer and closer, death comes slowly, slowly and every step he takes towards me doubles the speed of my heartbeat as he rides on my fear.

He's at my door.

He's entered the threshold of my being. I see him. His skin's smooth and milky white as though he hasn't got one drop of blood in his body, but he looks forever youthful like a teenager.

Death's almost stunning. He's dressed in fine silk and his feet never touch the ground as he moves elegantly like he's about to dance to some mellow jazz. What he's doing seems like the dance of death. I know it is because I've seen it in a movie with Aaliyah, called *Queen of the Damned*.

I hear his voice for the very first time, calling like a fountain of smooth, running milk: "Come and dance with me."

Although it's the most beautiful voice I've ever heard, I refuse his offer. Then he becomes like my father, angry, raining down lashes on my back. His screams spew hot lava and I can smell my skin burn as my flesh parts like the Red Sea with every stroke.

Oh so angry, he's lost that beautiful smile and looks straight through me. His eyes are red hot, burning like a furnace that's been burning for a thousand lifetimes. He has four rows of teeth, 20 score 4 = 80 + 80 = 160, with both top and bottom teeth sharpened to pinpoint razors. His silk becomes drapes of the souls of men, women and children of 1,800 generations, including those that I'd stolen on my path of destruction. His fingers are the teeth of what I can only describe as dragon's claws and on his chest is his name: Death.

He asks me once again, "Would you like this dance?"

When I refuse the second time, the beast extends his right hand to the dark sky. On the inside of his right hand is the name Heaven and on the back of his left hand, which he's pointing towards the ground, is the name Hell. The clouds open and there's a bright ray of light.

I'm saved. God hasn't turned his back on me!

The most beautiful angel descends and his right hand is extending a sword of burning fire. It's pointing directly in front of him, although I can't set my eyes on him cause the sword is as bright as the sun. The creatures speak with no words. I can't hear their voices, but I know the beast's asking the angel my fate. We wait for a while, then the angel points his sword to the ground and I know my fate's eternal damnation for all the wickedness I've done.

The clouds smear the sky in red, thick blood. The beast now pays raw, undiluted attention to me. He roars out loud as though for a split second he feels sorry for what's about to happen. But he has a job to do and the way I've lived my life it's going to be a job well deserved. All I want is one more chance, but that's a chance I never gave any of my victims. Why should I deserve better? I have one more breath left in my frail, deserted soul and this is what I say: "Smiley ... Help me ... Help me."

I hear the beast scream my name like the tsunamis of Asia and the bombs of Hiroshima and Nagasaki all rolled into one. I hear the screams of the lives that I stole from mothers, fathers, sisters and brothers, the children I left fatherless, the mothers I made widows; all of these sounds mix into a single, flat line so loud that if the rest of the world could hear it, the devastation would be immense. Calling me by my surname, Phipps, with the massive roar of a thousand lions entering battle with mankind, his hand comes down on me fast and hard. I scream a thousand times in two heartbeats and my legs kick out, trying to keep him away, but to no avail.

"Please, no, please!" I hear my voice say in a distant whisper. I feel four sharp slaps to my face.

I think I'm dead until I finally open my eyes to see a face that I haven't always been glad to see. It's Smiley and about 20 others standing over me while I'm laying in the middle of the road, my legs and arms lashing out like I'm getting attacked by a swarm of African killer bees.

Smiley's smacking the hell out of me, slap after slap after slap like he's loving it.

"Calm down, Snake calm down! It's OK bro, I've got you family, you're OK, just breathe bro, breathe, whatever it is, it's not real bro."

I open my arms and fling them around Smiley. I don't say a word, I just hold him tight like my life depends on it. His neck clicks with the force, but I just can't let go.

"Snake, it's OK bro, let go you're killing me! I'm going to take you home, it's going to be OK fam. Get up, let's get back in the car." I get up and feel for my shank; it's still in my waistband where I left it. I get into the car fighting the sleep I so desperately need, but I know I can't sleep till I get home.

****

I don't for one minute want to go back to Hell again. As a matter of fact, from tomorrow it's God time cause if there's no place like Hell then where I just came from is a walk in the park. But it's a walk I don't want to take again and it confirms to me that all my life I've been walking around with my eyes wide shut. We reach my doorway; all I want is a nice, hot shower cause I feel as dirty as shit. "Yo Snake, I'm going to stay here tonight man. You're not in no fit state to be alone," Smiley says, all concerned.

"OK Smiley." And trust me I say that with a lot of relief cause I really don't want to be alone. I walk into my yard, but Smiley stays at the door. He wants to come in, but he just stands there looking at me and that smile that gets on my nerves is totally gone from his face. Rah man, was I that bad in the car? Is he too scared to come in? I look back and say something that I may or may not regret for the rest of my life.

"Yo bro, what you standing out there for? Come in bro, about you're acting like you don't know me."

Then he smiles at me and glides into my yard. His feet never touch the ground, he moves so elegantly as though he's about to dance to some smooth jazz, but what he's doing is the dance of death. I know that cause I've seen this dance before. A vampire can only come into your house if you invite them in. And I just invited one in. Without hesitation, I reach for my shank, pull it out and start shanking like my life depends on it.

That's the last thing I remember then I wake up.

****

Now, I just want to ask, have you ever had a dream that seemed so real? You know, ones like winning the lottery, eating a sweet, linking one gal, or the worst one – when your wifey cheats on you with your best friend? When you wake up you realise it's just a dream, but for the next five minutes of your life you totally believe it's true. You check your bank account or look for your winning ticket, you try to keep the taste of that sweet in your mouth, you look for the girl you was linking or you totally hate your wife for at least an hour after waking up. None of it's true, but you stay pissed off for the rest of the day. You get totally pissed off at yourself, you ask yourself *Why the hell did I have that stupid dream in the first place?*

Trust me, I'm glad this dream was just that: a dream.

I jump out of my sleep. Damn, man, I'm sweating like a real crackhead and my heart's beating hard like that dickhead Patrick when me and Smiley jacketed his chain and money. Now I'm looking at my garms to see if there's any blood on me, but there isn't any, not one drop. I grab at my neck. Did I get bitten by Smiley? I hold my breath ... man, my neck's safe. My garms have no sign of anyone getting shanked last night, although I don't remember changing into this black Nike t-shirt and grey Nike joggers.

All I know was that dream was the worst I ever had and you better know this, I'm never, ever, ever watching them bloody vampire movies again; my head can't take that kind of shit so I guess it's MTV Bass from now on.

I don't know what Wayne gave us to smoke, but it's going to be a big hit with them crackheads out on the road. As for me: never again. I'm sticking firmly to the weed from now on cause that shit made man feel like I'd been hit by a damn train. I try to wipe the sleep out of my eyes. Last night must've been crazy cause I've still got my eyes wide shut. I'm there, laying on my sofa feeling like total shit.

Smiley must've left cause he's nowhere to be seen and you know he's a mad man cause after a crazy night out he's always up early playing Fifa with that dumb ass smile on his face. I don't know how the hell he does it, but I'm glad he ain't around. All he'd do is mess up the place and end up pissing me off. Right now it's just time for me to be upset, you get me.

Raas man, damn! I feel like someone just force fed my bladder with a whole load of water. I'm dying for a slash; I'm going to explode.

I need to get to the toilet, but I can just about feel my legs and I can't for the life of me shake off that dream I had about shanking up Smiley. I mean, don't get it twisted; I ain't got no problem shanking a man, the only thing is cleaning up afterwards cause it's bloody messy work and as you all well know by now, I hate mess. I'd never shank Smiley; he's my dog and my right hand man for life, even though he's a prick most of the time.

Damn, man, for real though, what the hell was we smoking last night? I'm trying to get to the bog before I piss myself. My dick's on fire like I fucked some grim reaper last night and caught a bad case of the clap. Man, I need to piss real bad, so now I'm in sprinting mode!

After what seems like an hour of running in the Olympics, I reach the toilet and gasp as I release a yellowish river. Just as I start getting into the flow of things, the flipping front door knocks.

Knock, knock, bloody knock.

First, it's soft, but I'm not stopping cause I'm on a flow. Then those little knocks turn into big ass bangs. Knock! Knock!

What the hell is man doing banging down my door like some fed? Whoever it is must be out of their cotton picking mind, fam.

"Wait! I'm bloody coming!" I yell, totally pissed off. They're kicking the door. What the fuck! I'm not going to answer that till I wash my hands and I tell you something, if that's Smiley with his silly ass jokes, I'm going to break his teeth.

When I rush over to the sink and start scrubbing away, I glimpse myself in the mirror real quick and something catches the corner of my eye. *Nah way man, this can't be real.* I rub my eyes.

Is that spliff still in my system?

Am I still seeing things?

If not, then what the hell is Smiley doing in my bath?

Why the hell is he covered in blood with my shank protruding from his chest? And it looks like Smiley ain't smiling no more. I can just about hear one last bang as the door flies off its hinges. That's when all hells breaks loose. I look up only to realise I'm surrounded by pigs and at least three submachine guns pointing at my head.

They call out, "Armed police!" Duh, I can see that.

"Get on your knees and put your hands on your head. Now! Where are the drugs and the guns? Where are they?"

Still in shock, I fall to my knees and pray in my head, *Please let this be a bad dream, let me wake up, please, for God's sake, let me wake up!* The police are still shouting, but their voices sound like fly-by mosquitoes, you know that annoying buzzing you hear when you're just about to get some shut eye.

Fuck the drugs. How the hell did my boy end up in the fucking bath?

Then it dawns on me … last night wasn't a dream at all.

****

I'm sitting in front of the judge, looking at 25 to life with no parole. Smiley's dead and I'm dead inside. It's crazy, but not as crazy as what's about to happen next.

Chapter 3
What Goes Around,
Comes Around

I'm walking through A block – that's where all the murderers and rapists are on lockdown. It's madness, people screaming and shouting, some calling me a cunt and all sorts. I walk to the rhythm of the keys that dangle off the chubby screw belt as he leads me to my cell. I stupidly think *It's cool, there's going to be a lot of man in here that I know from the ends.*

I'm right.

As I walk past the cells, I see at least eight of my dogs from the strip, but every single one of them turns their back when they see me. I call out to them, but they act like I'm not even here. The screw's agitated. "Quit talking and keep walking. This isn't your estate building, so keep it shut." Kmt, fat bastard.

Do they know something I don't know?

There's one cell I walk past and something inside me draws me to look. When I do, I see a very distressed Patrick. Damn, this guy has grown! He rushes to his cell door window, smashing into it head first and he smiles as though it's his first smile in a year. *Bloody hell, what have I got myself into?*

My mum warned me my past would catch up with me and I always shrugged it off. Well, look at me now. I finally get to the box that's going to be one of my hotel rooms for the rest of my miserable days. As the screw stops outside my cell, I notice a crude smile on his round face. My brain starts ticking cause I know that look. It's the same look I used to have when I was going to jack some prick.

Damn, man, can this shit get any worse?

He looks at me with an even bigger smile. "There you go son, sleep well and see you in the morning. That's if you make it." Then he shoves me into the cell and locks the door. What does he mean *If I make it*? Why won't I make it? I'll soon find out.

Chapter 4
Patience is a Virtue

I'm looking down from the top of my bunk bed to see the gift dad promised me. My fingers caress the Stanley blade my dad left me before he got out of this shithole. I can hear his deep voice saying, "I'm going to send you a present and when it comes, go straight for the throat, son."

I hear the hatch open and the screw shouts: "Oi! Wake up! Your present's here." Little does he know I'm already up and ready to rock and roll. I jump off my bed, all excited like a kid that just got the news he's going to Disney Land. I feel so powerful as my feet hit the cold, concrete cell floor. The whole planet shakes under my 6 feet, 18 stones frame. How I've grown! I raise my eyes to see the can I'm about to open and on that can there's a name: it's called Snake.

****

I've just been flung into a cell. I hear the door slam behind me and the keys lock the metal door for the first night of my sentence. As reality hits me that there's no way out, fear sets in. My legs start shaking like booty meat as I see the size of the guy that jumped off the top bunk. He's standing in front of me and looks like a monster. Now I know what that screw was saying when he talked about surviving.

I swear I know this dude.

The best way to find out is to ask, but he looks like he wants to rip my head clean off my shoulders. You know what? Fuck it, I'm going to ask him.

"Yo bro!" I say, nodding my head in his direction, trying so desperately to look hard. "Do I know you cause you look familiar?"

Now this guy doesn't say a word, he just looks at me hard. Two minutes go by. He's standing there, sweating like a rapist, then out of the blue his mouth finally opens.

"Yeah bro, you know me? How can you forget me? Look at me good." He poses like he's about to get snapped by paparazzi. "I tell you what, I'm going to give you two minutes to remember me, then I'm going to give you another two minutes to pray for your life. And trust me, you better pray hard fam."

****

Stop. Let's go back a few days before Wayne gave us that crap to smoke. Now imagine you're a fly on the wall in Wayne's kitchen and maybe you'll understand what happened to me and Smiley once upon that night.

Chapter 5
The Plot

"Delroy, we need to do this in a way we can't get caught and I've got the best idea to sort out them little pricks."

"OK Wayne, what do you suggest? Come on, spill the beans."

"Now you're talking. There's a new drug on the market called Ketamine, well it's not that new, it's been out for a while, but it's been a bitch to get hold of cause it's a beast from hell. Back in the day it was known as SK or Special K. That's when it was known to be a hallucinogen. It was really a tranquiliser for animals. I've never touched that shit, but I saw lots of old school friends on it. Why they'd want to take that crap, only God knows. It made them act totally crazy and they'd see things that weren't even there. All they'd do is scream and freak out and some would just look and act like they were crazy.

"I never understood where the fun was in taking that shit, so I stayed well away from it. I didn't even want to put it out on road cause trust me that would be a sin. But I got some especially for your two boys, so here's what we're going to do Del. We're going to roll one up in a big spliff, but we're going to bush it with crack skunk and a bit of crystal meth just for small measure.

"I gave Snake some guns and bullets to stash in his pad for me, so when they smoke that shit all we have to do is tip off the old bill and sit back cause they're going to be proper fucked. They won't even know what year it is let alone know the police are kicking off their door till it's too late. Old bill finds the guns and bullets, they get nicked and do hard time and we make sure they go to the right prison, get put in the right cell then Carlton can deal with them personally."

The plan's amazing.

"Bloody hell Wayne, you went on a bit, but you're not as dumb as you look!"

****

You see what them cunts did?

This beast of a guy speaks again, "Time's up. Well, do you know who I am now?

Under my breath I say, "Yeah, I do." He flips out and there's nowhere for me to run or hide.

****

"What did you say? I can't hear you?" My head's hot and I can taste blood at the back of my throat. But before Snake opens his mouth again, let's just say I cut a long story short. I aim for his throat. No need to cover his mouth as he can't breathe, let alone scream. I do my job then just sit back to admire my handy work. It's the first time Stanley's consumed a life by my hand, but, trust me, it won't be the last.

One down, one to go.

It harshly dawns on me: after fulfilling the only thing that's kept me alive in this shithole, I'll be spending the rest of my natural life in a box and I can't bear the thought of that. I have to bust out of here and I have to bust out tonight.

I slowly take off my shoe laces and tie them around each of my forearms, just under the elbow to stop the blood running to my hands, then I start to jog on the spot, running like my life depends on it, my legs going faster and faster.

I don't remember starting the run and I don't get tired. I just keep running. I drop to my knees in press-up position and knock out press-up after press-up. I can feel the blood trying to bust out of my veins. My heart's beating hard and fast as though it's got arms and is trying to claw its way out of my chest. I know it's time to get out of here; my blood's pumping crazily like acid through my veins.

I climb back up to my bunk bed and lay there staring at the ceiling. There are cracks that I never noticed before; I guess the dirt marks must've camouflaged them well. Now I speak to Stanley, "Yo Stanley, one more job to do son." I open him up and he sounds so beautiful, like a Beethoven symphony:

click ... click ... click. I've heard that sound for years as he's my only friend and the only contact I've got left with my dad.

I put Stanley on my wrist and press until I open my veins.

I untie the laces I wrapped around my arms with a smile on my face, knowing I'll be a free man soon. The blood's so desperate to get to my hands it gushes out my body like a busted water main. I watch as it hits the ceiling, turning the dirty off-white paint to a nice shade of red. *Now this is what a ceiling is meant to look like, a beautiful work of art.* As I drift away, I know that Snake's long gone to Hell and I'm right behind him.

We'll be together pretty soon and I'll have all eternity to kick his ass.

****

A wise man once said:

"A drug is neither moral nor immoral; it's a chemical compound. The compound itself is not a menace to society, until a human being treats it as if consumption bestows a temporary license to act like an asshole." Frank Vincent Zappa

What Made Her Like That?

Chapter 1
My Arrival

Knowing it was the last kiss and cuddle that I'd receive from my dear, beautiful mamma broke my little heart. I knew that pain would last for a lifetime.

OK, let's start from the beginning. I remember standing at the dockside looking at this massive boat, well it was a ship really, but I called it a boat. It was the longest boat I'd ever seen and it was going to be the longest journey of my life. I think the boat was meant to be white, but it was filthy. I just stood there, contemplating, *How does something that spends so much time in water remain so dirty?*

There was a thick, black line running from the back end of the boat to the front, but it was hard to tell the back from the front because they both looked the same to me. Heavy, grey smoke poured out of two long poles that stood side by side as though they were husband and wife, not wanting to be apart.

The smoke kept coming thick and fast, maybe that was why the ship looked so filthy. There were at least 150 little square windows and below them the name *Isabella* was painted in black down one side, so I guessed the boat was a lady. I couldn't help but think that's no way for a lady to dress (little chuckle)! Yes, mamma was right: first impressions do last and I wasn't impressed, not one bit.

Bwaaa ... that noise was irritating ... *Bwaaa.* The horns blew like the wind that made my dress sway from side to side. Yes, they got on my last nerve, but I hoped they'd make that noise all the way to sunny England just so I'd stay awake and not mess up my braids and my beautiful dress.

Yes, I had to stay awake and if the horns didn't keep me up, I knew that irritating little man with his tight, black jacket, receding hair line and two missing front teeth would do the job. In fact, I knew he'd do the job perfectly well.

As I boarded the boat, I heard his stale, croaky voice say, "Get in your hole," in a reedy English accent. "Get in there and don't come out unless you need to eat or piss!"

How rude, I thought to myself as he shoved me into a little box room with a slim bed which I could just about sit on, let alone lay on, but that was fine by me. At least I knew I wouldn't fall asleep. "This isn't the slave ship Jesus," I mumbled under my breath; we learned about the slave ship Jesus in history class and I think he knew about it too as he looked back at me with death in his eyes.

"Just don't come out because I will not be responsible for you if you fall overboard," he said as though he would've been responsible for that action.

He didn't have to tell me twice and anyway I had so many things to keep me awake and play with in my little pink bag that matched my dress. There was some bun and cheese, fried dumplings filled with ackee and salt fish and a nice, cool drink of carrot juice. Mamma made me everything to keep me occupied and my belly full, so I knew I couldn't fail to maintain the way I looked.

The worst thing was the way the boat moved; it made me want to be sick. It felt like the food from this morning that mamma took so much effort to make was going to come back up all over my pretty dress, but that was out of the question. That would definitely defeat the purpose of trying to keep my dress clean, so I had to buckle down and suck my belly in. But I tell you this: I'll never forget that feeling of sea sickness as long as I live.

****

I stepped off the boat in the long, pink dress that mamma had taken five, hard months to make. I could always hear her whispering, "Shit! Blasted hell, that hurt!" as she pricked her finger with a needle on a regular basis. Yet she'd done a great job this time around – all the other clothes she made for me weren't that appealing. Actually, they were far from nice, but this dress was the best ever and maybe that was because even though we never had much, mamma was a very proud West Indian woman. By the time I got off the boat, my beautiful pink dress was a shabby looking piece of cloth with at least 15 bows, 1,808 sequins and 12, shiny, pink buttons that shimmered as the light hit them from different angles. Well, how else was I meant to spend my time on that horrid journey? I couldn't even rest my head for not wanting to mess up my neat braids.

Mamma always told me, "Rebecca first impressions last!" and she was right. Silly me, thinking the streets were paved with gold; that impression was bound to last.

But someone lied to me.

Me and mamma used to sit up all night and she used to tell me about a place called England. It was like an adult's fairy tale.

She'd light a candle that brightened up half my room and was kept on my little bedside table. She'd cuddle up close to me under my shiny, pink sheets. As you can tell, pink was my favourite colour (little giggle). It was like she was reading from a book as she told me the good things and the bad things about England. She told me about all the areas she used to live and the big, red buses with so many windows which were like houses on wheels.

Yes, she knew a lot about England as she spent two full years of her life there before she came back home, pregnant with me and looking back I think she was grooming me to taste some of sweet, sweet England, the place where I was conceived. I guess she wanted me to see it for myself, or maybe she was trying to get me away from my best friend Chanttel.

I was always told the houses were made of candy of all different colours and the people's clothes were vibrant and eye-catching.

My dear mamma told me so much about England over the last three years that I used to have the wildest dreams about it; they felt so real, I couldn't wait to get there. So you can only imagine how disappointed I was when I got off that boat.

I gazed around with a huff and a puff then disappointment settled in.

The first thing I noticed was the cold that nibbled at my bones just like the way me and mamma used to sit at the table on Sundays biting away at the big, old chicken bone she used to cook so well.

I was so cold, all I wanted to do was sneak back on the boat and hide deep in her belly so she could drift me back home to the sunny side of life, but instead I stood in England as the rain filled my little white shoes. My pink ankle socks drank it up like one of those fluffy cats I used to feed milk to in my garden back home.

I looked around and on my left side, behind some metal fences, I could see a lot of unhappy white faces watching all the black faces descend from the boat like black ants. Their faces were as cold as their country as they stood there in black, brown and grey suits. Meanwhile, on the other side of the fence we wore black faces and all the colours of the rainbow. It was like we'd brought a little bit of Dominica with us. "Get back on your banana boat and go back to the jungle!" I heard them shouting, but I paid them no mind as mamma had warned me about that part.

Chapter 2
My Introduction

Oh OK, my name, how rude of me. My name's
Rebecca Elisa Jenkins. I was 13, dark skinned and
sweet when I came to England. The slight squint in
my left eye made me look kind of cute because it
complemented my big smile; it was a bit of a shy
smile, but it was a smile no doubt. I loved smiling and
people always used to comment on my pearly white
teeth. "Oh my God," they'd say, "Did you bleach
them?" *How silly is that?* I thought as my smile grew
broader to hide the fact that I felt they were talking
nonsense.

Mamma always put my wavy hair in four,
long plaits that reached near the middle of my back
just so I could look my age. But with my body already
developing, I was conscious of the amount of clothes
I needed to wear. Mamma told me before I left
home, "Rebecca Elisa Jenkins, always cover your
blessings to avoid prying eyes," and I was used to
that kind of stuff so no-one was surprised at how shy

and timid I was. I was so used to older men trying to grope or touch me in some way, I just hated the smell of their cologne, but I always felt safe around mamma. However, she was no longer there to protect me. In fact, I never really understood what she meant by *Cover your blessings,* but I'd soon find out.

As I stood there looking at my cold surroundings, I got lost in memories of my home across the sea; I was so deep in thought that all the sounds of scuffling feet and loud voices soon drifted away, but one voice stood out and made me feel like I was back home again in sweet, sweet Dominica.

"Rebecca! Rebecca!" The voice sounded kind, with a slight accent almost like mamma's. "Oh, there you are!" I felt a sudden, warm hand on my shoulder as the voice I heard shouting my name softened.

"Hi Rebecca, I'm your aunt Beverly. Let me look at you." Holding my shoulders gently and scanning me up and down, she said with a smile, "You're such a pretty picture. Your mamma told me so much about you." She held my head in her large, soft hands and narrowed her eyes. "Oh, poor baby! Did something fly in your eye?"

I gazed up at her; she was such a tall lady, almost frightening, but her tender voice extinguished the fear inside me.

With one of my big, kind of fake, but gentle smiles, I said, "No auntie, I've just got a slight squint." Sympathy spread across her face. "Oh dear, but it's quite cute. And look at that smile, it's just like your mother's."

I watched her as she carried on paying me compliment after compliment. It was my turn to analyse her; she was very light skinned with heavy mummy breasts. I think it ran in the family because all the women in my family, including me, were 'gifted' with big breasts, but I would soon wish that I was as flat as a pancake. Anyway, my auntie was well dressed in a long, flowing white frock with a white hat that covered her dodo plaits, you know, those *I'm in a mad rush, can't be late* plaits. She looked as though she was going to church. I could see where mamma got her first impressions saying from.

She held my hand and in her soothing, welcoming voice she looked down at me and said, "Come on Rebecca, I'm going to take you home. I'm sure it's nowhere as nice as your house, but it's home."

We got on a big, red bus where I fell into a deep sleep that was well needed. I wanted to stay awake to see the sights, but auntie's chest was so comfortable that all that mattered was sleep.

I heard mamma calling me, "Wake up Rebecca! We're here baby!" but it wasn't mamma at all.

Yes, I'd made it to England. We got off the bus and took a slow walk to what was going to be my prison for God knows how long; the sensation of the boat ran through my bones like I was floating on the deep, blue sea. Then I felt my auntie tap my shoulder and she stopped me dead in my tracks. "Rebecca, there's someone I need to tell you about."

Oh no, this didn't sound too good. I just kept quiet, hoping for positive news.

"Your uncle Samuel lives with us; he's not a very nice man most times, but all I want you to do is stay out of his way and he'll be OK. Can you do that for me?"

My squint twitched, "Er, yes auntie I can." I mean, did I have a choice? What kind of question was that? At that point, I really wanted to turn around and go straight back home.

"OK, good Rebecca. Let's go inside." I walked through the gates and up some short stairs. The house was massive; it had at least six windows in the front and stairs leading down to what looked like a basement apartment, the brick work had no colour at all, but the door was, yuck, purple. Whatever possessed someone to paint their door that colour was beyond me. We walked through the front door and up another flight of stairs.

I could smell the musty, old brown carpet and damp marks showed through the brown and cream flower patterned wallpaper; one corner of it had peeled and was slowly finding its way to the floor. I didn't feel good about this house, not one little bit.

"Come on Rebecca, not far now" my auntie confirmed. "You must be hungry and tired."

I was very tired, but the smell that emerged from the room when she opened the door knocked the hunger out of me: paraffin. I knew that smell because my uncle back home used it to clean oil off his car engines. I hated the smell with a passion because that same uncle tried to grope me with his filthy hands any chance he could get. Anyway, let's not talk about that; I'm in England now and that's all behind me.

I had a new life and I intended to make the most of it. I walked into our little front room and that's when I saw him sitting there as miserable as sin. He was short, much shorter than my auntie, but he was very well built around his shoulders. His afro was neat, as though he'd spent an hour patting it into place. He just sat there with his little pot belly popping through a well pressed, white shirt, hitching his short, bristly beard, gazing at me steadily.

"Samuel, this is Rebecca," my auntie explained like he didn't know I was coming.

Before I could say a word he stood, pulled at the brown braces that held up his well pressed brown trousers and with a huff he walked towards the door. "Ha! Another mouth to feed! Little girl, just stay out of my way." Then he was out the door like I was a bad smell; talking about smells, this is where my story gets deeper.

Chapter 3
That Smell Again

It was that smell again; the whiff hit my nose like that strong scent from the paraffin heater and even though I'd smelt it constantly for the last two years, it always seemed too close for comfort. Yet 'comfort' was all he wanted. I repeatedly asked myself, "Why me? Isn't my auntie good enough?"

I jumped out of my sleep again, so confused like a moth fluttering around an open flame as I had for the last 24 months of my miserable life. My innocent, young body contracted as I retreated into myself. My eyes quickly filled with tears while I felt his body on mine, touching me, breathing heavily and sucking my left breast like a baby feeding from its mother.

He woke me up in the only space I had in the corner of the single room which was our bedroom, bathroom, front room and kitchen. I didn't want to think about how long he was there this time, even though my mind kept prodding at the question. All I knew was my breast was sore and it hurt like hell, so he must've been there for quite some time.

Damn, I must've been totally knocked out.

I had that feeling in my belly again, you know, the seasick one … I didn't know when that feeling would ever leave me alone.

This sort of thing happened for a total of two years and eight months, but every time hurt like the first and I felt more and more dirty every day that passed. Not being able to bathe as much as I was used to made matters even worse as we had to wash in the same room that we slept, ate and everything else in. I felt so ashamed of my body; I didn't for one minute want to draw more attention than I already had to myself.

He finally lifted his ugly head. I thought it was over, but then he brought his face really close to mine. "Sshh," he whispered in my ear with a strong, deep Jamaican accent and the pungent smell of stale rum on his breath. I should've been used to that smell as I was completely addicted to the devil's water myself. It was a good way to help me sleep. Well, it was the only thing that made me sleep and took my mind away from all the madness. How low

I'd fallen! But that night I was about to fall so deeply into darkness, I knew I'd never see the light of day again.

Yes, I knew that smell well because when the pain inside got the better of me I started to sneak into Samuel's little, old, brown cabinet that sat neatly on the right side of the wall of our room. It was about the height of my waist with a key that squeaked as I turned it, so I had to turn it with a lot of loving, tender care, like my life depended on it – if I woke anyone in the room I'd have been one dead Rebecca. Luckily, the hazy street light that trickled down the side of the thick, black curtains and the paraffin heater's golden, reddish-blue flame helped to guide my hand nicely towards the key.

On top of the cabinet was a single draw that had no key, just a black latch, and underneath was a little swing door that was dark ebony, a bit like my skin. It was smooth to touch and every opportunity I got to open it seemed like a comfort; it helped to make me numb for a few hours and take me out of this hellhole called England into my own little world. I think you know the world I'm talking about: the one where children are loved and looked after just like I was back home, living with mamma, untouched, not frightened and not abused.

Apart from the time that Samuel sent me to get his black leather case, no-one was allowed to go near that cabinet let alone touch it, not even auntie. Mmm that little case; he loved it as much as I loved my innocence. I was the only one with direct access to it. He used to say in his old, rough Jamaican voice, "Rebecca, go fetch my case!" I hated his voice with a passion, but I just loved to turn that key. It made me happy to see my comforter any chance I got. Two swigs, that's all it took to put me into a deep sleep and deaden my pain just for a bit. But as time went by, I felt like I couldn't live without it so two swigs led to four then five as my body became used to the potency of the clear, dangerous liquid.

By then, I was drinking so much that it got to the point where I had to mark the bottle with my finger before I drank my share, then I'd refill it with water, getting the level right, and wipe it down till it shone. The worst part was when I had to eat raw garlic and onions to kill the smell of rum on my breath. I ate them till my throat and eyes burned; it felt like I was breathing fire through my eyes and nose, but it had to be done. I always thought I'd get caught, but most of the time that bastard was already drunk out of his skull before he got through the front door, so he didn't even notice the watered down liquor. Yet if he ever found out, I would've been beaten fiercely and I knew it would've been bad as I saw the damage he did to auntie on a regular basis. So when I heard him fall up the stairs, I used to exhale with relief as I knew I'd go another day without the beating of a lifetime.

Anyway, back to Samuel's pride and joy. When he opened that little black case and stuck that needle in his arm, he was dead to the world. I wondered what that needle was as I watched him sitting on the wooden chair, unzipping the case slowly with such love and excitement. When he burnt that stone, the smell was so terrible it made onions and garlic smell great. I was totally intrigued by the effect it had on him. I watched with excitement as he wrapped a belt around his arm real tight and slapped at it, trying to bring up a vein. Sometimes, when he was too drunk to find it, he'd call me: "Rebecca, come here! Push the needle in that big, blue vein. But listen, if you miss I'm going to bust your head till the white meat shows, you understand me."

I had to be on point. I had to control my fear which made my eye squint harder than ever. I couldn't miss the mark and I never did. When he loosened the belt and I squeezed slowly on the needle, it was goodnight as though he'd dashed himself off the roof of his life. It was a pity the bastard didn't hit the ground hard. *What was it?* I wondered. Mmm ... whatever it was totally put his lights out; his eyes rolled as though they were sinking into the back of his head and it made him sleep like he was dead.

I'd be so lucky.

But they were great times as me and auntie could walk around our little room like the queens we were born to be. We loved it when he was there but wasn't there as we took turns to slap the hell out of his disgusting, fat face. Sometimes, we got carried away and had to pull each other off him; auntie said: "Rebecca, get me the red pepper sauce." I used to run to our little makeshift cupboard with a big smile then she'd tell me to look away as she rubbed the sauce on the end of his you-know-what. It was so exciting to see when he woke up screaming like the cats outside our window that used to have fluffy fights; it was great as I knew he wasn't going to trouble me at night.

But that night was different.

My belly dropped as I heard his voice again, "Ssshhh! You don't want to wake auntie, do you, because you know she won't like that."

I could almost taste the smell of the white rum on his breath and the hairs of his rough beard were too uncomfortable to bear, like sharp, black pins pricking and scratching my smooth, dark skin which was quickly fading as my abuse of rum spiralled out of control.

The effect of the white rum I drank from the cupboard earlier had already worn off, so I just closed my eyes and took myself back home, remembering when I was playing on the makeshift swing that mamma had taken so long to make for me. Swinging higher and higher, I loved that little old swing. I loved the feel of the breeze blowing through my long hair and the smell of the mango tree that graced my garden with its beauty.

I remember mamma as she tried to throw the rope over a branch of that tree. She tried over and over again until she knocked a mango off a branch and we watched as it came crashing down, hitting her square on her head. Then we looked at each other in shock and couldn't help falling to the floor, lost in crazy laughter.

"Why didn't you just move mamma?" I said, and she looked at me and rubbed her head. "That mango can run fast innit?"

How I loved those days, there were lots of jokes.

But the memory wasn't enough. The smiles started to fade and that's when I knew I'd have to find another way to blind myself to my pain. I hated mamma for sending me here. I mean, what did I do to deserve this? Was I a bad child? Was I not good enough to be at home with her? I heard my inner voice screaming, "Mamma, I hate you! I hate you for what you did to me!" Then I felt a sharp pain in my privates; it was a pain I'd never felt before. I returned to reality in total shock. "Stop! Stop! That hurts! Please stop!" I cried as I grabbed at his fat hand and tried to back myself up on the mattress as he illegally inserted his stubby finger into my vagina.

Then I heard that dirty old man whisper. I just about heard his voice beyond the groans and shuffling as he touched himself.

"Shhhhh, let go of my hand. I'm not going to take you now, I'm just going to loosen you up for your 16th birthday then I'm going to make you mine."

He let out a gasp; it was over and very messy. As though nothing had happened, He shuffled across the room, back to his rightful bed like nothing had happened. mumbling to himself. "It's our little secret and if you tell anyone ... if you even think it out too loud, I'll make sure you wished you'd never got off that fucking boat. Now clean up the mess before you go to sleep."

He didn't even know auntie was looking straight at me and with the help of the dimly lit heater, I saw the twinkle in her eyes as tears began to wet her pillow. I knew she was disgusted at herself for letting this happen, but I knew she couldn't say or do anything as the beatings were real bad even if he just ran out of rum. If his dinner wasn't hot enough, there would be food stains all over the wall where he smashed his plate against it in one of his hissy fits.

Still in pain, I put my hand down the side of my mattress and pulled out the towel I kept for such nights; I started to rub away at my skin, just trying to get his scent off me. I rubbed and rubbed and rubbed some more until between my legs became red raw. I tried to go back to sleep, wishing I was dead, hoping I wouldn't wake up again, just pondering how I was going to get rid of the mental pain and get myself out of that mess.

The stinging made it hard for me to relax let alone think and knowing I was going to be 16 in two weeks' time was the worst feeling of my life. I had to find a way, any way, to stop the pain. I had to find a way to take his mind off me. I hated myself, my body, my long braids and my breasts. It must've been my fault. What other reason did he have to violate me? Maybe that's why mamma got rid of me, that's why she sent me here to be punished. I didn't even go to school, at least that would've given me a little bit of breathing space.

What the hell can I do? Think Rebecca think, I said to myself harshly in confusion. After what seemed like a lifetime and a half, *Ha!*, I had an idea. I was sure it would work, but I had to wait till the morning when everyone had left the house then I was going to end the pain once and for all. I was going to make him see another side of me, a side that would make him never want to touch me again. I had to force myself to sleep even though I loved it because it was the closest thing to death. All I wanted was for day to burst through the thick, black curtains that kept out all lights so I could fulfil my plan, but it was the longest night ever.

****

Ha! Great! It was finally 7.35am and I don't think I slept a wink. Everyone was up and getting ready for work. Auntie walked over to my bed and gave me a kiss.

She held my hand and looked deep into my eyes as though she was looking straight through me, trying to tell me something using only her mind, then her words came.

"Rebecca," she said softly in a whisper. "I'm sorry, I'm so, so sorry; I know what he's doing to you and I'll fix this. I promise you, I'll fix this if it's the last thing I do, just be strong. I'll think of something."

I lay there embracing her and for a split moment it felt as if I was back home with mamma, her big arms around me so warm and protective as she held me against her breasts. Her smell was like fresh baby powder with a hint of cocoa butter. I breathed it in and wished for home. Auntie loved giving me cuddles when he wasn't around and I accepted them as they were as innocent as a young baby just born.

I looked up at her and said in a fearful, low voice, "Please help me, please auntie. Don't leave! Stay with me! I don't know how I'm going to do this on my own anymore!"

I held her so tightly; tears flowed down my face like the waterfall that me and mamma used to wash our feet in at the hottest time of the year. The water was so cool, we always used to end up having a water fight or one of us would get pushed in.

Then I heard his voice and I felt my auntie pull back in fear; I could see the alarm in her eyes. Damn! What had that man done to her that made her fear him so much? She was a big woman, but he had her scared like a little child so how the hell was she going to help me?

"Get off her, she isn't a child! The damn girl is soon going to be 16! Get up and get your fat ass to work, woman. Move!" he snapped as he pointed his pudgy finger at the door. In all my days, I never saw her move so fast; then again, thinking about it, I never saw anyone her size move so fast.

Samuel's voice fell into a whisper as he pointed his grubby finger at me. "You better make sure that when I get back from work this place is clean and tidy. Do you understand me, you stupid little bitch?"

Then he proceeded to tip over a table on his way out.

Dread bled into my bones, but I was still comforted by the words of my auntie and for a split second I felt as though a big weight had been lifted off my shoulders because I knew she was about to help me by any means possible – I could see it in her eyes. But my bubble soon burst when I heard mamma's voice: "Rebecca, a promise is a comfort to a fool, never, ever forget that." I knew I had to help myself because no-one was going to do it for me. If I depended on someone to help me, I'd lose the drive and passion to help myself. I couldn't let that happen because I was the only person I had. I had to stick to my plan.

Everyone had gone, but I waited for 20 minutes just to make sure they'd left properly because my auntie always forgot something. Her poor little brain just about coped with the stress. My heart was beating triple time, so scared, so, so scared of what the outcome of my actions were going to be. My stomach fell as I felt the big boat smashing against the waves and sweat appeared from nowhere, covering my entire body.

When I knew the coast was clear, I rushed to my auntie's sewing machine. I knew what I was looking for. Yes, her pair of long, sharp scissors.

I stood there just looking at them, my eyes blurring in and out of focus as ten minutes passed which felt like an eternity. I was scared as hell, thinking, *Am I doing the right thing*? One hundred and one thoughts rushed through my head. The room was very dark and the curtains laid flat over our windows as though they were a dress tailor made for a princess, cuddling her body, letting drips of light down the gaps along the sides. I could smell the morning hour and barely heard cars go by as the world went mad, rushing to work to earn a crust. The smell of the paraffin heater attacked my nostrils as my eyes came back into focus. I had to do it and I knew it was going to hurt like crazy, but it needed to be done.

I gripped the scissors in my hands and took a slow walk over to the small sink that sat neatly in the far corner of our room, pulling the light cord as I went. The light revealed the tears rushing down my poor face as insanity set into my bones. I prepared my mind for the pain I was about to endure. My body went numb and my legs felt like jelly as happier days flashed before my eyes. I held the scissors tightly; my breasts had to go and they had to go that day. I held on to them, not caring about the pain I was about to inflict on my growing body; I knew it was going to be worth every bit of agony as they'd brought me unwanted attention.

First things first. I looked into the tainted mirror above the sink, grabbed my braids and hacked away at them. Lumps of my soft, curly hair fell as I watched myself. I lost it. I flung the scissors into the sink and started ripping away at my hair, yanking it out at the roots, followed by hard punches to my face. I screamed at myself, "Bitch, bitch! You dirty, little, good for nothing bitch!" The way he touched me kept running through my head and I hated myself for it.

Next, the skin from my face quickly filled the tiny gaps under my finger nails. I peeked into the glass to admire my work and that's when I met him – *Hello boy!* – then I rammed my fist into the mirror, smashing it into pieces. My hand poured with blood, but I couldn't stop there. I had to get rid of my breasts. I ran across the room and looked deep into my auntie's material basket, just grabbing and throwing cloth over my shoulder.

"Haaa! Too small, too short, damn there's got to be something here … Ha! There it is!" I pulled out a long piece of elasticated cloth, it was about four feet in length and eight inches wide, perfect for what I wanted. I stood up and proceeded to pull my nightie down around my waist, then I took off my raggedy, water-washed bra.

I was about to get rid of my breasts once and for all.

Tears of pain filled my eyes as I struggled to breathe and I wrapped the cloth tightly around my chest. The pain was so bad, but I had to keep going, I finally finished, just tucking the last bit in to secure the cloth. I pulled off my nightie then ran across the room again like a cat gone wild and dragged one of my auntie's baggy, old, grey cleaning trousers and a blue t-shirt from the dirty laundry basket.

I flung them on and felt them swallow me up. I walked over to the little brown cabinet, catching a glimpse of myself in the broken mirror. I stopped to look properly at my transformation; it was cruel to be kind, or, should I say, cruel to survive.

I'd achieved what I wanted, so I reacquainted myself with my new self.

"Hello boy," I said with a bitter smile followed by laughter and that's when it hit me: lovely, well-spoken, innocent Rebecca was dead. Boy had taken over.

I thought, *He isn't going to want me now I have no hair, no tits and I look like a boy. Unless he's a fucking batty man, I think I'm safe.* Anyway, where was I going? Oh yeah, the cabinet. No, I didn't want the rum. I needed something more, something to really take me away because when everyone returned I knew it was going to be the worst time of my life. Fear, exhaustion and anticipation overwhelmed me as I turned the key and reached into the cabinet. Then I saw it sitting there, looking at me. If it had had a face, it would've worn a massive grin as it welcomed me. I needed something to dull the beating I was going to receive in a few hours, that's if I wasn't dead by dead so, without thinking, I snatched the little black case out of the place where it sat neatly. It called me. I heard it and kindly obliged.

My plan was to inject myself and before I passed out I was going to take a big shard of broken mirror and slit my wrists. I put a piece in my pocket. It was time.

My heart raced as I smelt the bad smell of the burning stone while I melted it in the charred, black spoon Samuel always used. The mixture of crack and paraffin was unbearable. I thought I'd be used to it, but obviously I wasn't. That was about to change. I was so confused. Did that bastard remove the belt before he shot-up or did he leave the belt on then shoot-up? Then it all came back to me, like he was training me to shoot-up myself. I remembered his deep, terrifying voice: "Small surface veins, don't shoot at 45 degrees, put the needle almost flat. That's how you hit. You only hit at 45 degrees if the veins are deep. Do you understand me? Mess up and see what I do to you! So you better get it right." OK, belt tight, slap vein a little, prick, shoot, then release belt.

I felt my vein swell and puff up after I missed it a couple of times, but it didn't stop me. It was my first time injecting heroin, but I felt I truly understood the drug, as if we became one. It was done. My eyes rolled to the back of my head then there was complete darkness; it was the best feeling I ever had since I reached this God forsaken country. I was free.

The heroin rush came quickly and engulfed my whole being. It stayed and got stronger and stronger. It made me fall back onto my mattress; I was dead to myself and my surroundings. It was like falling from the sky and landing on a pile of the sweetest marsh mellows. Then it felt like the sky had fallen on me, a brick wall of warmth and euphoria speeding at 300 mph, hitting my battered body.

I can't explain the rush; it was simply amazing, like the taste of a bottle of 100 per cent proof white rum multiplied by 100 in the matter of a second and it just got stronger. Then came the vomiting, one retch after the other. I had to try to turn myself on my side as I felt myself drowning and choking on my own sick – even though I wanted to die, that really wasn't the best way to go. Being sick was a bit of a bummer, but I felt invincible, powerful and truly happy, so it was well worth it. It was so good that I totally forgot to slit my wrists. I was happy with the result, but little did I know I'd just become a slave to a thing called addiction.

Anyway guys, I'm drifting away nicely, so I'll tell you the rest of my story when I come down.

Chapter 4
Don't Take It, It's Mine

I came down sooner than I wanted to. All I felt was a thud and I could taste blood in my mouth as I woke up sharply only to see Samuel standing over me. Another thud. His fist connected squarely with my face. I gagged and tried to stop myself from choking as my two front teeth flew to the back of my throat.

"You silly little bitch, what the fuck do you think you're doing, touching my things?" I tried to back up in fear, but my body was in shock and it just wouldn't allow me to move. Then he lowered his voice into a whisper as though he was trying to seduce me.

"Oh, I know what you're doing. You think your smart, don't you? You think cause you tried to make yourself look like a boy, I'm not going to give you what you have coming to you? You think cause you cut off your hair, it's going to put me off and I'm not going to take what's mine. Is that what you think? Answer me! Answer me!"

I froze as I felt his rough hands around my throat and his spit and bad breath in my face as he tore at my clothes.

I felt no pain as I was still numb from the heroin that I'd shot into my system and what came next made me glad I'd decided to take that path. It was a narrow path full of twisted lanes, but it was the right path in this case because he was soon inside me, robbing my innocence as easily as that drug had taken me away.

OK, now let's take this a little bit deeper for all you girls reading my story. I'm not going to walk you through my violation as my heart's weak and I can't bear to think about that day again. If it even crosses my mind, it makes my stomach turn and want to heave worse than when I was sailing on *Isabella*. So, I'm going to make this short – you must read between the lines.

You know what it feels like losing your V for the very first time. You may have lost it to a boy you thought you loved, or to some asshole who talked the talk, but couldn't walk the walk, so it was totally shit. Or you may have lost it because all your friends lost theirs and you felt left out. Even if your first experience was crap, or it was the best feeling in the world, at least you had a choice in the matter.

Trust me, it's nothing like losing it unwillingly, especially if you learned how to abuse drugs that very same day.

Anyway, let's just say he didn't last long. I thought it was over, but he lasted longer the second and third times that he entered me. When he was done – *Can you believe the bastard?* – he just said, like it was all in a day's work, "Get up and clean yourself!" His voice was low, I could hear the shame and he couldn't even look me in my face. That, to me, spelled weakness.

He repeated himself as he clenched his fists, trying to be forceful like he was attempting to hide all evidence before my auntie got home, "I said get off the fucking floor and clean this raas clart place up." But I just laid there in the foetal position, in shock, trying to get my head around what just happened, attempting to get any little comfort from myself that I could. No tears, no words; I don't even remember breathing. I just laid there, still, like an abandoned, abused, stray street dog as he launched kick after kick into my legs and back. Until this day, I don't know if it was addiction, or the fact that I'd just been seriously violated, but I didn't feel a thing, just calm …

It's funny, mamma always told me, "After the storm must come the calm," but in this case the storm was brewing. It was about to erupt and tear down anything and everything in its path. The blows kept coming harder and harder, but they meant nothing to me; what really mattered I could never get back, I could never pick the man I wanted to share this precious moment with, it had gone, all gone.

One of the best moments of a young woman's life had slipped through my fingertips just because that old man couldn't control his actions.

Mamma used to tell me to pick my man like I picked mangos off our tree. She always said: "Rebecca, pick a good man, like you pick a good mango; make sure he's sweet to you and ripe and ready to be a husband, father and friend because if your man's spoilt he will only spoil you."

I used to show her a beaten up old mango and say, "What? Like this one mum?" That made me laugh so much, but I'm not laughing now.

When I started to pull up the trousers, blood ran down the inside of my bruised thighs.

I stood up like a giant among ants and looked him straight in his eyes. I don't know what happened and I don't even remember reaching into my pocket, but there was a lot of blood gushing like water from a tap from a deep wound on the side of his neck.

The mirror cut deep into my hand as I gripped it with undiluted anger; it was my turn to mount him and penetrate him against his will as I stabbed again and again until there were no lights left in his eyes.

I uttered no words, just exhaled with each strike until I ran out of breath.

A little before he blew his last breath, I leaned over him and whispered gently in his ear, "Who's on top now, bitch?"

With one last stab, I stood up to look at my oil painting; I felt like a real killer and I refused to take any blame for it.

Have you ever smelt warm blood mixed with the stench of a paraffin heater? Not nice, not nice at all.

Wait a minute … Something on the floor caught my eye as I glanced to the right. It was my new friend, due to be my very best friend indeed, and my only friend real soon. I kneeled to pick it up and pain started to throb between my legs. I had to shoot up one more time to numb it before it really kicked in.

I picked up the case and opened it with high hopes that there was at least one stone left. I couldn't open it fast enough, but when I finally did I was very happy to see there was a stone left. I got a bit too happy and excited, though, because it flicked out of the case and rolled neatly under Samuel's leg.

Damn, man, I had to get it. I crouched and blood covered my hands as I tried to lift his leg. I didn't know blood was so sticky, it didn't feel that way when I used to help mamma drain the goose at Christmas.

Anyway, I lifted his leg and guess what fell out of his pocket?

Yeah, you guessed right: it was silver foil all neatly wrapped up and inside were six stones. That would keep me going for a little while as well as the money he had on him.

It must've been pay day! I grabbed the packet and ran for the door, coated in blood. I had to get away. I galloped down the dusty stairway, jumping the last three steps, and headed to the front door.

No sooner had I got there than I saw a large figure standing in front of the patterned glass windows. The key entered the lock and the door finally opened. It was auntie.

I stopped dead in my tracks, but somehow managed to slip a hand in my pocket to hide the only friend I had left. It's funny how that happened isn't it? It was like my hand had a mind of its own. Anyway, the door opened and I froze.

"Rebecca, what the hell happened to you?" my auntie cried as she dropped the plastic bag full of apples, bananas and fresh mangos on the old, dirty carpet. I stood still; the shock and realisation of what took place settled in.

Auntie slammed the door shut behind her as if to say she didn't want anyone to see our business, not that anyone would care. One thing my auntie had left, and held tight with both hands, was her pride. That was something I lost a long time ago. She started to grab at me curiously, searching for the fine-looking, long braids that were no longer there.

"Rebecca, talk to me!"

Before she could finish, I finally found my voice. "He raped me," I whispered. I lowered my eyes in shame as she fell to her knees, holding her head in her soft, brown hands. "He raped me again and again and again! He raped me, auntie!" My tears flowed fast, but it was the first and last time. "He'll never hurt us again."

I hung my head as if burying it in shame. My auntie began to question me; she held my shoulders and shook them a little. She checked my body, looking for any major cuts.

"He did what? What have you done? Where did this blood come from? What happened to your hair?"

I could see she was about to go into shock as she fired question after question, then just like that she shook it off and became fully focused.

"Where is he Rebecca?"

I looked her stone cold in her face: "He's dead."

"What?" she grabbed my hand pulling me back upstairs crying, "Oh no, oh no, oh my God!" Her grip was tight and firm around my wrist; I felt like it was about to break as she pulled me up the stairs.

We got to the top of the stairway and we both stopped as if we'd seen a ghost; my body was totally numb, my auntie's big frame shadowed me like a block of flats as I peeked around her at the off-white door in front of us.

She stretched out her hand towards the handle and kept one hand holding me back.

"Just stay behind me Rebecca," she urged, and just as she opened the door we heard a faint groan. Damn! What the hell! He was still alive, but he couldn't be! I must've stabbed him at least nine or ten times.

My heart ran races in my chest as I jammed my fingernails deep into an open wound on my hand. I didn't feel a thing.

Then came another moan.

My poor auntie pulled the door shut. "He isn't dead. We have to go in, just stay behind me and don't look at him. Do you understand me?" she said as her eyebrows met. I shrugged and nodded my head in agreement, but I really wished he was dead because if he'd survived things would get so much worse for us.

Anyway, the door was opened and we walked in. The smell was horrendous. You could just about see the light shining along the sides of the heavy, black curtains but the light coming from the heater shed a bit more light on the situation. My auntie stepped over to Samuel as he laid in his own blood, trying to catch a breath.

We could just about hear him, "Help me!" those were his words.

"Die, why don't he just die?" I said. "Auntie, just leave him, just go! We can be free now." Tears filled my eyes again, following the tracks of the dry tear marks that I'd prepared earlier. "Auntie, just go!" I begged. "I did this, I'll take the blame! Just go!" Then a pain hit me in my belly; it was a real bad pain like I'd never felt before.

I fell to my knees as my auntie's old work trousers soon became soaked with the blood that was running down my legs. "Auntie, help me, please help me," I begged, then I saw a look in her eyes that I'd never seen before.

"Rebecca, I'm going to help you. I promised my sister I was going to help you and if it's the last thing I'm going to do in this miserable life, I'm going to do just that. But I need you to be strong; I need you to get up and wash the blood off yourself."

I was confused. "Why do I have to do that? Why don't you just run?" Her face completely changed as she snapped, "Rebecca! Just do as I say!" She held her head as I jumped back in fear.

"Rebecca, please trust me. If you can't trust anyone else, just trust me." She didn't have to say another word. I pulled myself up off the floor, removed my clothes and washed myself off in our little, old sink then I grabbed a black bin liner and filled it with whatever I could find as I watched my auntie from the corner of my eye. I saw her reach for the shard of mirror I used to stab Samuel.

She screamed, "You bastard, you dirty, filthy bastard! Die! Die!"

I watched as she stabbed him time after time using her full body weight as her hand came down. Then she wiped his blood over her face and clothes and turned to me with her soft voice, "You're free now Rebecca, I want you to run away. I need you to become a woman. Don't trust anyone. You're going to have to grow before your time and it's going to be hard, but this is your life now. Go to Forest Gate, I'll find you, I promise. I don't know how you're going to cope, but trust me, being alone's better than being in prison."

I crumbled inside; if only I knew my future because compared to the steps I was about to take out there in the big wide world, prison would've been a five-star hotel. Tears flowed down my face, stinging my wounds as they wet my fresh t-shirt. I thought my V and my freedom were the only things that mattered that I lost that day, but I realised how much I really loved my auntie, especially after what she did to give me a new life. It made me see she was going to go through any means to keep me safe.

I made sure that, to the best of my ability, all traces of blood were off my skin. I didn't want prying eyes on me; it was bad enough being black – that made people study my every movement as it was. I wrapped my hand in a piece of cloth to stop the blood flow then I checked if I had everything I needed.

I think you all know what I mean.

I took a slow walk towards auntie for a last, big cuddle as I knew I wasn't going to see her for a long while; I could see her curved figure still standing over Samuel and as she moved she was like a flickering flame that heated our room.

"Don't come no closer," she said in a low voice as she stretched out her bloodied hands in front of her to keep me away. My heart sank like an old fishing boat full of holes.

"You'll get blood on you. Just leave, go away as far as you can! Look under my mattress, you'll see three envelopes. Take them, there's cash in them that I was saving for a rainy day and now it's raining harder than I could ever imagine."

I walked over to the bed and lifted the mattress, patting away, looking desperately for the envelopes. "Auntie, they're not there."

"They are. Just look and you'll find them." I found the cash deep in the back of the mattress. But it wasn't enough, I needed one last cuddle, I needed to smell and feel my auntie for the last time. I made another attempt and walked slowly towards her.

"Rebecca, just go!" she snapped at me. I heard that command loud and clear. I rushed towards the door then I heard a thud and a desperate cry as she fell to her knees. I wanted to turn back. I wanted to turn back time. Should I have let him abuse me and get away with it, or did I do the right thing? Not knowing if my auntie was dead or alive, I carried on walking down the steps. Jumping the last three steps at the bottom was so natural to me, it was the only time I got to be a kid, but it was the last time I'd ever jump those steps and as for being a kid, well, let's just say that came and went within the blink of an eye.

Chapter 5
Cry Freedom

I stood on the top steps outside my old front door and glanced to my left, then to my right. There it was: a road. I'd seen that road many times before, but this time I was fascinated and it was about to swallow me up. The cold breeze brushed freely across my face, waking me up like a gentle friend just passing by. I called that breeze Freedom as I breathed it deep into my lungs, exhaling slowly. It felt so great, I had to inhale a second time.

The roads weren't paved with gold, nor were the houses made of sweets and beautiful cakes. But beauty was in the eye of the beholder and my eyes told me that sweet taste was called Freedom. I looked at the sky; there where clouds in shades of grey and shades of white. There was no sunshine, just bitter cold, but the warmth I felt inside was that of being free.

I could hear the pitter-patter of tired feet walking on my left. It was that old woman from number 36 who I saw every time I had to run to the corner shop for a pint of milk or some plain flour for auntie to make the dumplings that I loved so much. But each time I saw her for two years, wearing that same, old, dusty coat and crappy brown shoes, she had the audacity to give me bad looks like I'd done something to her. If only looks could kill, Samuel would've been dead a long time ago.

Funnily enough, her glances were more comforting as you could hear her mind wondering what happened to my beautiful, long hair and shiny, well-kept, dark skin. I had to come to terms with reality: there was nothing to look forward to out there, but there was one thing, something I longed for and that was freedom. Did my auntie tell me freedom came at a price? Er, let me think, mmm ... no, she didn't and I was yet to find out that freedom came at a price no money could buy. I walked away and didn't look back; I had some money and more importantly I had my comfort in my pocket. Damn, that was my bus. Next stop: Forest Gate.

****

Three months passed and I didn't hear anything from my auntie; I was living rough, sleeping in doorways, often getting pissed on by drunken yobs or being told to move. Food only came after Queens Market packed up for the day so I wasn't eating much and every time I put something near my mouth I just wanted to choke it back up. But what I couldn't understand was why the hell I was putting on so much weight. I just got fatter and fatter. Anyway, food was the last of my problems. What I needed was a stone. You know, the one I melted in that little black spoon? My blood was itching and I clawed at my flesh to scratch it, but to no avail.

Damn! I needed to make money. I couldn't even go into shops no more to steal cause they all knew me and as soon as I walked in they were on my case like flies around shit. I was 16, but looked like 50. I was a fat smackhead.

My hair still hadn't grown back. I didn't think it ever would, my two front teeth were missing, and to top it all off, I was living on the street. If only mamma could have seen her beautiful Rebecca! Trying to get in touch with mamma and her seeing me like that were out of the question.

I looked across the road. *Hold on is that? Yeah, it's him.* I made a dash across the road between moving cars, not hearing the shouts – "Get out the bloody road you silly black bitch!" – and horns blowing. Oh fuck them! I didn't have time to argue, I just kept running, slapping the bonnets as I desperately tried to get to the other side.

"Oi, Jason wait, please wait!" but Jason looked up and as soon as he saw me he just diverted. Jason was my dealer, he was only 22, but his dad put him to work the streets at the tender age of 13. He was a white guy, kind of tallish, about 5 feet 8 inches, and slim; his hair was a mousey brown colour and his eyes were a very dark shade of brown, almost piercing black. Jason was usually well dressed in the latest gear, but he was always hooded up and that made him look very shady.

I ran behind him, tugging at his jacket. "Jason help me out, I need something man!" He just looked at me harshly, but couldn't hide the fact that he had a soft spot for me. Then he said in his east end accent, "Rebecca, what the hell!" as he proceeded to prod my belly. "Why the hell are you getting so fat? Oh and the answer to your question is no, I can't keep giving you shit for nothing, man. My old man is livid and he wants his dough and I can't keep making excuses for you."

Before I could beg anymore, he lifted up his Adidas jumper. "Look. Every time I go home short, this is what I get."

Damn, man, Jason's dad was really laying into him. His belly and ribs were covered in bruises and it was all my fault. I felt sorry for him, I really did, but I was a fiend, a scumbag, a ghost and I had to get a fix by any means possible. Begging for money wasn't helping at all. I wanted to keep away from that cause every time I begged some guy, he always wanted me to work for the money and that was out of the question. I promised myself, it didn't matter how low I got, I'd never, ever allow a man to touch me again. Although Jason was a real nice guy, if he ever tried or even contemplated it I knew I'd have to hurt him; I was glad that he saw me as just poor, little Rebecca, the smackhead.

"Jason, please man, please. I'll pay you back, I promise. I just need a fix and I need it now." My blood was itching, I needed it and I was prepared to kill for it, but I wasn't prepared to fuck or suck for it.

I looked at Jason hard. He backed up a little bit. "Rebecca, I'll tell you what to do. Meet me later at Studley Road, number 36; I'll give you some of my stash, but you're not getting anything from me now and nothing comes for free so you better back the fuck up cause it's not happening. I don't know how much more beatings my body can take."

I could see the look in his eyes; it was the same look my auntie used to have when she was about to take a good right hand from Samuel, so I had to let it go even though my blood was itching and I was as hungry as hell for the fix. I knew I just had to let it go: the look on his face brought back memories I'd rather not remember.

And what did he mean nothing comes for free?

I brushed it off and made my sad, puppy dog eyes and said, "OK Jason, please don't let me down." I extended my right hand as though I was begging for food. Jason just looked down at me and pointed in my face as he walked off. "Just be there!" I called. "What time J?" I mean, it would help if I had a time innit?

Without looking back he shouted, "Number seven Becks and don't be late," then he disappeared into the Friday shopping crowd.

OK, so I had three hours to kill, if they didn't kill me first. I didn't know how I was going to cope but I had to. I wanted to eat, but I felt crazy sick and all I wanted to do was shoot up. I kept feeling little thuds in my gut like something was moving around inside me. I found the nearest doorway and that's where I sat, rocking away, trying to control my thirst for my friend and trust me it was hell, total hell. The closer I got to the time to meet Jason, the worse it got; it was just like when you want to shit, the closer you get to the toilet, the harder it pushes to come out. LOL, you know what I mean.

"Have you got the time please?" I asked a passer-by.

"Yes it's time you got a job, coming to our country and littering our streets."

That didn't bother me, I got that all the time. I got up and started walking weakly; it was just down the road, but I knew it would take 30 minutes to get there.

Chapter 6
Home, Sweet Home

Anyway, it was seven o'clock when I reached the house. It was an old house with boarded up windows and the bushes overwhelmed the path way; rubbish wasn't the word, it was like a dumping ground, a total wreck, so I guess sleeping in doorways was great compared to this shithole. The walls were painted a yellow colour and the window frames didn't matter because you couldn't even see them. This prick, he lied to me just to get rid of me! No-one could live like this.

"Jason!" I called out. "Jason!" *Damn, he has to be here* I thought as I placed my hands on top of my head. I needed that shit, man. I could feel my track marks itching and my blood boiling. I needed my nurse and I needed it urgently. *Fuck it. I'm going inside*. I pushed away the bushes to uncover a pathway and an old, black front door. Not knowing where to touch it, I tried to look past the cobwebs for the clean spot. *Damn man! Just get inside!* I thought out loud as the door squeaked open. I entered and to my relief Jason was standing there beckoning me with his finger, gesturing to follow him. That boy loved to wag his finger like any old dog's tail.

"Rebecca you're late," he said, rolling his perfect, dark brown eyes, "so don't talk, just come this way."

Not knowing where he was about to take me and not really caring, I followed him. All I wanted was a fix; I had to feel my friend run in and around me. I had to go to that place where nothing or no-one mattered, you know, that place where I wasn't judged, that cool, calm place where I could relax and let go. I had to let my friend take me to a place that I didn't know. I walked through the dusty passageway; I could smell the damp, rotten smell of wood.

My nose followed the smell. To my left, there was a set of rotten stairs; underneath there was a cupboard door. I walked through the narrow passageway. Graffiti replaced the wallpaper and the old floorboards sang songs of memories of those that walked there before me. I looked up the stairs then I heard Jason.

"Don't even think about going up there. Them stairs can't even hold the weight of a cat and by the looks of how fat you're getting over the last three months, you don't stand a chance!" he laughed, but I didn't find it funny.

"Look Jason … "

Jason put a finger to his lips. "Sshh Rebecca, trust me, you don't want anyone to know about your new home or the old bill will have you out of here before you can get a good night's sleep, if you get my drift."

I was in total shock, still walking to my destination to see my nurse. "What do you mean 'my new home?'" Then I just shrugged it off. "Look, forget that. Did you bring some for me or not?"

Jason walked over to a door, then looked at me with a smile and wiggled his long finger again. "Come in here." I walked towards the door.

Why would he do that? I didn't understand; I walked into the room and even though it was a complete shithole, he'd managed to make it look like home. There was an old sofa and a table with a kettle and a camping cooker sat nice and neatly on one side of the room.

I looked down to see a shag pile rug; it wasn't completely clean, but it was a nice rug. There were no windows as they were completely boarded up, but he'd put up some curtains that gave it a touch of home.

Then I had to stop and think *What was that smell*? It made me feel sick, but in a nice way, it was a smell I hadn't smelled in a long while. Was it rice and peas and curried chicken? Where the hell did he get that?

To the left of the room, I saw a set of candles burning brightly and a cast iron bath the steam was coming out high and fast and it totally stopped me in my tracks.

I took another look at the sofa and there were clean clothes sitting there with my name written all over them. Damn! What had he done and why did I feel like that? What had taken my mind off that slave master who'd held me captive for the last few months of my life?

I stepped back and asked myself *Is this love*? Well, I'm not having it, not in this life or the next. "Jason what's your game?" I snapped at him "and why the hell did you bring me here? Have you got the stuff or not? I'm dying here so stop pissing about."

"Calm down Rebecca," he said firmly, but softly, as he walked towards the sofa. "I've got it, but before I give you anything, you got to do something for me."

I felt so desperate. What the hell could I have that he'd possibly want?

"Look Jason, just give me it!" He rolled his dark brown eyes and lifted the right side of his well-shaped lips.

"Er, no Becks, you want something, I've got and there's something I want you to do for me before I give you what you want. You don't get something for nothing in this world, girl."

"OK, what do you want? What have I possibly got that you would want?" I snapped, totally not caring who heard me.

Jason paused for a couple of seconds as though he was trying to work out some hard maths or some crap like that.

"All I want you to do is get in the bath and wash yourself. Put on these clean clothes and eat this food then I'll give you what you want." He raised his eyebrows, "Deal or no deal? It's up to you."

I begged him, "Please, I don't want a bath; I don't want any food, I just need to shoot up and I need it now."

"No Becks! My way or no way!" he snapped.

"Jason, why are you doing this and why do you even care? I'm just a smackhead ghost, look at me." My voice got louder. "Look at me!" I watched him as the candlelight flickered against his pale skin and waited for his answer.

"Rebecca, you may not know this, but I come from a big family of three boys and four girls, my youngest bro is Wayne...Wayne Brannon. My old man can't wait to put him out there on the roads. He says my blond her blue eyed boy is so hansom he could sell crack to the queen with them eyes. Anywayz I know a pregnant woman when I see one."

I burst out laughing. "Jason, what the hell are you talking about?" He couldn't be saying what I thought he was saying.

"Rebecca you're pregnant. Why do you think you can't eat, ha?" He waited for an answer but got no response.

"The amount of shit you inject, by rights you should be getting the munchies like a freaking monster."

Still, he got no response. "OK, I see you have nothing to say," he said, growing frustrated at my rudeness.

"OK, why do you think you're getting so fat and feeling sick all the time?"

He looked at me and my eyes settled on his elongated neck and well-shaped eyebrows that nearly blended in with his hair. "Becks, you've got a bun in the oven, trust me, and I'm going to look after you because you have no-one else." I freaked out because, thinking about it, he was right and it dawned on me: I'd never get rid of Samuel. Although he was dead, he'd always have a part of me and that made me sick to my stomach.

"Rebecca, I don't know when and how you got a bun in the oven, but I do know this," he paused for a beat, "I'm going to take care of you from now on, both of you, because it's too late to get rid of it now even if you wanted to. So don't try and stop me or I'll stop your supply before you can spell cat. You can spell cat can't ya?" and before I could say a word, he walked out the door, talking as he left. "Get in the bath, eat and I'll be back in half hour; I need to pick up some stash." He stopped to look over his shoulder, "You better eat it all. That's the deal because if my old man finds out I'm doing this, I'll be brown bread, son or no son. So I'm walking a thin line here – don't let me walk it for nothing."

As he walked out, I heard the floorboards sing their melody then the door slammed shut: he was gone. I never knew I was pregnant, but as soon as I did I had a definite hatred for the bastard child inside me. I wanted it gone, but I knew if I even tried to get rid of it Jason would have no reason to look after me or supply me with drugs.

Er, did I say drugs? I became conscious of the fact that I was a total addict, of course I was, so I couldn't get rid of it. Every now and again, when I got real upset, I'd just punch myself in the belly hoping that it would die at birth, but that little bastard just kept on kicking stronger and stronger.

Anyway, five months passed and I was still living in that squat, but it wasn't that bad as Jason stayed with me most nights. I grew fatter and fatter while Jason was still there by my side, looking after me, administering my heroin.

He was in total control of it, only feeding me when I got real low. I felt myself getting stronger and stronger to the point that I thought I no longer needed it and that was fine by Jason because most of my veins had collapsed. It was hard to find a spot to inject.

"Yo, Becks! I'm going to get some food OK? I won't be long."

"OK J!" I went to give him a hug, but as I touched his back, he cringed in pain and his legs buckled beneath him. "J, what's the matter with you?"

He fanned me away with his long, slender fingers and tried to brush it off. "It's cool Becks, it's just some boy that owed me some money; I made chase and fell, it's nothing really."

I looked at him. "If it's nothing then show me."

He pulled away like a spoilt kid, "It's nothing Rebecca, just leave it!"

Damn, I must have really been in love with this guy. Knowing he was hurt hurt me, so I totally flipped out. "I said show me!" I don't know where I got the strength from, but I spun him around, ripping up his t-shirt. "Oh my God, who did this?" I snapped at him, "It was your dad wasn't it? He did this because of me." I fell to my knees, "It's me, isn't it Jason? Talk to me!"

Jason kept his head down, looking in the other direction so he'd keep his secret with his deep, brown eyes. Then he looked at me, "Yeah it was him .... Every time I come up short, he slashes me with a blade, but I don't care. I can take it Becks, I'd do anything for you. Just because you're on drugs don't mean anything; you're the nicest person I've ever known and I know now that I'm totally in love with you." Our eyes filled with tears as our lips met for the very first time. It was the best feeling ever – no-one had ever made me feel like J did. I breathed as though I'd never breathed before. I smelled scents I'd never smelt before and I felt as though my useless life was complete, it was going somewhere. We broke our embrace reluctantly, still hand in hand.

J held my head and looked deep into my eyes. "Becks, I've had enough of this; I'm going to go and tell my dad I'm not doing it anymore. I'm going to get a job and look after you and the baby. I can't live like this no more." But I didn't like the sound of that. His dad was an animal and by the looks of J's back it seemed he'd go to any lengths to keep him on the streets and the money coming in. To him, J was like a drug prostitute, but his brother was the one he really liked touching. Anyway, that's another story that J told me. Yes, his dad was a right animal, just like Samuel, so I had to stop him.

"J, don't go, please, I don't like the sound of that and I don't think he's going to let you walk away that easily." I placed my hand softly on his face. "I'm nearly clean and off the stuff; just a little bit longer and it will be over, then we can go away together. Please J, this don't feel right. I have a bad feeling this won't go the way you think."

However, Jason just looked at me; his eyes glazed over like the cream doughnuts that he always brought home for me to eat with my dinner. He tried to hide it, but I knew fear and it was written all over his face. "Becks, it's OK. Trust me. I'll be back before you can say 'J, I love you'." He put his hand on my belly and with a big smile and a little rub, he spoke in a soft, sweet, childish voice, "Bye little man, I'll be back soon. Be a good boy and don't kick the hell out of mummy, OK." The baby always gave me a massive boot when he did that.

"Damn, J, he kicks hard. How do you know he's a boy anyway?"

J couldn't help but smile. "Becks, well if that's a girl, judging by the way she kicks you, she must have big feet!"

Then he walked away. I waited until he reached the front door then I called out to him: "J!"

"Yeah, Becks?"

"I love you!"

Smiling from ear to ear he just said, "I know you do Becks, but I love you more." Then he was out the door and I had a funny feeling he wasn't coming back.

My legs left me as I wobbled towards the old sofa to try and break my fall. I got pissed off with myself: *Why the hell do I feel like I'm still on that damn boat?* Maybe it was because all that time I was pregnant.

****

Two days passed. No drugs, not much eating and no Jason. I had a gut feeling there was something wrong, not nearly wrong but really wrong. I had to go out and find him, so I walked back to the only place I knew he'd be. I reached Queens Market and my heart skipped a beat; I was properly upset when I saw Jason standing there crossing hands with a punter. Why did he leave me worried sick about him? Why didn't he come home and tell me what had happened? Why did he say he loved me knowing he wasn't coming back for me? I needed answers, no fuck. I wanted answers and I wanted them fast.

I walked up behind him and tapped him on his shoulder. "Jason, where the hell have you been?" I said sternly. He turned around, but everything seemed to slow down like in those old black and white films when someone's about to get killed. I jumped back in fright as I saw it wasn't Jason at all.

"Oh, sorry, I thought you were … " he cut me off sharply.

"I know who you thought I was, Rebecca." The way he called my name sounded just like when Jason used to call me. It sent shivers down my spine and I don't mean the shivers I got sleeping on the cold streets of London. They were like the shivers I felt when I first tasted Jason's lips.

"I thought you were dead," he said as he stood there analysing me. "Jason said you overdosed."

I stepped backwards and took a good look at him as he ranted on. *Did I know him?* He looked pale as hell, as though he was getting high on his own supply. He was so pale his blonde eyebrows blended neatly with his skin. It was obvious he was a dealer – trust me, I knew a dealer when I saw one. I couldn't help but stare at the scar that ran down from the top of his left eye patch to the side of his lip, it was a perfect half-moon. He was very scruffy – didn't he own an iron? – and the one eye I could see was deep blue, offsetting his thin, mousy hair nicely. He was about six feet two or thereabout and around fifteen stones. I looked at his big hands as he waved them around while he ranted on. There was a tattoo across his right knuckles with word 'Hate' and across his left knuckles I expected to see the word 'Love', but no, he had 'Hate' tattooed there too. *Weird man*, I thought. I had no love in my life, but, damn, he must've had a rough time. Then the shock came.

"Are you Jason's brother, Biffa? You are, aren't you? Where is he?" My voice grew. "Where is he and how do you know about me?"

Biffa glared at me. With a sarcastic huff and a shrug of his broad shoulders he replied, "Yeah, I'm Biffa, I'm the ugly side of Jason. You see that stripe?" He pointed to the scar on his face. I followed his finger as he ran it down the scar. "Yeah, the stripe you've been looking at for the last two minutes, do you know where I got that? Nah, I guess not. I mean, how are you meant to know that if my little bro Jason didn't tell you?"

I just cut him dead in mid-flow. Wrong move Becks. "Oh, so you are?" But before I could finish, he grabbed me by my face and squeezed like he was making every attempt to crush my jaw. Everyone walked past and looked straight at me, but no-one even tried to stop this guy from trying to rip my face off. Pregnant or not pregnant, they didn't even bat an eyelid. He had a serious reputation.

"Listen to me, you fucking little smackhead, and listen good!" He glanced up at the people walking by as they just looked away. "And don't look at them cunts, they're not going to help you. You see when I'm talking, you shut your fucking mouth and just listen. Do you understand me?"

I nodded my head like a little puppy dog, you know, like the ones you see on the dashboard of old Ford Granadas.

Then he returned to a whisper, "This is how it is. You see that scar on my face you were admiring so much? When I was 15, I was working the streets for my old man. Every day I stood outside this sports shop and every day a pair of pure white Gola trainers was looking at me and I was looking at them like big, fat cream cakes. Well, one day I made up my mind. I just had to get them trainers and the only money I had was my old man's.

"Let's just put it this way, as soon as I got home and walked through that door, those wicked, pure white trainers became bright shade of red. Yeah, that's right. My old man opened me up nicely and took one of my eyes with him. I never played with his money again.

"You see, what we are to our dad is just workers and when you fuck with his wonga, he'll fuck with you, family or no fucking family, and that's why I thought you was dead because Jason tried to protect you. He knew my dad was going to come and open you up like he did his back and my face.

"But now Jason's swimming with the fish, wearing concrete boots somewhere in Southend on Sea. There's no such thing as family in the drugs game; the only family we have is called money."

It seemed like the only words I heard were "Jason's swimming with the fish" as my heart crumbled. Jason was dead and it was all my fault. If he didn't try to help me, if he didn't fall for me, if I didn't fall for him, if fucking if. Damn, what have I done? I was lost in ifs and buts, but the slap that followed soon snapped me out of my daydream. They say the best dreamers are the ones that dream while they're awake because they make things happen but I say that's bullshit.

"Look at me," Biffa said through gritted teeth. "This is how it goes. One: I can tell my dad you're still alive then he'll pay you a visit and no doubt he'll kill you. Or two: we can do it the easy way – what dad doesn't see, dad doesn't have to know. I'll keep our little secret to myself and he doesn't even have to know as he thinks you're a stiffy anyway. The decision's totally yours. I tell you what: I'll give you five to think about it … Live or die? It's up to you."

Without giving me any time to think and with his lips pressed together like a ventriloquist, he blurted out, "OK, time's up. This is how it's going to be. Jason was in debt to my dad, you were in debt to Jason, but now he's brown bread so because I'm giving you a lifeline, you're now in debt to me. Capish?"

"What do you mean?" I stuttered.

"What I mean is I'm taking on my dad's debt. So all the free shit that dickhead was giving you, you're going to have to pay me for it unless you want me to tell my old man you're still alive, then you know what will happen don't you. Yeah, that's right, he'll send you to meet your nigger lover boyfriend, no questions asked."

He stood there looking at me with a slight smirk on his face, knowing I had no choice but to do as he said.

"So what will it be then? Me or my dad? Oh, I forgot I asked you that before didn't I? Silly old me, it's all them drugs, they mess your head up." The words just flowed through my head like some Bob Marley tune. What the hell was I going to do? I was silent, totally lost for words. With a roll of his deep blue, beady eye he said, "That's what I thought, good decision Becksy girl. You don't mind me calling you Becksy girl, do ya?"

I looked to the ground; I didn't even respond to his stupid, dumb ass question. I just wanted the ground to open up and swallow me. "Yeah, but how am I going to pay you back?" I said totally confused. "I haven't got no job, no money; I'm pregnant and I live in a squat."

Biffa put his hand on my shoulder and squeezed while he grinned. The smile was so big, I could smell the strong weed on his breath. "Oh Rebecca, Rebecca, my sweet, silly little Rebecca. You're going to have to put my money where your mouth is and I got some good friends that would like to do the same."

At first I didn't get what he meant, but then it dawned on me. "No I can't," I snapped. "I'm pregnant! How can you do this?"

Then he slowly slipped his big hand around the back of my neck and pulled me close. His grip was tighter than the last time and much more forceful. "Look, shut the fuck up! You're staying at Studley road innit? I'll be there in a couple of hours for my first deposit, go home and get cleaned up and if you try to run, if you even think to run you better run that thought out your head. I will find you and I will kill you. You get me? Now fuck off!"

He pushed me hard to the ground, not caring about the lump I had in my belly that was in full view of the world. I dropped, hitting the pavement hard and for some reason my first instinct was to protect my unborn child. As much as I hated it, spending time with Jason made me learn to love and appreciate my unborn burden, not just for me, but because J couldn't wait to spoil him.

I heard Biffa shout "Run along Rebecca!" and he laughed, poking his tongue inside of his cheek, making sexual suggestions. I dragged myself off the floor and walked away scared out my head, not knowing if I should run away or just do as he said.

****

Back at home, I sat like a prisoner waiting for execution. I wanted to feel my baby move because it gave me comfort and a reason to carry on, but I felt nothing. Three hours passed then I heard someone pulling at the front door. My head snapped up, not knowing who it was or what to expect. A tall figure entered the room; it was Biffa. He strolled in all bold and proud as he looked back over his shoulder, pointing at the front door like he cared.

"Tut, tut, tut," he said, raising the right corner of his mouth. "You really should get a lock on that door, it's dangerous around here Becks." He let out a little giggle. I didn't find it funny and only Jason called me Becks. But what could I say?

"OK, it's time to put my money where your mouth is." He strolled over to where I sat, undoing his flies as he came closer. He placed his thumb firmly over my eye and pressed hard.

"Now, if I feel any teeth, not that you got much anyway, but if I feel anything I don't like, I'm going to pop that eyeball straight out your fucking head then you'll need a patch like mine. Do you understand me? Open wide." Then came the violation.

As you know, I'm not going to go into that, you're going to have to read between the lines.

"Now swallow and say thank you," he said, just about able to stand on his feet. "I said, say thank you," he snapped as he grabbed my face.

I had no choice. "Thank ... you." Oh my God, not again. Why me? What did I do in my life to be treated like this? I was violated at fifteen. I was pregnant with a child I didn't want. I'd been through hell and back, now I'm being abused again and God knows how many times more. I promised myself I wouldn't let another man touch me unless I wanted them to, but it looked like there would be a lot more touching than I predicted.

He started to put himself away. "OK, that was good for a smackhead. You start work tomorrow. I've got a friend that's going to pass by and I need you to be nice to him."

I sat there, trying to get the taste out my mouth; I just wanted to brush my teeth till my gums bled. "What do you mean, be nice to him?" I asked, confused about what he meant.

"Just be fucking nice!" he barked through his crooked teeth. Then he stopped, "Oh yeah, I got something for you I nearly forgot." He dug deep into his side bag and pulled out a needle. Before I could say a word, it found its way deep into one of my veins then it was goodnight Vienna. That stuff travelled through me like nothing I'd ever felt and just before the convolutions, pissing and shitting started, I heard Biffa's voice: "You'll love this shit, it's good, pure heroin."

I was totally knocked out and woke up the next day covered in shit, piss and sick but they were minor things because I was totally hooked on the shit. I was back to square one, but this time this would prove to be the God of anything I'd ever shot into my veins. A small part of me tried to resist, but a big part of me wanted some more. Little did I know, I didn't have to wait too long. I heard Biffa coming through the front door and I was like a kid in a candy store.

"I've got one of my friends coming over to see you in an hour," he said, like I'd already accepted his business proposal. "He just broke up with his girlfriend, so make him happy and make sure you wash yourself, you stink … and don't fuck up."

I knew what his so-called mate was coming for and if it was what I thought it was then I needed to get off my head. The only person that could throw this dog a bone was standing right in front of me. I had to get some heroin because I knew I couldn't do it without my friend.

"Biffa, I need something. I can't do it without it, I just can't!" I could feel my blood itching; it was something I hadn't felt in a long time, but that stuff entered me and it made itself a resident, rent free.

"Nah Rebecca, I need you normal, not all monged out!" he yelled, but I just had to get some, one way or the other. I needed it badly and I needed it before I was penetrated by Biffa's so-called 'sad friend'. So I got on my knees and started crawling over to him, unzipping his flies as I looked into his eye and begged: "Please Biffa, please, just a bit. I promise I won't take it till after." Next, my mouth was full and my syringe was full, so you could say the mouth is the best tool of persuasion. That was a tool I had to use a lot in the near future as I became completely addicted.

Months flew by like days and Biffa had me working the streets hard, as he called it, putting his money where my mouth was. Dirty old men in flash cars, some married, some single and most didn't give a shit that I was pregnant. I remember the last guy who pulled up in a smart, brown Triumph which was polished to the nines. He pulled over, all shy and vulnerable, leaned over to the passenger's side and wound his window down.

"Excuse me, er, how much?" he said in a posh English accent. He was a young-looking, well-groomed white guy; his jet black hair was cut short at the sides and the top was combed neatly to the left, revealing a side part. His lips were thin and bright pink, like he was either blushing or he'd put on a thin layer of lipstick before he left his mansion. Damn, the man was hot. He was so polite, I couldn't help but wonder why a nice guy would want a smackhead like me. He could've got any girl he wanted and I was totally fucked! I stank and dressed like a tramp, I even had the smackhead limp. To top it off, I was nine months pregnant and God only knows how many diseases I was carrying in the back of my throat. But money is money and drugs ruled this black chick, so I had every intention of taking his niceness for weakness.

"Fifteen pounds," I replied, jumping into his ride without hesitation while charging him three times the going rate. I guess what Biffa didn't know Biffa couldn't miss. "But I only do blow jobs as you can see," I said as I pointed to my lump. He nodded in agreement, totally shy.

It was his first time, but it wasn't mine and I knew I had to get him off fast because since morning I'd been getting mad pains in the bottom of my belly. I didn't know what it was; maybe it was all the punishment I gave my gut every time I thought about my useless life. The pain was so bad, but luckily it went as fast as it came.

"Drive around the block and I'll tell you where to stop," I told him, as I pointed in the direction I wanted him to go. Scared and confused, the guy put his foot down and stalled the car, jerking it violently.

"I'm so sorry. Are you OK?" he asked, but it was too late for concern.

The pain came, pain I'd never felt before in my life, followed by a gush of water that poured out of me.

I grabbed onto the dashboard, not wanting to move. I needed mamma more than I'd ever needed any type of drug, but she was nowhere to be seen. I knew that little bastard was coming and it was coming faster than I could say, "Drive da damn car! Get me to hospital now!"

The poor guy firmly pressed himself up against his door in fear and disgust then put his foot down like he was the old bill.

"I'm not from around here! Which way? Which way do I go?" he yelled.

"Go left, now turn right!" I shouted. "Top of the road, turn – ah, it fucking hurts!" I don't know how we got there but we reached Forest Gate Hospital.

He turned on me. "OK, we're here! Get out the car!" What a surprise; this shy guy who was about to lose his virginity to my mouth had turned into a crazy dickhead. "Get out of my fucking car!" he snapped again. He opened his door, legged it round to my side of the car, opened my door and dragged me out, dashing me onto the cold, concrete floor. I felt the gravel bury itself deep into my hands and knees; the last things I recalled were the shrieking of tyres and the smell of rubber. Then darkness settled in. I passed out.

****

I felt a gentle pat on my face; I started to come round, but soon wished I hadn't. Oh the pain! The pain was so bad.

"Wake up Miss Jenkins, we need you to push! Come on, push Miss Jenkins, push, push!"

I'd never in all my miserable years felt pain like that, I couldn't do it. It felt like it was impossible for any woman to push a basketball out of her pussy, regardless of how many cocks they'd had in there.

"I can't!" I yelped at the nurse. "It hurts, it hurts, get that little bastard out of me, he's trying to kill me, just cut it out!" I've never felt pain like that before and I never wanted to feel it ever again.

"No-one is trying to kill you Miss Jenkins" the nurse said politely. She was trying to comfort me, but I didn't care for her comfort, all I wanted was for the nightmare to end. "I know it hurts, but I need you to push. I can see the head – push!" Her brown eyes lit up like it was her first time delivering a baby. She was so excited, but all I wanted was my best friend; the pain was so bad and there was blood everywhere, I couldn't control my bowels and I lost command of all my strength and senses.

"I hate it! Get it out! Get it out of me!" I snapped as I held firmly on to the side of the bed.

"One last, big push ...!" she shouted. "Push ... Push! Harder!" *How fucking hard did the bitch want me to push? Was she crazy?* I thought as I felt my pussy split. I screamed in agony and gave one more push. It was finally out.

My head collapsed back into the pillow and I exhaled. All I could think was that bastard child that made my life a misery for nine months was out and I no longer had to punish my belly every time I felt a thud.

The nurse brought me back to reality. "Oh great, you have a beautiful baby boy." She tried to hand him to me, but I just wanted to get the hell out of there.

"Look, I don't care. Just get him away from me," I shouted, with the tiny bit of strength I had left.

"Come on Miss Jenkins, you can hold him now if you want."

"I said get that bastard away from me!"

My hand came down hard and fast. All I wanted to do was hit the pipe or get my hands on the nearest syringe. I needed Jason, but I was alone, so alone and my best friend was in Biffa's back pocket. All I could think about was when would we meet again; heroin was my best friend, my only friend. He was the only one who truly loved me, so I wanted to embrace him like I was embracing my long lost mother.

I heard the nurse cry out, "Oh my God, I think his arm is broken!"

I just wished he was dead. That bastard Samuel had raped me and put him there. I didn't want for one second to be any part of him, let alone have him suck on my breasts as his dad did most nights for over two years. I faintly heard the doctor say they had to rush me to theatre as I was losing a lot of blood. I passed out yet again.

Chapter 7
Back to Business

Someone tugged my arm the way mamma used to when she woke me up for school in the morning. Was it all a bad dream? I opened my eyes slowly, just wishing it was only to see a nurse standing over me. It was real. My mind snapped at me like it was my fault I was in that mess.

"Miss Jenkins, wake up. You have a visitor," the nurse told me. I was so groggy and tried to open my eyes, but they just kept closing. I heard her voice again, "Wake up Miss Jenkins," as she shook me once more. I was awake. The same nurse that had delivered my baby stood over me with that same fake ass smile she wore when he slid out, then I realised where I was.

My throat was dry, so dry that it hurt and I didn't even have spit to lubricate it. "Water," I croaked groggily. The nurse brought me the glass of fresh water that was sitting on a side table to my right. When I reached to grab the cup, I felt a sharp pain in my arm. I was used to needles, but I felt this needle deeper than any needle that had ever penetrated me. I looked at my arm and saw that I was hooked up to a drip. My eyes followed the tube that was connected to the needle embedded deep in a vein. My first thought was *How did they find that vein?* because I couldn't have found it in a million years. The tube end connected to a bag that was hanging nicely from a metal frame; the bag had clear liquid inside.

My mind wandered around the space. I saw that I was in a little private room, lying in a nice, soft bed. To my left was a little window. The white blinds kept the daylight from hurting my eyes and the powerful smell of strong Dettol hung in the air (I knew it was Dettol as I used it to rub the skin on my breasts and between my legs after Samuel touched me).

"Miss Jenkins, you have a visitor," the nurse repeated, yanking me out of my thoughts.

Who could it be? No one knew I was there, then it hit me: it could only be Biffa.

How the hell did he know where I was? I didn't need that nutcase around me. I was too tired, too sick and I needed to rest. I knew what he wanted; he wanted to put me back on the road asap. I knew that because I was bringing him at least £1,000 a week, so he must've been missing his pocket change. I mean, why else would he come?

Not to bring me flowers and a slap-up meal like Jason would have. I had to think fast. OK, I had it. I had a reason why I wouldn't and couldn't go back on the streets.

No sooner than I had the idea, he walked in wearing white Gola trainers, dark blue jeans, a white Fred Perry t-shirt and an army green bomber jacket.

"Alright Miss Jenkins, I'll leave you both alone for a bit," said the nurse.

She must've thought we were an item, but still looked over at Biffa with a concerned expression on her face. "Sir, please don't stay long as she has lost a lot of blood and needs her rest."

Biffa played the nice guy. "OK nurse, I won't be long."

She left the room with a smile then all eyes were on me, well, at least one eye was.

"Damn, Becks, you've finally got rid of that lump," Biffa said as he sat on the end of my bed like we were friends "and that means more money on the roads for me." He smirked as he rubbed his hands together like he'd just got out of the cold and was trying to warm them, "So we need you to get up on your feet asap cause every day you're here, you're losing me money and we can't have that now, can we?"

What the hell was this guy on? Was he serious? "Biffa I've just had a baby, I can't even move let alone work and I must've paid off my debt by now, so all I want to do is go to rehabilitation, get my son and start a new life for both of us."

That was my big plan: to get off the roads and as you can imagine, Biffa wasn't happy, not one bit. He grabbed my face hard, putting his massive hand over my mouth. I felt a sharp blow to my stomach, which totally took the wind out of me. I doubled up on the bed that was going to be my prison for one more week, but if Biffa had anything to do with it you could call that week one day.

He lifted his patch and I saw his eye for the very first time, what was left of it. He gazed into my eyes and whispered through his teeth, "You're a fucking smackhead. Furthermore, you're my smackhead and you stop working when I tell you to. Your debt ain't over till I tell you it is. Have you got that?" He raised his voice a bit louder, "Have you fucking got that?"

I had no choice. "Yes Biffa, I understand." He still had that grin on his face.

"Good. I knew you wouldn't let me down, so tomorrow you leave this shithole and go back to a bigger shithole, hit the streets and bring home the bacon."

The guy must've really lost his damn mind. "But Biffa, I'm still bleeding heavily and I look worse now than when I came in."

"Then you fuck in the dark! Use your brain Becks," he said as he poked me on the side of my head with his index finger. "Oh yeah, and as for rehabilitation, it starts right now." He grabbed my jaw and squeezed. "Open wide, now stick out your tongue." Terror crept through my body like cold ice, filling every muscle, every vein and every thought. "Good girl!" Then the needle pushed deep into my tongue and its contents went straight into my system.

Before I passed out I thought, *I've got to get out of this shit before it kills me*. Jason helped me to learn that no matter what you go through in life, it's always worth living and I needed to do just that, live my life to the very end.

****

One year passed. I'd never seen my son, although I thought about him a lot and when I slept I often had dreams about him. I wasn't doing too well. Biffa constantly had me on the game and fed my habit to keep me sedated, so I didn't have the strength to run even if I wanted to. I still got those seasick sensations; I thought they'd pass after having the baby, but I guessed they were there to stay. I waited for crumbs to fall from Biffa's table, so I didn't eat much and the last time I weighed myself was in hospital a year ago. I was nine stones then; judging by the way I looked 12 months later, I'd say I was about seven stones if that. I didn't know how or if I was going to see another year. I really didn't. I was like a petrol tank; I kept getting filled up then used up.

Yeah, I was still in the squat. The government tried to kick me out, but smackheads have rights too, I think they call them squatter's rights or something like that. I placed my head between my knees, thinking *How, how, how am I going to get out of this?* I knew I'd never see my baby and I knew I'd never be the same, but I needed to try. I thought about auntie only sometimes, but mamma's face was a vivid image in my mind. Thinking was hard to do some days as it really hurt my head. But I just had to. *Think Becks, think. How am I going to get away from this guy?*

The idea came in the form of Jason's voice: "Don't even think about going up them stairs because they can't even hold the weight of a cat and by the looks of how fat you've been getting over the last three months, you don't stand a chance."

I got it. I must've been about nine stones around the time he said that. Biffa now looked about fifteen stones, so if he went up those stairs, they'd definitely give way then he'd end up in the cupboard underneath. That sounded like a plan and a lot of pain. So I found the biggest bag I could get hold of, went outside and started walking from one end of the road to the other, opening gates and stealing milk bottles. First, I walked down on right side then I came back on myself on the left side. I had to be vigilant, I couldn't let Biffa see me, let alone catch me out of my cage only to ask what I was doing.

It was a long, hard road to travel for a smackhead, trust me. I was tired as hell carrying that bag, but I finally got back to my squat. I dragged the bag over to the cupboard door under the stairs and opened it wide; the stench of damp walls hit me hard. Bloody hell, it was unsettling. I pulled my old t-shirt over my nose to mask the stink. I started smashing every bottle; each bottle I smashed reflected a time in my life I hated and, trust me, there were a lot of hated moments and a lot of broken glass.

The floor was soon covered, but it wasn't enough. I ran into the front room and snatched anything sharp I could find. Razor blades, needles, knives and forks, I tried to find anything that would do damage to the flesh of a cunt called Biffa.

Now that part of my plan was executed, it was time for the major execution. I had to get up the stairs without falling through, but more importantly I had to get Biffa up them as well. Ok, no time to waste. I walked to the bottom of the stairs and took a good look up as it was probably the last time I'd ever get to see them again. Becks, you've been through worse, so this has got to be a breeze, I told myself.

I stepped on the first step and felt my heart beating like a good one. The step sang. I jumped off quickly. I stood there contemplating, *What should I do?*

I could hear Jason's smooth voice, "OK Becks, come on girl, you got to do this, your life depends on it."

"You know what? Fuck it! If I die, I die," I snapped at myself.

I tried again. One step, then two. Jason spoke again. "OK Becks, nice and easy, easy and nice. Good girl." My heart pulsed through my fingertips. I got to the third step then lost all concentration, I just wanted to hear Jason's voice again. I fell into a deep daydream. "Wrong move Becks."

There was a loud creek then … Crash! I fell through the stairs, separating my finger nails from my fingertips as I tried desperately to grab at the steps to break my fall. Splinters from the rotten wood and rusty nails ripped through my flesh. I hit the floor below but before I hit the glass beneath me there was a loud crack: my ankle snapped like a twig.

The pain was immense, but what was left to come would make me feel like I was having fun playing hopscotch in Dominica.

My body and face slammed into the broken glass beneath me and it penetrated deeper than Samuel ever did. Shards entered my breast and face, but the killer blow was the razor blade that dissected my jugular vein.

I was left there bleeding to death, choking on my own blood and just before I blew my last breath I heard Jason. "Becks, snap out of it!"

I clawed my way back to consciousness only to find myself on the top of the stairs. Damn, that was a hell of a daydream. I had made it to the top. Now all I had to do was wait, so wait I did. Three hours went by and I started to get the shakes. I had to focus, I had to bypass the thirst just for a bit longer, I fell asleep at the top of the stairs.

Then I heard my name. Was it a dream too? You know when you dream that someone's calling you, but then you open your eyes and they really are calling you?

Yeah, well, it was one of those dreams and the honking voice was Biffa's. It just got louder and louder. "Oi, Rebecca! Where the fuck are you?" he snapped. Now this was the plan: I had to get that 15 stones guy so mad that he came running up the stairs, but if I got him mad and my plan didn't work I was going to be one dead smackhead. I stood at the top of the stairs and called down to him.

"I'm up here!" Biffa looked up the stairway, crimson faced, totally pissed off. "What the hell are you doing up there?" he shouted as he held the end of the banister "and where you been? I ain't seen you out there making my money!"

Anxiety stroked my bones. I murmured as though I wanted him to hear, but didn't really want him to hear: "I don't work for you no more."

Chapter 8
Rage

"What did you say?" he barked. "I said, what did you fucking say? You better get your black ass down here before I come up there an show you what pain is."

My mouth, my fear and my anger grew some balls and got the better of me. I knew if I made him angry enough there would be no way on God's Earth those stairs would hold his weight. "I said I don't work for you no more, so do one you cunt. Oh yeah, by the way, before your dad carved your face did he play with your ass?" My heart beat triple time. If that didn't make him angry enough to fly up the stairs then nothing would.

Yeah, Biffa was angry and I mean crazy angry. His face turned bright reddish orange, as he flew up the stairs like a bull in a china shop. "Y-you what you fucking bitch? You're fucking ..." He sped up the stairs like a man possessed. His last word echoed as he crashed through the stairs: "Dead!"

I watched as the stairs gobbled him up like quicksand; the rotten wood opened its belly and devoured him like a well cooked meal. After the dust had cleared, there was silence. I had to get down the stairs, so I walked part way then leaned over slowly and looked into the hole only to see bits of Biffa's clothes, flesh and a tuft of hair between the grooves of split wood. I tell you something, I hadn't smiled like that in years. I heard Jason's voice again: "Good job Becks, that's my girl!" then it disappeared like it never existed.

I had to get to the bottom, but I didn't want to end up on top of him so I did it the only way I knew how. After walking down what was left of the top steps, I jumped the massive hole that was left, just like when I was beautiful, clean, well-spoken Rebecca. I strolled over to the door, stretched my hand and grabbed the round, wooden knob.

As I opened it, memories of that last day with Samuel crashed through my mind like waves in high winds against the rocks back home in my beautiful country.

I reached for the handle and pulled. What I saw was a sight for sore eyes, but not as sore as Biffa. He lay there in pools of blood and chunks of flesh, and judging by the way his eye was dilating there was a strong possibility he wasn't going to make it. He let out a faint groan as he took a last look at the smack head that ended his shitty wicked life. If looks could kill, I would've been struck down by the hand of God himself.

I slowly stretched over to Biffa's back pocket, finding enough smack to last me at least three months, well two months minimum. I must say the money he had in his pocket just kept coming. I closed the door, mumbling "Die you bastard, this is for my Jason." I grabbed my prepacked bag that was hidden neatly behind the couch in the front room and headed for the door. Hearing the floorboards sing to me for the last time was a weight off my shoulders.

Next stop was auntie's house. Jason managed to get me off the crap once, but the stuff I'd graduated to was ten times stronger and if I was to ever get myself clean and see my son again, I was going to need someone ten times stronger to get me off it. The only person I knew who could do that was my auntie. Regardless of the past, I was going to have to think of the future, so it was back to Paddington for me, where it all started.

I limped on to the bus. Oh, I didn't tell you about my limp did I? Well there's not much to say about that because limping comes as part and the parcel of being a smackhead. Then again, I told you that earlier, didn't I? Drugs can also fuck up your memory.

Anyway, as I was saying, I got on the bus with my old, tatty clothes and my scruffy ruck sack. Everyone held their noses and all sorts. Well, I guess I was a wee bit pongy. I felt low and so weak, but I had to change my life. As they say, 'You try to change your life and your life changes you'. Yes, my habit got worse. It just spiralled out of all control and when you have a relationship with Mr Heroin, you can't have a relationship with anyone or anything else.

I remember when I returned. I limped past my old house on the other side of the street, glimpsing it from the corner of my eye, hoping not to get spotted. I must've walked up and down at least ten times just waiting to see if my auntie came out, but she never did. How disappointed I was, even though I didn't know the outcome of what happened in the house the day I left. I had to go and knock. I walked up to the gate, trying my best to disguise the smackhead limp and straightening up my clothes as though I was wearing a stylish dress. As I got closer, I couldn't help but think *Nothing about that house has changed, nothing at all.* The only thing that had changed was the way my heart beat faster than ever. I wiped away the sweat, you know the sweat that all addicts get, then reached for the big, black knocker on that horrible, purple door. Why would anyone in their right mind want to paint their door that nasty colour? I asked myself again.

I knocked, but no-one was there, so I decided to take up residence on the cold, concrete floor, just behind the porch wall; that's where I curled up and fell into a deep sleep as time flew like the end of days. Mamma always told me, "You'll know when it's the end of the world because years will feel like months and months will feel like days." Now I understood what she meant.

I felt a hand tugging at my tracksuit and heard an old, croaky voice. Was I still on the boat coming to England? Was it all a dream? Damn! No, it wasn't "Rosy, Rosy get up!" I couldn't believe it, I thought my auntie had come home. My eyes opened wide, but I still couldn't make out the raggedy figure that stood over me, calling me a name I'd never heard before. "Rosy, she ain't here you know."

I gazed up to see an old, white woman with tea stained teeth looking down at me. "My name isn't Rosy, I'm Rebecca," I croaked. "And who isn't here?" I asked, still half asleep and slightly whacked out of my head from the shot I took earlier.

"Your old girl, she ain't here and you look like a Rosy to me," she said as she pointed her bent finger at the purple front door. "She's doing porridge."

I was confused. "What do you mean, porridge?"

Then that old woman, whom I'd never seen before in my life, rolled her eyes. "Rebecca, you've been gone for too long girl. Your old dear on a government holiday. You know, she's doing time for killing her old man. I dare not say it, but he was a right bastard." She looked at me hard after that little outburst. She seemed to know Samuel very well. "Do you understand now?" She looked at me with half-raised eyebrows. "She got ten to life. Look, get up and come with me, there's nothing that a warm bath and a cup of rosie lee can't fix. You'll feel right as rain in no time."

What did I have to lose? I had nowhere to stay, no auntie to save me, no son, no anything so even though I didn't know who the old hag was I'd have been a fool to turn her down.

"OK," I said, trying to pick myself up off the cold floor, brushing off my clothes like butter wouldn't melt in my mouth. But let's not talk about things in my mouth for a bit because I had enough gear to last for three, maybe two, months. I could keep my mouth clean. Anyway, I got up and we started walking back to this old lady's house. As we walked, she started nattering over her shoulder at me while she led the way.

"Rebecca, I know you're on the drugs and although God loves everyone, and he's the only one that can judge you, in this case I'll be the judge of you." She didn't even look back, she just kept walking and airing my dirty knickers in public.

"Don't you ever get high in my house, or you'll be out as fast as a shot. I've got a shed that my old Frederick used for his gardening and smoking his cigars, you'll be safe in there. It's not good to hang your dirty linen in public."

At that point, I rolled my eyes. I wanted to ask if she realised she was putting my dirty clothes and everything else through people's letter boxes, not even on the washing line. I wanted to snap at her, but then I just got to wondering, *Why is she telling me all this?* She only offered me a cup of tea, not a damn hotel room. I was stuck in confusion as she yapped on.

"So if you need to shoot up, you can go in there," she was talking, but my mind drifted away as I listened to the click-clack-clicking of her aged shoes. Then I realised who she was ... Do you remember that old woman who used to give me nasty looks? Yeah, *that* old woman! How the chickens came home to roost! I gasped as she spun around, wagging her finger.

"Did you just hear a word I said?" she shouted.

"Yes Miss, er, miss!"

"Just call me auntie; I've always wanted to be one of them. I didn't think I would've had a black niece, but beggars can't be choosers," she chuckled, but I knew it would be a long friendship because she wasn't that bad after all. We walked to her front door. She couldn't put the key in the key hole, "Damn thing," she muttered under her breath. So I took the key and tried, but I was shaking so much I was useless. She patted my hand and giggled, "Give it here, you're worse than me!"

We walked into the house; it smelled like old people and cats, but it was where I stayed for the next few years of my life.

I did my best with all that was going on around me, you know the prostitution and all that kind of stuff. I wasn't injecting anymore as I had no veins left. I was like an old tea bag, full of holes. But I did try my best, even though I was a bag of bones, to sell my ass, vagina or mouth for a rock and my adopted auntie tried to look after me the best way she could. So, as you can imagine, I was devastated when she passed away. I didn't even know her real name, all I know is when her son that no-one ever saw came to throw her things out, he threw me out with them. Then the house went on the market and was sold.

I waited and waited to meet Samuel and judging from the suicidal thoughts in my head, that day would come sooner than I imagined. I visited my dealer and asked him for my last shot; I had no money as no-one, not even the tramp that slept in Queens Market scavenging food out the bins or the guy that played the films in green street Odean cinemas, would come near me, so it had to be for old times' sake. I finally convinced my dealer it would be my last fix. I told him I was getting out for good and he agreed, just out of pity. He accepted he had to help to put this sick dog down. I told him I needed pure, undiluted heroin and it was done.

Chapter 9
Ten Steps to Heaven

I walked slowly to my old house, passed through the gate and headed to the top of the steps. I stood there and I looked to my left then to my right.

My future was unclear, just like the black sea at night that brought me here in the belly of that big, old boat. There was a road. I'd seen it many times before, but this time it wasn't with fascination because I knew it took me to the end of nowhere, swallowing me up like the rotten stairs took Biffa.

The cold breeze freely brushed past my battered face, waking me up like a gentle friend just passing by. I once called that breeze *Freedom*, but I came to know it as death. The roads weren't paved with gold, nor were the houses made of sweets and beautiful cakes, but I hoped heaven was ... aah, I exhaled.

I took in the sky. There where clouds in shades of grey and shades of white. The sun was shining, but all I saw was the darkness that was about to consume me.

I walked down the stairs, trying to jump the last three steps like I did when I was beautiful, young, innocent Rebecca, but I fell and that's where I sat as I went through my ritual for the last time. Belt tight, insert needle, release belt then press. The pure heroin didn't even want to take a break, it just rushed through my veins like a hot knife through butter. I'd overdosed; it was unpleasant, but at least I was free.

****

A pair of strong hands scooped me up from the concrete. My limp, lifeless, frail body covered in sick levitated off the ground as the hands of God carried me across to the other side.

Sun rays bore down on me stronger than Biffa ever did and penetrated my dirty rags deeper than Samuel ever could. As the saying goes, the sun even shines on dog shit, making me no different to anyone else that I came across in my sickening, crappy life.

It doesn't matter if you drive a big car, or live in a big house, or sell your body for drugs because when we die, we're all the same. Think about that the next time you see a drunk or crackhead having a kip in a doorway. Don't be a dickhead, be kind.

Anyway, all my problems were long forgotten as I met my son in a dream. I had to give him a message to keep him on the straight and narrow, but my message was crudely interrupted.

My message to him was: "Son, know your children like you know yourself. Don't be like your mother. Be a better person, so your mother can wish she was like you."

Oh, I wished I'd had the chance to finish my conversation with him, but I awoke in total pain, holding my belly, laying on a mattress in a room covered in darkness, with sick, piss and shit as my only company. I was going through cold turkey and lost all track of time. Worst still, I wasn't dead. However, what I was about to experience made me wish that I had died with every blood cell, every vein and every breath I had left.

All I wanted was my best friend. I needed to feel him running through my veins or travelling up my nose, kicking me straight in the back of my head. But like everyone and everything, he left me too. I started begging my auntie for a shot, yeah that's right, and every now and then, I tried to bite off my tongue so I could bleed to death. I needed a fix. I saw auntie, bigger, stronger and more confident than ever before. She'd returned and found me like she promised!

No … that was a hallucination. Yes it was … no, it wasn't …

I learned how a downfall can reach the strongest part of your soul, especially while auntie punched my chest when my heart gave up at least twice. I was willing to go, but she had no intention of letting me. I had no choice but to get back on that bike called life's a bitch; I rode that bike and rode it and rode it and rode it some more until that cunt called downfall became the strongest part of me.

Let me give you a brief encounter with my cold turkey.

Auntie was set on withdrawing me from heroin. Listen good, as this is cold turkey. She gave me supplements when I couldn't eat and eight clonidine pills when I got high blood pressure or had panic attacks, and trust me, I got a lot of them.

Sometimes, when the attacks got so bad, she'd give me four Ativan pills, so you can imagine I was totally of my head and that was just ten hours after I tried to die. I felt the soft, cold flannel on my forehead as my auntie tried desperately to cool me down.

****

OK Rebecca, you need to rest now. Let me tell them the rest of your nightmare, so hopefully they won't make the same mistakes we did.

Rebecca must have been injecting for about 10 years and judging by her weight and how she looked, naturally I was scared to raass.

Oh sorry, excuse my French, but I really didn't think she was going to pull through. Ten hours after she tried to kill herself, poor Rebecca wasn't feeling much besides depression, but I had to stay close by to make sure she didn't try to do anything stupid again. I tried to help her relax, talking to her about when I was back home living with her mamma, my beautiful sister.

Hold on, this room is getting really smelly from the sick and everything else, so hold on and let me crack the window open a bit. As I was saying, Rebecca was dying for a shot, but there was no way on Earth she was going to get one, even when she screamed at me and tried to attack me, blaming me for everything that had happened to her. I knew she didn't mean it, yet I couldn't help but think she was right.

I wasn't about to make the same mistake twice, so I had to be cruel to be kind. The aches in her legs started to get much worse, which was good in a way because at least that was the first sign of withdrawal symptoms. After reading those books, I knew they'd be followed by major discomfort in her stomach and I wasn't surprised when she started hallucinating. Rebecca would scream, "Get him out of me! My stomach feels like it's going to rip apart! Get him out of me!" I couldn't help but hold her and sob in silence. What else could I do? I couldn't show her any weakness.

One day later, the punching, kicking, sweating and runny poo started; she had no control over her bodily functions, none whatsoever; she couldn't stay in one spot, she just wanted to move, but her legs hurt too much. So I picked up what seemed to me like a bag of bones and moved her around. She was so frail that if she dropped, hitting the ground could've been fatal. I held her strong and we paced up and down the room, her poor body was so restless.

She started to get the jitters, shaking like she was getting little electric shocks in random parts of her body. Then came the nausea and at that point it was real bad. I read up on all of this in prison, but there were some things that no book prepared me for. She couldn't eat at all and whatever I put in her mouth just made her gag. But she had to eat and take in fluids or she wouldn't last the next two hours, let alone the next two days. So, naturally I was scared to death. If that was how it was after one day, how the hell would we cope when the hell peaked in two or three days?

I couldn't imagine how much worse it was going to get.

Oh, and I forgot to mention the hot and cold. At 24 hours, despite being drenched in sweat, Rebecca screamed and screamed, "Auntie, I'm freezing! Help me, please! Auntie, help me!"

She was freezing; it got so bad that I had to lay under the covers with her, holding her close till she'd push me away when she got too hot. "Auntie, it hurts! It hurts so much, it feels like spikes digging into my flesh, just give me a hit, please, I beg you, just one more hit and I promise to be good, I swear I will." Her voice faded, "I promise auntie, I'll never be bad ... again." Then she drifted back off to sleep.

Now, even though I was the nurse, the auntie, the rock stone, depression and unbearable darkness finally covered me as I fell to my knees and begged, "Oh God, help me, help me, *please* give me the strength."

Then I heard a voice: "I never helped you before, so what makes you think I'm going to help you now?"

I knew I was alone. But if I felt so bad, how the hell do you think poor, sweet Rebecca felt? I had to be strong for her and for my own sanity because sometimes I felt like placing a pillow over her face and pressing down firmly to put her out of her misery. But I couldn't bring myself to do it, not in this lifetime – maybe in another because I never, ever want to go through that again.

It took Rebecca at least two months to get back on her feet and at least a couple of years to feel strong enough to leave the house alone without relapsing.

Chapter 10
The End of an Old Day

OK auntie, I'll take it from here.

Thanks to the most beautiful woman I know, my life had just begun. I was up, eating and getting stronger each and every day and no-one, not even God himself could take this life from me again.

Next step: find my son. He must have been around 15 years old and in school. If it was the last thing I did, I was going to find him and beg for his forgiveness, regardless of the outcome. I knew he was living right under my nose the entire time in Forest Gate and I knew what school he went to: Forest Gate School obviously because they sent all the black kids there.

I didn't know what he looked like, but I hoped he looked like me and not the sperm that created him. Anyway, it wasn't going to be hard to point him out as there weren't a lot of black people around that neck of the woods with one arm. Yes, he had one arm because of me. I could vaguely remember the nurse saying they had to amputate it when I flung him on the ground straight after he was born.

Tears filled my eyes as I called out to my auntie, trying to put on a brave face. "Auntie, I'm ready," I said as I stood at the front room door, watching as she read the newspaper. She looked up at me with motherly love.

"I know you are Rebecca and it's been a long time coming." She got to her feet and walked over to her coat which was hanging on the back of one of the wooden chairs that stood around our matching dining table. She slipped her hand in her pocket, looking at me and talking as she did. "I have something for you that I've been saving for this very moment." She reached into her pocket and pulled out £300 in crisp £10 notes. "I saved it for you, especially for this day," she said with a smile as she handed the cash to me. "Go and get your hair done and buy some new clothes; it's not much, but it will help you to look decent so you can find your son with a bit of pride. Remember: first impressions last." She raised her eyebrows as she extended her hand, "Yes, to you it's a lot of money, but don't abuse it. You're strong enough now, so do the right thing."

I reached out my hand to take the cash and couldn't help but fall into her arms, laying my head on her chest. Words weren't enough, but I think she understood the intensity of my embrace and I knew what she meant by her words. I wasn't about to cross that road again because I knew if I did, I'd surely die.

I walked out the front door, hoping it would take me somewhere better than all the other doors

I'd left behind. Next stop: shopping then the hairdresser. Finally, I was ready. I still didn't look as pretty as other women because heroin has a way of living in cracks and wrinkles that scares you; my limp was the constant reminder I needed of my relationship with it. But I tried my best and my best was all I could do. I had a new grey, tweed coat, a slick kilt and black satin blouse; I looked so good in my shiny black shoes, they were a little bit tight but they'd do.

My hair was too damaged to do anything constructive with, so the hairdresser fixed me up with a wig and it was real hair so it passed. I don't know what anyone else thought about the way I looked, but I loved it! For the first time in my life, I felt like a real woman. I buried my hands deep in my pockets, not wanting to scuff my new nail polish, but when my hands were warm, it gave me that extra sense of security. As I reached Forest Road, just around the corner, not far to go, I had a sense, a very strong sense, that I was about to see my son.

I was just going to cross the road when I suddenly stopped. Worry struck. What if I see him and he doesn't want to talk to me, or he hits me or, worse still, what if he spits on me like those white folks used to when I slept rough in doorways? So scared, my heart pumped fiercely as I crossed the road. Well, I thought it was my heart racing. There was no pain as it hit me, the ancient, blue Volvo that sped out of nowhere. I didn't even see it coming, but I did get a glimpse at the young black boy and girl driving. I couldn't help thinking the boy looked a bit like me when I was younger.

There was a violent tear in time and objects zoomed by as if they were part of a flip book animation. The collision felt like a slow motion, black and white movie that mamma used to watch every Sunday after church, but I wasn't watching cowboys and Indians, I was watching myself. I had no control over what was about to happen. I lay there for what seemed like forever, almost dead in the centre of a circle of onlookers.

When I opened my eyes for the first time, people came from all angles to try to help me. I felt nothing, so what was all the panic about? But then the pain exploded. Broken nose, broken jaw, broken collar bone, a punctured lung, a massive gash that exposed the top of my skull, not forgetting the brainstem injury. The killer blow was death.

Before the Volvo smashed into me, I remember thinking *Why do they go so fast*? and that thought echoed on the wind which rushed past my face while I soared through the air. I heard my bones snap over and over again as I slammed down on the bonnet then bounced off. My wig flew in one direction and my shoes seemed to sprint from my body. But that wasn't the final blow. The car's front wheels ran over me, closely followed by the back wheels and it just kept going. I guessed I'd never get to see my son after all. Before I took my last breath, I could just about hear sirens as the ambulance dashed to my aid.

Bwaaa ... Bwaaa ...

"Move please! Move out the way! Let us get through please! Give us some space!"

Their distant voices were background noises, but I clearly heard their feet scuffling as they rushed towards me. Rough hands gently patted my face. "Can you hear me? Can you hear me?" When I failed to respond, the pats turned into two, sharp slaps that violently jerked me out of my slumber. Slowly, slowly, my eyes gradually focused on that irritating man with the tight, black jacket, receding hair line and two missing front teeth.

"Wake up little girl, you're in England now! It's time to get off my ship."

"It still looks like a boat to me," I muttered under my breath.

****

A wise woman once said:

"My sleep wasn't peaceful, though I have the sense of emerging from a world of dark, haunted places where I travelled alone."
Suzanne Collins, *Mockingjay*

Reflections about *Twisted Lanes* from those who have lived the tales

Thank you to the inmates of Pentonville Prison for sharing their thoughts.

I'm a prisoner serving time in Pentonville. I was in the block when I was given your book to read. It's a really good book; I was very drawn to it and read it in depth. The story line was so emotional, it felt so real, like I was living it.

Like I said, I couldn't put it down. It was really powerful and inspiring. It gave so much meaning to my life and so many others who have been through it. I give you thanks for taking the time to put pen to paper and sharing this with the world. I can imagine there are so many more people that can relate.

I'm going through a little rough patch myself, but reading your book made me realise we all suffer in different ways, some greater than others, and it could happen in a blink of an eye. Your book captured my spirit; it had me up in the early hours of the morning speaking to another prisoner at the door who'd already read it and it was so deep that it really touched us both.

If my opinion helps, I'd love it if you could pass down your book to the kids at school. I really think they need it in these dark times; they're lost souls. It will not only send a message, but it'll properly impact their lives and help to open up their minds to what's really going on around them, the unknown, so they can notice their actions and the consequences that follow.

I don't know how long it took you to write this book, but I like what you did with it. I hope it doesn't end there.

* *

This book is very intriguing: I couldn't put it down, it kept grabbing me proper. I couldn't stop laughing and, best of all, I couldn't stop reading and I can't even read good.

It made me want to write a book about my life, plus it really relates to my own life growing up in Leyton and Leytonstone and learning how to trim in Garvey's on Leyton High Road. It was like reading my own life story! I loved it.

I really enjoyed reading *Twisted Lanes* because it's very realistic; it's very true to the streets and life in this day and age, very funny and gripping. It would be a wicked series.

* *

It's insightful; it shows how different backgrounds are interrelated. The lessons of the story are about peer pressure, ('priorities'), anger management, absent parents, and 'loyalty'.

* *

Twisted Lanes ties into the nature versus nurture debate.It shows how you sometimes play a factor and your upbringing also plays a factor, but it doesn't eventually determine your fate/destiny.

* *

I think the book's a good way of showing people how important it is to be a parent and not just have kids. The title is perfect because it's twisted for sure, but it takes something like this for people to realise how much time you need to put in to your young.

* *

I enjoyed the book very much and I found it very interesting. The author wrote the book in a very exciting way that really means twisted lanes, as it's written so twisted that you read one page and you will want to read more and more. So thrilling and fascinating.

I highly recommend that people pick this book up and read it. They won't be disappointed at all.

* *

I think the stories are relatable and I can picture them while I'm reading. I like the way the different sections of the story all lead to one main story as well.

Many of the experiences of the characters in the book relate to me and some of my past situations are similar to those of Carlton and his father Delroy.

For example, when Snake and Smiley give Carlton packed drugs to sell, only for him to be robbed by Jacka, I've seen and been part of similar things where people's desperation can be used against them to take advantage.

Scars from 'road life': Delroy was rejected by his mum and lost an arm because she was on heroin and was not in her right frame of mind. I can relate because I have scars from people living a similar lifestyle.

Once, when I was about to leave the house for college, my dad found a phone in my jacket pocket. He asked me where it came from. When i told him I robbed it, he head-butted me in the face and buss my eyebrow.

Moral of the story: have patience and work hard for what you want because if you try to take easy shortcuts, things can go wrong. Slow money is better than no money.

Drugs are bad: Snake's experience when he smoked the spiked spliff reminded me of people who have smoked spice and had fits and passed out, or other kinds of paranoid delusions which make them act crazy and unpredictable. It gives you an idea of how powerful these substances can be if abused.

* *

Your story kept me glued to the pages and I'm not book person. However, it's kept me entertained, I enjoyed it! It also made me feel as if I was there at each scene.

I'd really be grateful if I could read more of your stories. Keep it up and I hope to come across more of your work in the near future.

Thank you for giving me the opportunity to want to read books.

Twisted lanes Teens edition is now available for on Amazon (suitable for 14yrs upwards)

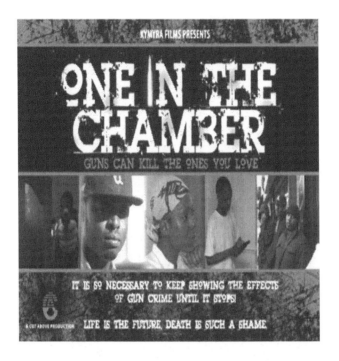

Watch Patrick Phipps's short movie *One in the Chamber* on YouTube. Search for 'one in the chamber full film'

My *Little Book of Empowerment* is a powerful handbook by Patrick Antony Phipps. After many successful years in business, he has undeniably been loved by some, hated by others and betrayed by many. His decision to write *My Little Book of Empowerment* was based on the desire to share solutions and methods for dealing with problems that can occur in life and business.

Patrick shares the many mistakes that he has

made along the way and hopes that this book will work to transform them into positive lessons that will help to empower others to combat problems with better solutions in the future. It also shows how some negative circumstances can even be avoided completely.

My Little Book of Empowerment contains Patrick's instructional methods for you to follow in your daily life. Committing these new methods to your subconscious mind may be empowering, or even life changing.

Some of the methods within this book may at first seem manipulative, conniving or even negative, but when it comes to dealing with the business world, a harsh place, people will find that there is at least one chapter in *The Little Book of Empowerment* which will teach them something valuable that they need to know, or will help them to combat a difficult situation in the future.

There will be circumstances in the book that you can relate to and you will be able to reanalyse how you would deal with them in your own life, as well as find out ways of detecting when someone else is using a negative strategy on you and how you might best turn it around.

So, as small as this book may seem, the potential power that it holds within its pages could be transformative, making it a journey worth taking.

Now available on lulu.com

If you've been affected by the issues raised in this book, please ask for help. Here are the details of some organisations that will be able to provide support.

http://rapecrisis.org.uk/
On this site, you'll find out how to get help if you've experienced sexual violence along with the details of your nearest Rape Crisis services, information for anyone supporting a sexual violence survivor and information about rape and other forms of sexual violence for survivors.

http://www.talktofrank.com/
Call 0300 123 6600 for emergency help, or a confidential talk about the effects of drugs.

https://www.childline.org.uk/
Call 0800 1111 to get help and advice about a wide range of issues, or talk to a counsellor online.

REJECTION IS A LIE...

R I S E

D. U. OKONKWO

A young artist paralysed by past rejection.
A life shackled by lies.
A truth waiting to be discovered.

At age eleven, Ria Ofor was caught in a fire that left
her face scarred. Devastated by the apparent
rejection by her father, Ria, now twenty seven, is a
gifted sculptress but lives a semi reclusive life.
Avoiding art galleries and their consequent publicity,
she scrapes a living through online sales of her art.
But when she's hit with a repossession notice on her
home, it rocks the shaky foundations she's lived on.
On borrowed time, Ria must land a gallery
contract in order to survive. That means stepping out
of her comfort zone and coming face to face with
what she's spent the last sixteen years trying to
avoid: rejection. But competition for lucrative gallery
contracts is cut-throat and Ria soon discovers that
some artists will stop at nothing to keep the spoils of

London's glittering art world for themselves. Torn between the events of her past and the lies threatening to destroy her future, Ria is faced with a decision that could change her life forever.

Printed in Poland
by Amazon Fulfillment
Poland Sp. z o.o., Wrocław

51388131R00204